OWEN
STORM ENTERPRISES BOOK 3

B J ALPHA

Copyright © 2024 by B J Alpha

All rights reserved.

No part of this book may be reproduced in any form or by any electronic or mechanical means, including information storage and retrieval systems, without written permission from the author, except for the use of brief quotations in a book review.

This book is a work of fiction. Characters, names, places and incidents are products of the authors imagination or used fictitiously.

Any similarity to actual events, locations or persons living or dead is purely coincidental.

Without in any way limiting the author's exclusive rights under copyright, any use of this publication to "train" generative artificial intelligence (AI) technologies to generate text is expressly prohibited. The author reserves all rights to license uses of this work for generative AI training and development of machine learning language models. No audio files can be produced without the authors written consent beforehand.

Published by Alpha Team Publishing

Edited by Dee Houpt

Proofread by Mackenzie Nice Girl Naughty Edits

Cover Design by Acacia At Ever After Cover Designs

Photographer Michelle Lancaster @lanefotograf

Model Cooper Black

AUTHOR NOTE

WARNING: This book contains sensitive and explicit storylines.
All content information can be found on my website.
www.authorbjalpha.com
This book is recommended for readers ages eighteen and over.

BLURB

OWEN

I've always wanted her, to protect her.

Laya Kavanagh: sinful, seductive, passionate ... and my best friend's little sister.

Unattainable in every sense.

She deserves better than me. A manipulator, a monster.

I'll always protect her, even from myself.

After pushing her as far away as humanly possible, my hell becomes a reality.

She's married, pregnant, and living her dream life.

But what if she discovered it was all a fantasy, a charade masking the epitome of the devil in disguise?

What if she needs me to protect her?

I'll claim her and her baby, make them both mine. Just how they always should have been.

Because Laya is my everything, now I have to prove it.

LAYA

Owen James Stevens, a dark, broody man covered in ink, was my everything.

I've watched him from afar, drooled over him from a distance, and when I came of age, I handed myself to him on a silver platter.

Only, my heart was broken, and I was tossed to the curb.

I moved on with my life, creating a dream.

But it's a charade. Because beneath the surface of my new life lies an underbelly of darkness.

When evil strikes, I run.

Owen Stevens isn't just my crush, he's my soulmate.

My protector.

And when I need him the most, he claims me.

But at what cost?

DEDICATION

To every reader who wants their hero to fight for them at whatever cost, Owen is for you.

PROLOGUE

LAYA

AGED EIGHTEEN

Pushing my shoulders back, I stare into my vanity mirror and straight into the eyes of Owen James Stevens, my brother's best friend. At ten years my senior, he's forever been out of my reach. I've always been too young, innocent, illegal.

Not anymore.

I apply another layer of the bright-red lipstick I know drives him insane, then roll my lips together.

My eyes once again snag onto the photo pinned to my mirror. It might be of me with my brother and his three best friends, but I only see *him*.

For as long as I can remember, I've only seen him.

When he did everything in his power to avoid me, I

always tracked him down, craving his attention with an all-consuming need.

Even if he pretends like he didn't let me kiss him when I was seventeen after telling him I saved my first kiss for him, I still only see him. The way his heart had beaten wildly beneath the palm of my hand was burned into my soul, and I chipped away a little of his denial of our mutual attraction. For a split second before he pushed me away, he was mine and I was his.

Then he acted like the biggest ass in the world and left me feeling rejected once again.

But not tonight. Tonight, I'm eighteen and want more than a kiss.

I want him to be my first.

My first everything.

My last too.

OWEN

My pulse hammers as I glance around the foyer, contemplating whether I can slip away without my absence being noticed.

The mansion is heaving with partygoers and socialites, like a goddamn afterparty for a film premier, complete with red carpet on the stairs. I shouldn't be surprised Laya is beautiful, a social butterfly with an air of sophistication that money can't buy. Her body is chiseled to perfection, with olive skin and long waves of dark hair. Those luscious red lips of hers are naturally plump, not from the Botox shit her friends inject into themselves, and her fucking eyes, they're the brightest green you've ever seen. She's unique in every sense of the word, and with a promising career ahead of her in the fashion industry, the girl has it all.

My mouth becomes dry just thinking of her while waiting with bated breath for her to greet her guests.

I'd always assumed she wanted to become a model with looks as beautiful as hers, but she scoffed at the notion and scrunched her nose when I helped her practice for a mock job interview when she was fifteen.

Her friends sat gawking at me with rosy cheeks, but not Laya. She would throw her hair over her shoulder, straighten her back, raise her chin, and feign confidence whenever she was around me. I hated it. Hated how she felt the need to put on a display, but I hated it more because I understood it. She wanted to impress me.

Laya Kavanagh has had a crush on me for as long as I can remember, only now she's old enough to act on it, and my heart pounds erratically at the thought.

I've been feeling angsty all day, and she hasn't even made her grand entrance yet. I glance up the stairs again, my palms sweating while clutching the gift in my pocket I don't want anyone to see. Somehow, I made it to the bottom of the staircase, now leaning against the wall as if I'm not some creep waiting for a glimpse of her, a stolen moment I can present her with the only item I have left of my mother, the one I took from around her cold neck.

Flicking my eyes left and right, I triple-check my friends are out of the vicinity, then make a run for it. Grabbing a hold of the banister, I take two steps at a time and dash up to her bedroom.

My feet freeze at her door and the blood in my veins bubbles with trepidation, a knot sitting heavy in my stomach. Fuck me, what the hell is wrong with me? I scrub my sweaty palms down my pants as I stare at the door.

Jesus.

Maybe it's the fact she's no longer jailbait, that I'm standing outside her bedroom door. Somewhere I've no place to be.

OWEN

Knocking, there's a slight tremble in my fist. Shit, that's new too.

"Come in." Her voice is as sweet as honey, and I suddenly want more of it, as if I haven't heard it a thousand times before. I mean, she followed me around for years like a love-struck puppy. She even got herself the nickname of "Owen's helper" as a kid because she was constantly looking for an excuse to be by my side.

Her familiar scent invades me the moment I step into her room, causing me to suck in a sharp breath. My focus zeros in on her vanity and the abundance of familiar photos and cutouts of the future she longs for. When our eyes lock in the mirror, I swear she can see deep into my soul—every sordid truth, every longing, desire, and thought riddled with the sickening guilt that has consumed me for even allowing it to creep into my mind. Her breath hitches, as if unearthing those truths, stripping me bare, and I stand there frozen, finally allowing the pent-up feelings to spill from me.

Staring into her eyes, I know I have to do better, be better, for her. And I want it, I want that more than anything else in the world. I want to be worthy of her.

"Owen?" she whispers, and the softness of her voice shoots to my balls, and my cock thickens in my slacks at the sound.

My mouth becomes impossibly dry as her tongue darts out over her plump bottom lip. That fucking lipstick she doesn't need marring her precious lips when they're edible enough without it has my fists pumping beside me.

Who the fuck did she paint them for?

I long to wrap her thick brown waves around my fist and haul her back so I can devour her neck. Her hair flows down to her ass, accentuated in a little red dress molded to her body like a second skin, forcing a lump to clog in my throat.

Jesus, she's stunning.

"Owen. Are you okay?" Her concerned tone filters through my senses, and I squeeze my eyes shut at the intense pain lancing through my chest at her beauty.

I imagine peeling her dress from her, sliding it down her hips along with her panties, then I'd bend her over the vanity and gag her with her panties while I fuck her cunt ruthlessly.

"Owen?"

My eyes snap open, and she stares back at me. Those emerald orbs that haunt my dreams, scanning my reflection.

"Are you okay?" she repeats.

Okay?

I choke on a sardonic laugh.

How the fuck can I be okay? I'm standing in her bedroom with a raging hard-on. Every part of my body screams to take her, to make her mine. Yet my mind tells me not to do it.

There will be no going back.

I'm not good enough for her.

My best friend would hate me.

She would throw her life away to be with me. I know she would, and ultimately, she would hate me for giving in to this intense craving I have for her.

But in this moment, as she stares back at me with equal longing in her eyes, all my inhibitions slip away, and I simply don't care.

I want her.

LAYA

His gaze holds my heartbeat hostage. He stares at me with such potency I grip the vanity to stabilize myself. How I've longed for his eyes to devour me the way they are right now.

From the moment I set eyes on him, I've loved him, and not in the cute, crush kind of way that's been insinuated repeatedly over the years.

When I was little, my stomach would flutter and my body would tremble with an awareness of his proximity. I'd become his shadow, annoying my brother and his friends to be close to Owen, but I didn't care. No matter how many times they ridiculed him, he never made me feel like an inconvenience. As I grew, my feelings only intensified. The flutters became laced in desire, my trembles became quakes at his touch, and every sly glance he gifted me only gave my mind the reassurance I needed.

He's mine.

My dreams were dedicated to him, my thoughts invaded by him, and my future dictated for him.

I've loved him with every fiber of my being, with every beat of my heart, and every breath I take. Owen James Stevens has always been mine; he's just been too afraid to show it.

Until now.

His eyes bore into me with such reverence it steals my breath from my lungs, causing me to divert my gaze for only a moment, as my eyes are desperate to be back on his handsome face.

His thick thighs cause the fabric of his pants to cling to him, and his white dress shirt is pulled tightly across his shoulders, the top two buttons open, exposing his numerous tattoos, each one symbolic to him. I've memorized them over the years, even going as far as to watch him as he sleeps, sneaking photos of his bare chest and spending hours trailing my finger over the delectable photo as if it was real. Always so out of reach, yet always so close, my protector.

His wrist adorns his signature gold Rolex gifted to him by my parents on his twenty-first birthday, and beneath it sits the multicolored woven bracelet I gave him as a gift when I was fourteen.

He drags one of his thick fingers over his sharp jawline as he assesses me, and I chew on my bottom lip, wondering what he's thinking. Does he have the same lustful thoughts racing through his mind as me, or will he always see me as "Owen's helper" and a little girl?

Forever forbidden.

I turn to face him, and his gaze roams over my dress. My nipples peak with desperation, begging him to take me, and when he swallows thickly and his eyes fill with lust, I know he wants to do just that.

"Do you like my dress?" My voice comes out breathy, and my pulse races with the heightened tension, waiting for a response that never comes.

He releases a low grunt, and I sigh, knowing that's all I will get from him. That's all I ever got from him, never anything more, just the gruff noncommittal noise from somewhere deep in the back of his throat. I spin on my heels to face the mirror again and lift my lipstick as if I didn't just apply it.

All the while, the heat of his stare radiates from him like a furnace.

He steps up behind me, his chest to my back, and I pause with the lipstick midair.

Then he pushes his hard length against me, forcing my heart to still. "That answer your question?" His gravelly voice sends desire flooding through me, and Jesus, his cock is hard because of me.

I swallow, then he slides his thick hand around my throat, and my entire body freezes, shocked by his commanding touch. His touch a whisper against my skin, but still, it's there, he's there, touching me like never before.

The fire in my belly ignites, and a glimmer of the hope I always had sparks, creating a determination like no other.

I want him, and judging by his rock-hard cock digging into my back, he wants me too.

"Owen?"

"Shhh," he breathes into my neck, trailing his nose into my hair, forcing my heart to race as I watch him in the mirror. His eyes are hooded, his shoulders tense, and a tremble escapes him. That makes me realize how much he's holding back, and I revel in the thought.

He withdraws a box from his slacks and flips the lid, then pushes my hair to one side. With trembly fingers, he settles a beautiful white-gold necklace around my neck and an emerald pendant falls from it. Emotion overcomes me as my fingers graze over the stone—it's beautiful.

"You're beautiful, baby. So fucking beautiful it hurts." His admission makes my eyes fill with tears. His words, his actions, they're everything I've ever wanted and so, so much more.

He uses his body to cage me in, with one hand on my hip. His eyes are full of craving, his muscles coiled tight, and as his hand moves to cup my jaw, I jolt at his firmer touch. His blue eyes snap to mine as if seeking approval, and I bite into my bottom lip, forcing his focus there. Then his thumb plucks it from between my teeth where he leaves it resting. He slides his thumb back and forth over my lip, and when he swipes the lipstick roughly from my lips, my mouth falls open. Then he brings his thumb to his mouth and sucks on it, our eyes never straying from one another's.

OWEN

Two years later, she still tastes like cherries. The first time she stuck her tongue down my throat, I had to push her jailbait ass away, but she tasted of cherries then too. I gift the soft skin of her neck with a gentle kiss and her pulse races beneath it. I revel in the effect I have on her.

"Are your panties wet?"

She shudders at my words, and I smile as I kiss down her neck.

"I'm not wearing any." My lips still as I freeze, then lift my head to search her face in the mirror for a hint of a lie.

My cock leaks as I trail my hand from her hip over the fabric of her flimsy dress and down to her thigh. She sucks in a sharp breath when I slide it between us and over her firm ass. Then I push my hand under the material, ignoring the flash of goose bumps that erupt over her skin at my touch.

"Open your legs," I whisper into her neck, and shuffle back, allowing her the room to accommodate my demand. Her legs part, and I slip my thick, tattooed fingers between her thighs. Wetness coats my skin as I stroke over her slick pussy lips, and I hiss at her dripping arousal coating my fingers. Liquid heat surges through my veins at her desire. I strum her clit and relish the whimpers she makes as she pushes her ass against my cock.

My fingers twitch to push inside her, to feel her tight little cunt wrap around them, but my cock is more eager, determined to succeed in the war raging inside me.

I've already crossed so many lines tonight. The moment I stepped into her room being one of them, and now with her pussy juice on my fingers and her ass thrusting against my cock, I know I'm about to cross more.

There will be no coming back after crossing this boundary.

"Please, Owen …" The sound of her begging is so beautiful, so enticing and imploring, it sends a tidal wave of ownership through my veins.

"Who owns this cunt, Laya?" I grip her pussy and blow into her ear, delighting in the stuttered pant that leaves her perfect lips.

"You."

"That's right, beautiful baby girl. I own this little cunt." I strum her clit again, gifting her with my appraisal.

She licks her lips, which forces my balls to ache with a feral need for her I can no longer control, and a growl erupts from me.

"I saved it for you." Her eyes glisten with uncertainty, the weight of them holding a thousand wishes, each begging for me, and fuck, does she have me by the fucking balls. By my heart thundering in my chest, she has me.

Her words smother me, causing a cough to lodge in my

throat. "What?" Surely, she's not saying what I think she's saying.

"I saved my virginity for you, Owen." Her tongue darts over her bottom lip while my fingers rest on her pussy. "You were my first kiss; I want you to be my first everything."

Dumbfounded by her admittance, I squeeze my eyes closed. "Jesus, fuck, Laya," I choke out.

She doesn't know what she's asking, not from a man like me, and yet I want to be that man. Jealousy consumes me at the thought of anyone else experiencing her body when it's meant to be mine. *Mine.*

She turns in my arms, and my eyes fly open. My fingers slip away but remain wet from her arousal. Then she raises up on her tiptoes and wraps her arms around my neck. I stand there, frozen, unable to move a damn muscle because every one of them is wound painfully tight by her touch.

"I want your cock inside me, Owen."

My tongue sweeps out to dampen my dry lips, and she watches it. Her eyes become heavy, then her lips touch mine, her tongue seeking entrance, and I allow it.

Each gentle swipe is like torture as I allow her to explore my mouth, not moving a goddamn inch to encourage her.

She pulls back, but my lips follow hers before I stop myself, the thin thread between us becoming more frayed by the millisecond. "Touch me, Owen." Her hand slides between us, and my pulse quickens as she wraps her palm around my solid cock over my slacks.

As she strokes it, my fingers somehow become tangled in her hair, holding her in place as my lips meet hers again, and this time, it's me forcing my tongue into her mouth, me showing my consumption, my control.

She moans, and a surge of pleasure zips up my spine, the sound so intoxicating it seems surreal. "Harder," I grit out as she pumps me.

"Please, I need to feel you."

"Jesus. You don't know what you're asking for, Laya." I pull back, breathless and dazed, staring into her green orbs.

"I do. I want it." She squeezes me. "All of it. I want it to hurt, Owen. I want to feel you when I walk. I want every inch of my body to ache like my mind does without you. Burn me from the inside out."

I brush a wave of hair behind her ear. I need her to know I'm not like other men and don't do slow, meaningful fucking. "I won't just burn you, baby girl. I'll scar."

Her pupils dilate. "Then scar me. My body is your canvas to paint with your marks."

She fumbles with my belt, and fuck, I let her. Then she pops open the button of my slacks, and I snap my hand out to grip her wrist.

"Take your dress off."

She complies eagerly, letting her dress slip to the floor, then I bend and lift her by her ass. Her smooth legs wrap around me as I walk her over to the bed, all while breathing in her scent, her need for me, and I could drown in it.

I lay her on the bed and pull back to stand. Her eyes flash with a vulnerability I hate, but I pause to take her in. Her beauty is unimaginable. The way her chest rises and her nipples peak have me tugging my belt from my slacks. Then I turn, ignoring her soft whimper, and walk toward her bedroom door to flick the lock. Taking a deep breath, I exhale as I fight the ever-internal battle with myself.

Walk away! my mind screams.

There's no going back from this. My heart drums.

I spin to face her, and all the air is stolen from my lungs.

Make her yours.

LAYA

He stands at the foot of the bed; his sharp stare penetrates me with such desire that heat travels up and over my neck. Achingly slowly, his gaze roams over me, from head to toe, as if memorizing every inch of me. The longing in his eyes is imperative, sending a shiver and surge of arousal through my body. Has his need for me always been so great, and only now I am seeing it?

I watch with rapture as he disrobes and kicks his clothes to the side until all that remains is the folded belt in his hand.

"Open your legs."

His stare lands on my pussy, and he licks his lips, the lips which devoured me after waiting a lifetime for their willing touch.

"Put your hands on your ankles, Laya, and pull your legs up."

I move on his command, thrusting my legs up and holding them open.

"This what you want?" He fists his cock with his free

hand, and my breath catches. All my dreams are finally my reality, yet my mind can't play catch-up. "Fucking answer!"

"Ye-yes."

"Yes, what?"

"Yes, please."

"Fuck, yes," he grunts as his hips work in time with his fist. "I'm going to come on you, Laya. Would you like that, baby girl? For me to come on you?"

Oh, dear god. I want it so badly I can barely construct words.

"Ye-yes."

"Of course you would." He steps closer and raises the belt. Then before I can dispute it, the sharpness of the leather hitting my pussy makes my back arch off the mattress. "Always teasing me with your tight little ass." The veins on his neck protrude, and he slaps the leather against me again, the burn overwhelming as I squeeze my eyes shut but snap them open just as quick, not wanting to miss a damn thing. "Those perfect tits begging to be marked." His shoulders pull tight, and his jaw sharpens as if angry before slapping me harder, causing me to cry out. "Tormenting me." Holy shit, he admitted he wanted me too. I bite into my lip as another searing lash hits my bare flesh.

"Like fucking torture, not touching you," he grits out with such hatred that guilt slices through me at the turmoil I caused him. I welcome this lash; I take it willingly, if only to take away a sliver of his pain.

He throws the belt to the floor and kneels onto the bed. Then he sits back on his heels between my legs, and I raise my head to watch him jerk his cock. Pre-cum coats the bulging vein running up his length, and the thick head is purple, looking painful as his desire slides from his slit. "Fuck, yeah. Watch me coat your pussy with my cum, baby girl."

Sweat coats his forehead as his fist works faster and faster, and all I can do is watch with hungry eyes at his eagerness as streams of pre-cum land on my pussy, increasing the arousal leaking from me.

My pussy burns from his belt, but as my arousal slips from me, I crave his thickness. "I need you inside me, Owen. I want you to come inside me."

"Fucking Jesus," he hisses as his cum shoots from the tip of his engorged cock. The look of ecstasy on his face is like something I have never witnessed before. Every thought I ever dreamed, every stolen moment, nothing could have prepared me for his look. I'll never forget it. Pure, unadulterated rapture coats every feature of his perfectly handsome face, and I commit it to memory, to keep it forever.

As his breathing regulates, his eyes meet mine. My heart thuds with nervousness. Is this the moment he leaves?

He drops, resting his elbow at the side of my head, our eyes locking and our mouths a hairsbreadth apart. "You still want this?" He drags the tip of his cock through his cum and down to my hole where it rests at my entrance, teasing me with a promise of things to come.

"More than anything," I whisper.

His soft lips find mine, and one palm holds my head in place while he uses the other to guide himself inside me.

He swallows my whine as I wince at the intrusion, my vagina struggling to accommodate him.

He's big compared to any man I've seen in the porn I've watched, but it's given me a good indication on the size of a man's dick, and Owen is something else. I spent my teen years stalking him and watching him fuck other women—always on the sidelines, wanting more, hoping for more, but never being enough.

"You're too good for me, baby girl."

I move to shake my head and argue, but his hand holds me firmly. "But you're going to take every fucking inch of this cock like a good girl. Do you understand?"

"Yes."

He glares at me. "Yes, fucking what?"

"Yes, please."

He nods, seemingly happy with my response, then draws his hips back and surges deep inside me. My back arches off the bed on a choked scream, and his pupils dilate. A feral look of ownership crosses over him as he slams his thick cock through the barrier. "Fuck, I could come already. Your perfect little cunt is squeezing me so tight."

I moan his loss when he slides his cock out to the tip. "You see that?" I glance between us, his cock coated in a mixture of our arousal and my blood. I nod.

"Your pussy is mine, do you hear? Your blood is on my cock, mine. You've marked me too, baby girl." He grips my chin between his fingers, forcing my eyes on him. The enormity of what we've done feels monumental. We've claimed one another, not just with our bodies, but with our hearts too. "Do you understand?"

"Yes," I utter.

"Good girl. I'm going to come inside you, okay?"

"Ye-yes."

He settles above me once again, then narrows his eyes. "Are you still on the pill?"

Something about that makes my gut twist, but being too overwhelmed at finally getting what I've always wanted has me banishing the thought just as quickly as it came.

"Laya, hanging on by a thread here, baby. Are you on the pill?" His eyes implore mine.

"Ye-yes."

"Thank fuck." He slams his lips against mine as his cock sears into me. Each slam harder than the last as his thrusts increase speed with each moan I cry. Each one an aphrodisiac to the last. "I'll never get enough of you, baby." His words burn into my soul, bringing with it the solitude I've always wished for, yet only ever dreamed about achieving.

My hand finds his jaw, and I hold his mouth against mine, desperate not to let him slip away, to taste this moment, treasure it, and never let it leave me. My free hand clings to his powerful shoulders, my nails piercing his skin, yet I've no choice but to hold on and hope to never let go.

The slapping of our skin fills the room as his body brands me as his. "Fuck, so goddamn good." I preen at his words. "So goddamn mine."

I belong to him: my heart, soul, and now my body too.

Flurries of sparks swirl deep inside me, threatening to ignite into a torrent of flames with each twirl of his hips, each powerful slam of his cock, and each growl of his ownership. I moan into his mouth as our tongues tangle, our passion colliding into something prolific.

"Fuck. I'm going to come," he grunts as my walls

clamp around him like a vise. "I'm going to come, Laya." As his cock hits me deeper, he groans. "Tell me you're mine." The slam of his body is more forceful than the last. "Tell me," he growls, sending a shiver down my spine as my wetness spills between us.

"I'm yours." *I've always been yours*, I want to add.

"Fuck, you're coating my cock, Laya. Fucking beautiful, baby." Then he moves and stares down at his cock pistoning in and out of me, his gaze flicking back to my throat, and I know what he wants. I've witnessed it so many times before.

"Do it," I encourage, my eyes searing him with the same desire coursing through our connected bodies.

His eyes flare and the cords of his muscles appear taught, as if he's struggling, but then he wraps both hands around my throat and presses. I give myself over to him, trusting him wholeheartedly because my wounded warrior would never hurt me or break me.

His thrusts become erratic, and when a moan vibrates around his hands, his fingertips flex and his mouth drops open. A choked grunt escapes him as he stares at me through heavy eyes, then his cock pulsates deep inside me, taking me over the edge with him.

Our gazes are locked as I float into the abyss with him, the pleasure so overwhelmingly good I never want to be grounded again. He slows his pace, as if draining the last of his energy along with his cum.

Heavy breaths fill the room as he eases his hands from around my neck, and just like that, his face falls, as if realization hit him.

When his eyes flash with vulnerability and hurt, I

know I've lost him and that this night will become a scarred memory.

His fingers tremble as they graze over what I can only guess are the marks left behind by his fingers, and he rears back as if electrocuted.

"Fuck." He tugs on the back of his neck. "Fuck!" he bellows, staring up at the ceiling. While his cock remains deep inside me, his panicked expression sends a ripple of uncertainty through me.

When he drops his head forward again, his bottom lip wobbles, and my heart shatters.

He regrets it.

"Owen?"

He shakes his head and bites into his lip, then after a moment, he clears his throat. "I didn't mean to hurt you."

He thinks he hurt me. That's why he's reacting this way?

"You didn't." I'm quick to reassure him, so eager to keep him.

He shakes his head again, as if banishing my response, then slides out of me, and I can't help the wince that falls from my lips.

His eyes draw up toward mine, and he licks over his top teeth. "Exactly," he says, as if receiving the confirmation he needed.

"Everyone hurts a little when they lose their virginity, Owen," I bite back as he storms toward the bathroom door.

He reappears just as quickly, and I can tell with the furious gleam in his eyes that I've lost him, and the thought sends my stomach plummeting. "Does everyone have marks around their neck too?" he snipes out, throwing his hand out toward me.

My fingers find my neck while he throws a washcloth onto the bed, pissing me off with his behavior.

"Can you not be such an ass, Owen?"

He pulls his bottom lip between his teeth as steam practically blows from his ears, and I wipe away our cum coating my thighs.

"Not be such an ass?" My eyes snap to his. "I just fucked you raw, Laya. My best friend's little sister, while choking you out. Not to mention, I took your virginity." He scoops up his clothes and dumps them on the bed, then he buttons his shirt as if desperate to leave the room.

"You didn't do anything I didn't want." I shrug, my eyes pleading with him to see I want this.

"Right. Congratulations, you got what you wanted." He finishes buttoning his slacks, and I try not to cry with the way he's speaking to me.

Owen is never angry with me; he's always made me feel like he has all the time in the world for me, like we're in our own bubble. He's protected me from my brother's taunts and mindless teenagers bitching. He's always shown me he cared, even if it wasn't in the way I wanted.

My eyes narrow in on him, the way he's dismissing me and what we did as if it meant nothing, when only moments ago he told me I was his everything. Fury spikes inside me. "I don't want you to be an ass about it."

He scoffs and shakes his head again.

"We can speak to Tate. He'll understand."

He buckles his belt, and when he turns to face me, my soul crumbles into a thousand pieces. "You and me both know that's not going to happen."

My lip wobbles as emotion swirls through my veins, sending my heart into turmoil. "Wh-what do you mean?"

His eyes, usually so full of fun and laughter, are cold and calculating. "This was a one-time thing, Laya. You know that as much as I do."

I fist the sheet, tugging it toward me like a blanket of comfort to protect me against his words.

He slips his feet into his shoes and adjusts his watch, covering my bracelet once again, covering my existence.

I sit, frozen in shock at how I gave him my everything and he happily stole it from me.

"Make sure you cover the marks." He nods toward my neck, then turns and walks to the bedroom door, leaving me stunned as my eyes lock onto the blood-streaked sheets.

"And Laya?" He glances over his shoulder, his face void of emotion. "Put some fucking panties on."

Then, with a slam of the bedroom door, he's gone, destroying me.

My fingers tremble as I toy with the necklace and try to remain strong.

I know him.

This is not him.

He's running scared.

He'd never hurt me intentionally, and the thought of him losing my brother became too much for him to bear. That must be it.

Owen James Stevens told me I am his everything, and I believe him.

Taking another glance in the mirror, I double-check to make sure his finger marks are covered with the concealer.

My mom texted to let me know everyone was waiting for me to make an appearance. I bite into my lip at the ache between my thighs, a dull throb that reminds me of where the man I adore was only twenty minutes ago.

I'm determined to turn this night around. It's been momentous for me. I finally got what I've always wanted. Now I need to get him on board with it too. Taking a deep breath, I steel myself. This birthday will be one to remember for more than what just happened. It's the beginning of my future, our future.

I pull open the door, and as I walk toward the stairs, the guests erupt into claps, hoots, and whistles, party poppers go off, and my favorite song, "Black Magic" by Little Mix, fills the foyer as I beam at my mom's party organizing skills.

As I descend the staircase, my eyes lock onto Owen, and I pause mid-step. He has a woman tucked under his arm, her straight blonde hair and pale skin the complete opposite of me. He doesn't pay me any attention as he places a kiss on her forehead while she smiles back at him with a love-struck gaze. A gaze I recognize well, the same gaze on my face whenever I'm around him. My blood runs cold. How the hell can he stand to be around another woman when he just fucked me? My lip wobbles, and I try to shake their image from my mind, but it's stuck there, squeezing tightly at my chest while the background noise of celebration goes off around me.

A loud noise snaps my attention toward my father when he hits a microphone. "We're all here tonight to celebrate our beautiful girl turning eighteen. We're so incredible proud of you, Laya." Claps and shouts of "Happy Birthday" flood my ears, yet the whooshing sound of the turmoil of my heart is louder. "We also have another celebration tonight." I dart my gaze toward my younger brother, Dex. He stares back at me with concern, his eyes narrowed and scanning over me. We've always been close, so in tune with one another, as if we're from the same blood and not adopted. He knows my inner thoughts, my dreams, my obsession, and when I see his fists pump beside him, I know he knows something happened with Owen. I give my head a subtle shake, and he sighs. "Tonight, one of our boys has gotten engaged." I turn my focus toward Tate, who grins like an idiot. Nope, there's no way he's engaged. The guy is a manchild. Then I move to Shaw. He's not officially my brother, but my parents have always welcomed him as such with him being one of Tate's best friends. They all fall under the same umbrella as far as my parents are concerned. They're family. It's what always made me believe it would be easier than Owen expected for us to become an official couple. My family already loves him. "Congratulations, Owen and Samantha!"

I cling to the banister, but my knees buckle. My heart is torn from my body, leaving me a shell and unable to function. The room feels like it's spinning as I struggle to suck in air, the crushing pain in my chest too much to bear when all I want to do is scream and plead for help. I squeeze my eyes shut at the heartache, trying and failing to regain control. A loud noise erupts, and I snap my eyes open to witness Dex fly toward Owen, landing a punch at his jaw while my ass drops onto the red carpet.

Devastation, betrayal, and heartbreak rack through me.

All of it hits simultaneously as I struggle to breathe, my mind spinning with a tsunami of flashbacks. Every touch and smile he reserved solely for me has become debris. Nothing more than dust floating away like it never existed.

He was never mine.

It's clear now; I was just a fantasy he played out. He used me and discarded me like I meant nothing to him at all.

I gave him my heart, and he destroyed it. The flames that burned between us become ash as I stare through the bars of the banister and our gazes lock. The impact behind his stare causes a jolt deep in my chest, a scar lancing my heart. He's right, he's scarred me. Then her hand guides his face toward hers, and he allows it. Their lips touch while mine quivers.

He's gone.

My hand finds the necklace sitting like a weight around my neck, and I will myself to snap it away from me, to break it like he's broken me. But I can't because I love him.

I love him, and it hurts so much.

He was meant to be my everything, but he never will be.

OWEN

I cling to the counter and breathe through my nose, trying yet failing to regulate my breathing. A technique taught to me during my therapy sessions as a child, something that worked well until now.

"What the fuck is going on?" One of my best friends, Mase, storms into the kitchen, but I can't face him. I can't face anyone. "Since when were you getting engaged? And to Samantha? Did you learn nothing from my mistakes?" I can feel the anger emanating from him, but I'm unable to respond. I squeeze my eyes closed to the point of pain. All I can see is her heartbroken face, the look of resolution hurting more than the tears that spilled from those shimmering orbs.

I did that.

I caused her pain when I promised myself I'd never hurt her.

"Owen!" he barks, and I snap my eyes open to stare back at him.

Disappointment is etched on his face, and I hate that I

put it there. My only family are my brothers and best friends, and they're everything to me, but Laya, she's my fucking world.

"What are you doing, man?" His tone is softer. "You're breaking her heart," he mutters, and for the first time, he's letting me know he's aware of how I feel about Laya, even though I worked so damn hard to make sure nobody ever knew.

My mouth becomes dry, and I lick my lips, unsure of how much to divulge. "Her mom said she was offered a scholarship to Miami. She turned it down." Mase nods, as if aware of this already. "I know she turned it down because of me."

He leans closer. "Does it matter? She's wanted you forever, man, and no matter how much you think you hide it, you want her too."

"I want her to have a fucking life, Mase. Outside of me." I scrub a hand over my cropped hair. "Everything she does, she makes sure it's pleasing me."

He nods. "The girl is obsessed, I get it, but she loves you, Owen, and you love her too."

"You don't think I fucking know that?" My voice gets louder. "Do you really think I want to marry Samantha?" Her name on my tongue is bitter, and I wince when I become too loud, then lower my tone. "I don't want to hurt her, Mase." My voice is solemn this time, and even I flinch at the defeat in it.

"So, what? You push her away. I never saw you as a coward, Owen," he snaps, and I want to lash out, but I stop myself, knowing I wouldn't be able to stop, not when my emotions are so out of control.

OWEN

I grind my jaw and exhale. "I hurt her." I hold his stare, and he swallows.

"What?"

Tilting my head up to the ceiling, I exhale before settling back on him. "I hurt her, Mase."

His eyes flash with worry, and he shuffles from side to side. "How, Owen?" he snipes out, his concern for Laya, the girl who has always been like our little sister, shining through.

"I …" I can't find the words to say it. Instead, I say the one thing he'll understand. "My father."

His shoulders fall lax.

The kitchen door swings open, and Tate comes storming in, making me gulp.

Oh Jesus, does he know?

Oh fuck, I'm going to lose him too. I will lose everything.

"Why the fuck did Dex punch you?" His furious eyes flick over me, his body coiled tight like a viper waiting to pounce as he bounces on the balls of his feet.

My brain seems to be broken as it stumbles to piece together an excuse as to why Dex took his anger out on me.

Mase steps forward. "He has a thing for Samantha. Jealous, I guess." He shrugs. "Kids."

Tate reels back, and the anger in his face dissipates within seconds. "He does?"

Mase glances at me, then back to Tate. "Yeah, I think Owen is just as surprised as you are."

From the corner of my eye, I see Tate wince while I stare ahead, determined not to give away any of my emotions, the anguish inside me threatening to spill over.

"Shit. Sorry, man." He slaps me on the back, and I close

my eyes at his touch. The fact we're lying to one of the best men I know, betraying him like this, sits heavy inside my stomach, and the fact I screwed his little sister has bile rising in my throat in waves of guilt.

I'm so fucked.

I grip the counter tighter, my legs threatening to give way.

Like hers did.

The agony of knowing that makes it difficult for me to remain standing.

"And you kept the engagement a secret. Fuck, who'd have thought you'd be the first to get hitched? Congratulations, man." He steps back and focuses on the door to the foyer. "I'll catch up with you guys later. I need to check on Laya." I stiffen at her name. "Mom said she had a panic attack, probably been worshipped too much for one night." He chuckles, and in the reflection of the window, I see his eyes roll at what he thinks is Laya's dramatics. Not understanding my poor girl is hurting, and worse, I caused it.

"Catch you later." Mase gives him a chin lift while I can barely grunt in his direction.

As soon as the door closes, Mase steps closer. "Owen, please. As someone who has a lifetime of regret, don't let Laya be yours." He sighs heavily when I don't respond and heads toward the door. How the hell can I respond to that?

She will never be a mistake, even if I let her think she is. I know that deep in her heart, she won't believe that. Never.

And I refuse to be hers.

My head spins as I unravel. I did it. I walked away and

destroyed the only woman I will ever love. The only person to ever truly see me, yet she wanted me anyway.

The door closes behind him, and I sink to the floor.

I've destroyed the only thing good in my life. My body shakes uncontrollably, and I squeeze my eyes closed while dropping my head in my hands. Her emerald eyes flash before me, and my heart seizes in my chest, forcing me to suck in sharp stuttered breaths. Every moment we were together, every smile we shared, her laugh, every touch we ever had, her whimpers and moans, will forever be scarred in my mind. Forged in a love that only we share. A place in time where only we belonged.

Burned into my memory, engrained into my soul, Laya Kavanagh will remain my everything.

And I will forever remain in the darkness, loving her from a distance for an eternity.

ONE

LAYA

AGED TWENTY-ONE …

Scanning the club, I scrunch my nose. This is not what I wanted tonight, not at all. But Brynn is determined for us to celebrate my birthday in style, so she flirted with every guy she knew, screwed the barman, and now, here we are.

When I applied for colleges, I decided to forgo my maiden name and opted to use Jones. I didn't want to get offers based on my money and parentage, so I kept my life back home a secret, just like him.

Miami is everything I expected it to be: glitz, glamour, and money, yet I pretend I have none. Instead, I'm making my own way, forging my own path while erasing my past and carving out my future.

"Can you believe this place?" Brynn shouts, and I feign

happiness and deliver her a smile. "This club is amazing. Am I the greatest bestie in the whole world, or am I the greatest bestie in the universe?" She flutters her lashes, and I throw my head back on a laugh.

"You're the greatest bestie in the whole world."

Her grin is infectious, and she holds a champagne flute up toward me. "Drink up, we got the entire bottle." Her eyes light up with excitement, and I laugh. If only she knew I could easily afford the champagne we're consuming if I allowed myself access to my account set up by my parents.

Crossing my legs the other way, I try to relax, when inside, I'd rather not be here. I spent all day checking my phone, hoping for a birthday text from Owen, which never came. I'm tempted to check my purse again, just in case, but that reoccurring anger whenever I think of him flares inside me. God, I'm pathetic. I drink the champagne down in one gulp, making Brynn's face break out into a playful smile. "Yes, girl!" she hoots, throwing her fist into the air.

Slowly, her ass finds her chair again, and her mouth falls open. "Oh fuck, don't look now. Don't look now," she chants while darting her eyes all over the club and pouring champagne into my glass, but it sloshes over the side and spills onto the table, as her focus remains elsewhere. "There's this guy checking us out. He's in the fucking *VIP* section, Laya." Her eyes bug out, and I giggle at her reaction. Again, if only she knew. "Holy shit, he's coming down here." She fidgets from side to side, then smooths out her blonde hair. "Do I look okay?"

I bite into my bottom lip. "You look hot!" Her shoulders relax, and I smile at her as I take another sip of the champagne. VIP or not, my friend deserves a good time.

She's worked her ass off to get where she is, coming from a shitty home with junkie parents. She works two jobs to help pay for her college tuition. At the end of the semester, she will discover her tuition has been paid by an anonymous donor—me.

"Ladies, would you like to join us upstairs?" A smooth voice caresses my skin, and for the first time in a long time, my heart skips a beat, and I draw my eyes up to meet those of a drop-dead gorgeous guy. His Brioni suit fits him like a glove, tailored to his specification and showcasing his physique. The smell of his sandalwood aftershave sends my head woozy, and when I latch onto his caramel eyes, a dull ache throbs between my legs. His gaze drills into mine, waiting for a response. His dark hair is slicked back, his olive skin practically glistens, showing me how well-groomed he is, and his sharp jawline makes me want to track it with my fingertips. The man is stunning, and my ovaries agree.

"Abso-freakin-lutely!" Brynn exclaims, and I want to punch her in the lady balls for how desperate she's making us appear.

He tilts his head at me.

Brynn jumps up from her seat and takes hold of my arm, tugging me to stand. "She wants to come, don't you, Laya?"

Then I part my lips to speak, but his voice holds me captive me. "Laya? Beautiful, mi querida."

I can't help the scoff that erupts from me. "I'm not your darling."

His lips twitch. "Mm, you don't realize it yet, mi novia."

The Spanish rolls off his tongue like silk, and I can't help but quip back, "I'm not your girl either."

He throws his head back on a deep chuckle that has me smiling. "Come, Gonghu." He speaks in Mandarin, then holds out his hand to help me stand. When I slide mine into his, a flurry of excitement fills the empty void of longing as he pulls me toward him. His eyes flash with hunger, and this time, it's not unwelcome.

"Princess I can get on board with." I wink and drop his hand, then stroll past him, giving a little extra sway to my hips as I climb the stairs.

"What the hell? I didn't know you could speak other languages." Brynn's eyes bug out as she whisper-yells in my ear, making me giggle.

"There's a lot you don't know about me."

"Right." Her shoulders sag, and guilt hits me, so I stop and turn to face her.

"I'm sorry. One day, we will have a really good chat."

Her solemn face glances over my shoulder. "We do. The scary one is into you, typical." His eyes eat me up, causing heat to flush over my skin. "I liked him," she admits, then shakes her head. "It's your birthday, you have him." I choke on a laugh at her words, the way she speaks as if she's giving him to me when the connection between us is like a spark of electricity about to set alight.

The hot guy speaks to someone who looks like security or a bodyguard, given his thick build, instantly reminding me of Owen. I shake my head. I need something different, and this guy might just be what I need.

He nods toward Brynn, and I narrow my eyes, but when the bigger guy licks his lips, I smile because Brynn bagged herself a hot guy too. She just doesn't know it yet.

OWEN

We crash into the hotel room, and I try to tear his shirt from his chest while he lifts my dress and grabs my ass, leaving me with no choice but to wrap my legs around him. His fingers brush over my panties, stroking my wet heat, and I moan into his mouth with ferocity as our tongues scramble for control.

After learning my hunk, Carlos Andreas, was the owner of the club we were dancing in, Brynn puckered her lips and threw more disapproving glances my way. Thankfully, the guy from earlier made an appearance and whisked her off to the dance floor, leaving Carlos and me together. Something tells me it was an orchestrated plan, but I didn't have it in me to care. For once, I was actually enjoying attention from the opposite sex, and the fact he was gorgeous helped.

Carrying me over to the bed, he lays me down. He undresses while I pull my dress over my head. A gnawing feeling in the pit of my stomach tells me not to continue, but when an image of Owen with his fiancée flashes in my mind, I shake away the thought. They're no longer engaged, but I'm also all too aware of how many women Owen will have slept with by now—before and after he took my virginity like I was just another random girl. He fed me the lies I wanted to hear and did it spectacularly.

"Don't think about him. Just think about me." His soft lips nip at my skin, and his words pull me from my head.

Like a fool, I told Carlos I had underlying feelings for someone in my past, and to save his time, he might as well not bother pursuing me. He threw his head back on a loud laugh that startled me, then looked me in the eye and told me he was taking me to bed tonight.

Another bottle into the bucket of champagnes he ordered, and here I am, my body and mind at war with one another as his fingers continue to caress my pussy.

The bubbles from earlier have me dropping my inhibitions, but not enough to deem me not coherent. Of course I want him; he's gorgeous, successful, charming, and I'm a girl who longs to forget.

When he slides inside me, I cry out at the intrusion. Only having been taken once before over three years ago.

"Fuck, you're strangling my cock, mi amor." I dig my nails into his back, and he hisses as he thrusts inside me to the hilt.

When his fingers stroke over my throbbing clit, I've no choice but to lift my hips in motion with his so we buck against one another. "The most beautiful girl I've set my eyes on." His words wash over me as I try to banish the thoughts of Owen ravishing my mind, the dull ache when I think of him always there. Carlos lifts my leg to slide in deeper, and I feel it. Right in my soul, I feel it. Every part of me screams to stop this, that I'm betraying the man I love. Yet I know he doesn't love me back, not how I want him to, at least.

I close my eyes to lose myself in the sensations waving through my body. Bright-blue eyes flash before me, and my pussy clenches around him.

"That's right, mi amor, come on my cock." His smooth baritone voice feels like a bucket of cold water spilling over me, a reminder of who it is fucking me. The deep feral gruffness is missing, the weight of his heavy body absent as the void inside me remains just that. When I hoped Carlos would be the one to fill it, I know deep in my heart he never could.

The edge now feeling so much further away.

Carlos stills, and when I snap my eyes open, caramel eyes filled with lust roam over my face. "What did he call you in bed?"

"Wh-what?"

"The man you're in love with. What did he call you in bed?"

I turn my head away as a tear slides down my cheek. "Baby girl," I whisper.

When I think he's going to pull out, he surprises me by rearing back and slamming inside me harder than before. "Pretend it's him fucking you, baby girl." His grunts of pleasure fill the room and his hips begin to work again. "Fuck, baby girl. So damn good." My body betrays me as his words filter into my mind. With each thrust and swivel of his hips, I become wetter, and my pussy responds, clenching around him until I pulsate deep inside. "Fuck, yes. Yes, baby girl, give it to me."

My mouth falls open on a silent scream, and I squeeze the cum from his cock. He spills inside me while staring into my eyes, holding me hostage and forcing the air from my lungs.

He doesn't withdraw his cock, and for that, I'm grateful. Instead, he rolls us so I am on his chest. "I'm going to make you fall in love with me," he declares, and I chuckle into his chest while resting my head on the beat of his heart until it becomes steady and the soft sound of him snoozing fills the room.

A vibrating noise startles me, and I sit up, taking the sheet with me as I lean over the bed to grab my purse. I pull my phone out, and when I see the message on the screen, my heart plummets.

DOUCHE: Happy Birthday, baby girl. Always.

I drop my phone onto my purse as devastation racks through me, and I try to stifle the sob lodged in the back of my throat.

"Come back to me, mi amor." Carlos's sleepy voice makes my body pause, and when he tugs me toward him, I fall into his chest, ignoring the wetness coating my cheek and the sickness welling inside me.

His grip on me tightens. "You're mine now, baby girl."

His words hold a finality behind them that makes my blood still. It's a vow, a promise, one that tells me my life will never be the same.

TWO

OWEN

OVER A YEAR LATER ...

I'm sitting around the Kavanaghs' dining table, hating every minute of being here. Her absence has left a deep crevice in everyone's heart, along with a well of misery in mine.

"How old are the children you have staying here?" Emi, Shaw's new wife, asks.

Tate's parents have had an ever-revolving door of foster children over the years. After adopting Tate, Laya, and Dex from shitty backgrounds, they open their house up every summer to kids needing a break from the system. I glance out toward the patio and take in what they must see: a mansion with beautifully manicured lawns, tennis courts, a vast swimming pool, and a boating lake. They have a gym, a dance studio, a spa. This house is incredible, but it's more than that. Steph and Mark have made it a home, and we sure as hell have used it as such.

"Anywhere from four to eighteen," Steph replies, while I shove another forkful of vegetables into my mouth. Since my mom passed away, she's become the closest thing to a mother I have, and as much as I appreciate her home-cooked food, being here when Laya isn't and knowing I'm the cause of her absence makes the food sit like a heavy brick in my stomach.

The front door slamming shut has Steph shooting up from her chair and rushing toward the entrance as if she's expecting someone.

Hushed voices filter through from the foyer, and a prickle of awareness invades me. She's here. My heart hammers.

She's fucking here.

Shit, she's here.

I try to regulate my breathing, and each click of her heels heading in our direction has my heart thudding louder, and I will it to slow down, convinced everyone else can hear the deep thrumming filling my ears.

"Mom, it's fine. Jeez, stop fussing." Her soft voice forces me to suck in a deep breath while I try my best to keep my face impassive.

"Here we fucking go," Dex grumbles, making my eyes narrow on the little prick. He throws an arm over the back of the chair beside him, then glances at me and winks.

My eyebrows furrow. What the fuck is he going on about?

The moment she steps foot in the room, every muscle

on my body becomes taught. Jesus, my body is so in tune with her presence, it's like the ability to function is stolen from me.

My hand trembles as I bring my fork to my mouth, and I stare straight ahead, determined to keep this simple and my head on straight. I refuse to give away how I feel inside, like a fucking wrecking ball.

"Laya, this is Emi. Shaw's wife. Emi, this is my daughter, Laya." Steph introduces Laya to Emi.

"I'm sorry. I didn't know you were married, Shaw," Laya says, and I balk at that. Of course she doesn't fucking know, she's never here. Then, during her college breaks, she chooses to be anywhere but here.

"You wouldn't fucking know. You're never home," I grumble, unable to help myself.

"Well, I'm here now, and I have news." I squeeze my eyes shut on her soft voice. Why the fuck does it have to hurt so damn much?

"What news? Is everything okay?" Mark asks, and my eyes snap open.

"I'm married."

Gasps fill the table, then it falls silent. Instead of paying her the attention she craves, I shovel another forkful of green beans into my mouth, choosing to ignore the pain lancing through my chest like it doesn't exist.

Denial.

"And there's more." Her voice drones on while I try to control the rage inside me, the blood surging through my veins at an alarming speed.

"I'm pregnant!"

I pause with my fork midair.

Did she just say she's pregnant?

"What the fuck, Laya?" Tate explodes from his chair, and I'm unable to breathe, the room closing in around me, my chest caving in. I push back on my chair, sending it falling to the floor while I push through the clouds in my vision to get outside; I need fresh air. I need to fucking breathe.

She's pregnant.

The cold air hits me, and I reel back on my heels. I've never felt so out of control in my entire life. Sickness wells inside me, bile churning as it rises and sticks in my throat.

I grip onto the balcony railing and feel like I'm falling. "Oh shit." I close my eyes, willing it all to be a dream. "Please! Fuck!" I scream, not caring who hears. Not giving a damn for the first time, not giving a motherfucking damn who knows.

I breathe in through my nose and out of my mouth until the pulsating in my ears dampens and my pulse settles.

"Have you got something to tell me, Owen?" I still at the sound of Tate's firm voice. He's pissed.

But he doesn't know anything. He just suspects because I couldn't keep a lid on my damn emotions.

I suck in a sharp breath and steel my emotions as I turn to face him.

His fists bunch beside him, as if itching for a fight, and I get it. His little sister just announced to the world she's pregnant and married.

Fucking pregnant. Jesus.

Rein it in, Owen, rein it fucking in.

"No." I stare back at him.

"Then why'd you react like that?" He points toward the house, his face twisting.

I wait a moment before replying and school my features, giving myself time to think of the best response I can give him while throwing him off the scent. "I'm pissed. She's knocked up and married, and we haven't even met the guy yet. Aren't you?"

"Yes, of course I'm pissed," he snaps.

Just what the fuck is she playing at? Getting married to someone else? And pregnant? "Makes me wonder what she's hiding. She never brought him to meet you all. Right?"

Tate pauses, and I can see his mind whirling with the questions I just fed him.

He drags a hand over his jaw. "I want to know everything there is to know about him, Owen." And there we have it. He's given me full permission to dig a little deeper into his sister's private life. Like he could have stopped me anyway.

"You'll have it. You'll know everything there is to know about him." I can't hide the venom in my tone. I will leave no stone unturned about the little prick. Then I'm taking her back, taking them both back.

One way or another, I'll make them mine.

Tate sighs, knowing I have the contacts to make shit happen. Hell, I could find out what the prick last ate if I wanted to.

He stares at me blankly, and sweat gathers on my forehead.

It's as if he can read every damn thought and feeling I've ever had regarding Laya, and I hate it. "I'm pleased there's nothing between you and my sister, Owen. Because you don't fucking deserve her." He spins and heads toward the door, sending a familiar churning in my stomach.

"I know," I mutter as I stare at him retreating. "I know," I repeat, as if convincing myself I'm not good enough and every move I made was to cement that for her.

THREE

LAYA

I've spent the last hour explaining to my parents everything they need to know about my relationship and pregnancy. As much as I wish Carlos could have been here with me, I am relieved he isn't. My mom didn't mention that the guys would be here too, but she did say, "Family dinner," so I should have known better. They're all family.

My father excused himself to make some business calls, and now my mom sits beside me, resting her hand on my knee. "Are you happy, honey?" Her question jars me, and concern lies in her question, but I shake it off.

"Yes. I'm happy," I snap back, then feel guilty at the way her face falls. "I'm sorry. It was a big thing for me to face everyone."

"And Carlos couldn't make it?" The question isn't accusing, but my defenses are up, nonetheless.

"No, he's away on business." I keep my answer short

because I don't want the questions, the probing, and the undue concern regarding his business. Something I'm not entirely comfortable with myself but have little choice in.

My mom watches me, as if looking for a sign of uncertainty, something she won't find. Then she blows out a deep breath. "Well, I'm excited for you, honey. Where are you planning on giving birth? I'll make sure I'm on hand around your due date."

My shoulders fall. I want that more than anything, but in all honesty, I don't know where we will be. Carlos keeps his plans close to his chest and never divulges too much. It makes me angsty, but I have no say in it.

I bite into my lip. "I'm not sure."

She tilts her head, again with the fucking analyzing. Then she pats my knee. "Let me know when you figure it out, and I'll be there."

Then she stands and brushes the invisible lint off her skirt. "Owen's outside. You haven't seen him for a while. It would be nice if you went out and said hi."

My gaze flicks to Owen's back, his T-shirt pulls tight across it, and those familiar butterflies begin to flutter, and I hate it. I hate the reaction I have to him; I'd hoped I was past all this, but one look toward him and I'm a lovestruck teenager again.

The baby kicks and the harsh reminder of my reality returns. This baby is my future, and Carlos is a good man who loves me enough for the both of us. I'm determined to have the family I always dreamed of. My parents are incredible, but not knowing my blood parents has sometimes been crippling in my upbringing. There's nothing I wouldn't do to make sure my children have the best home life they can have, with two parents who love them more than anything, and Carlos loves us. There's no doubt in my mind about that.

Out of the corner of my eye, I watch Owen pull up a chair, then lean forward with his elbows on his knees and his head in his hands. My heart constricts at the way he holds himself, and I wonder what's going on with him. "I'll go speak with him."

My mom nods and leaves the room while I steel my shoulders and take a deep breath before sliding the patio door open and stepping outside. He doesn't react to my presence, yet I know he knows it's me. He's always known when I'm in his vicinity.

My pulse races with trepidation as he lifts his head and his eyes slide up my body achingly slowly, as if taking in every part of me.

A lump catches in my throat at the same time his Adam's apple bobs, the air between us like a tethered restraint ready to snap.

"What the fuck, Laya, a baby?" His deep voice sends a shiver up my spine, but the disappointment in it is clear, causing me to jolt.

His eyes latch onto my bump, then he squeezes his eyes closed and turns away. The pain etched on his face crushes my heart. Why the hell do I feel this way when it's him who pushed me away for a woman he broke up with only weeks later?

He sits up straighter, then tugs on my jacket, pulling me between his firm legs. Those muscular thighs of his look like they're about to break out of his jeans, and I clench at the thought.

His thick hand moves and rests on my bump and a strangled noise catches in my throat, making him dart his eyes up toward mine. He licks his lips, and his touch scorches through the fabric of my blouse. "Should have been mine," he mumbles before closing his eyes. "Jesus, I fucked up." He grits his teeth, then his eyes flare open. "You're going to divorce him."

I reel back on my feet, stumbling at his words, and with his free hand, he grabs my arm to stabilize me while his palm never leaves my stomach.

His words ring out in my ears. *"You're going to divorce him."*

How fucking dare he?

Then he scrubs a hand over his cropped head before nodding. "Yeah, that's exactly what you're going to do." I stare at him as he unravels, his chest heaves, and the vein on the side of his forehead pulsates. "You hear me? Get rid of him." The sharpness in his tone has me jolting, and I tug my arm out of his grasp and step back as anger surges through me like a volcano threatening to erupt.

"Don't you dare speak about him like that!" I spit back. "He's ten times the man you'll ever be, Owen." He clamps his jaw shut and rises from his chair, and I step back again, determined to put space between us. Anger combines with hurt, and I hate the way my voice quivers as I speak. "He loves us and would do anything for us." My chest rises rapidly. "Anything," I snipe out with conviction.

He swallows hard, and I know he took it as an insult, and it was meant to be.

He tilts his head to the side. "You don't think I would?"

A mocking laugh rumbles in my throat. "We both know you wouldn't."

My back hits a brick wall as he backs me up against the house. "Wrong." He cages me in with his arms braced above my head. "I'd do any-fucking-thing for you, even let you go." His eyes scan my face, as if looking for a sign of my feelings. He won't find one; I refuse to go back there. So I shake my head, unwilling to hear his words. They're meaningless now. I've moved on. No matter how much the warmth of his body invades me, no matter how close he breathes against my lips as he speaks. "You're both mine, and I'm coming for you. Both of you."

Through the intoxication of his presence, his words settle in my mind. He's talking like he owns me and our baby, mine and Carlos's baby. I shove him away, and it's not lost on me that he allowed it.

Always so easy to give me up. Why would now be any different, and why do I want him to fight for me when I've already made my choice?

Because deep down, I know Owen is embedded in my heart and soul, and as much as I attempt to move on, to live a life without him, he'll always be there.

"I love him."

He scoffs. "No, you don't, baby girl. Don't lie to me."

The sound of the name he used the night we had sex on his lips fills my bloodstream with annoyance, and I want to hurt him, hurt him like he hurt me. I want to rip his heart out and stamp all over it like he did mine.

"Oh, I love him, all right. I tell him every night when we have sex. Every time his hand touches our baby bump." As I rest my hand on my bump, his eyes snap to the action. "And he tells me right back." I step closer to him, so close I could touch him, but don't. I won't allow myself to risk him pulling me in. "I'm his everything, and he'd go to war for me."

He grinds his jaw from side to side and tilts his head to

glare at me. "But would he win?" There's something in his tone, an underlying meaning to his words, and I don't like it. It's as if he's saying he'd go to battle for me. But doesn't he see? There is no battle, he already lost. He gave up.

I spin to walk away, done with this conversation. Done with him.

"You've always been mine, Laya." His voice rises. "You're my first love, baby girl, and I'll make damn sure I'm your last."

I ignore his words, even as they crush me, because this time, it's me who gets to walk away from us.

"I'm coming for you, baby girl." He promises as I slide open the patio door, and a shiver rushes up my spine. It's a promise I'm not ready for.

FOUR

OWEN

EIGHT WEEKS LATER ...

The day she walked away from me was the day I made it my mission to uncover everything there was to know about the prick she calls a husband. Now staring at the information gathered on the screen, anger overflows my veins, pumping through me so strongly that it might rupture my flesh.

I will it to happen, welcoming the bleed out. Knowing she's starting a life without me, the life we should have had, pains me more than any physical pain you could endure. It guts me and poisons every cell inside me.

The piece of shit staring back at me on the screen is Carlos Andreas from Mexico. At thirty-eight years old, he's far too old for her, far more dangerous too, and the husband to the woman I love.

My eyes flick over the information I've already memorized, to drive me on my quest for happiness.

His best friend is Nico Garcia, head of a cartel family in Mexico, a known drug lord, and a piece of shit whose family has been linked to human trafficking.

Over my dead fucking body will I let this scum steal what's mine.

She might be pregnant with his biological baby, but that baby belongs to me. They're my family, and nothing will stop me from taking what's mine.

Not Laya.

Not Tate.

And sure as hell not Carlos Andreas.

I'll spill blood if I have to. I'll revel in it, even.

But I will have my family.

Laya and our baby will be mine.

I lift my phone and scroll through until I get to the name I want—Reece O'Connell. He's part of the O'Connell Mafia family, a good kid, a child genius, actually, with a mind full of knowledge at the family's disposal that makes him both useful and dangerous.

But there's a connection that Reece O'Connell has with Nico Garcia, his former would-be stepfather. Nico killed Reece's unborn sibling, forcing Reece and his mom to run and relocate under new names.

I know Reece has reconnected with Nico, something his father may not be aware of. Information I intend to use to my advantage because I'll do anything to get my girl back.

Anything.

"What the fuck do you want, Owen?"

I chuckle at the little shit's manners. He really does not give a fuck how he speaks to anyone. "I need a favor."

He grunts noncommittally.

"You owe me," I clarify, and he knows I'm referring to the shitshow that went down at his family's wedding, where he assisted with the escape of Luca Varros's wife.

"So I'll ask you again, what do you want? I have shit to do." His voice is sterner this time, and I shake my head at his attitude.

"Nico Garcia."

He grumbles something under his breath, then groans. "You want me to have him killed? You know I owe him too, right?" I know he owes Nico. I'm sure Nico won't let him forget it either. But the little shit is as valuable as the debts he owes and uses that knowledge to his family's gain.

"I don't want you to kill him." I hear the whoosh of air escape him. "He has a close friend I want a meeting with."

A loud chuckle erupts from him, and I pull my phone away from my ringing ear and glare at it.

"You want the girl back, right?" My pulse races and the vein on my temple thrums. Of course he knows about Laya; Reece O'Connell makes it his business to know about everyone, and it's times like this I'm grateful for it.

"I do," I confirm, hating the way my heart thunders against my chest at letting someone know my plans.

He balks, and I want to reach down the phone and wring the little shit's neck. "Reece," I warn in a tone that would normally make a grown man piss themselves.

He chuckles. "Lighten up, man."

Lighten up? Is he fucking serious? My girl is knocked up with another man's child and married to the fucker.

My head throbs, and I rub over the vein protruding along my neck. "For fuck's sake," I grunt as despair washes through me at how difficult Reece can be to work with.

He sighs heavily. "I'll have him call you later."

Surprise floods me, but before I can thank him, he hangs up, leaving me staring at the phone and asking myself if it was really as easy as that?

As relief filters through my body and my plan slips into place, I sit back in my chair, contemplating what I discovered on Laya's Pinterest account and all the work I have to do to help her realize this is for the best.

She will have everything she's ever wanted.

And me?

I will finally have her.

My office door is thrown open, and my thoughts are interrupted. Mase, Tate, and Shaw stroll in and throw themselves onto the chairs.

It's Friday, the day we have our meetings to establish all the shit we've dealt with during the week and what needs to be done within the business to prepare for Monday.

"So, thirsty Thursday is pointless now, right?" Tate asks as I turn my head in his direction.

When my best friends started this dumb bet to see who could get a blowjob every Thursday night, I never imagined the lengths I would have to go through to make it seem like I was actually participating. The truth of the matter is, my cock refuses to get hard for anyone but her, and imagining someone as her is not even an option. I simply don't want to. The fact I've been celibate since I took her virginity is my penance.

I lift a shoulder, not acknowledging his statement.

"Well, me and Shaw are off the market. Mase doesn't get any, so it's between you and Reed. Pretty sure Reed is winning." He grins toward me, and I smirk back. Happy to let him believe I'm out of the equation. We all know Reed needs more than one woman to satisfy him, whereas Mase, who is married, has been trying for years to have sex with his wife despite her openly cheating on him. Poor dude realizes they need to divorce, but she keeps on trying to win him over because he's worth a fortune. The bitch has tried to get with me multiple times, Tate and Shaw too. She probably realizes she wouldn't be enough for Reed, so he assures us she's never attempted him.

"Can we cut the crap? I need to get home early," Shaw grunts out. Since the self-proclaimed playboy married the Mafia princess because of knocking her up, he's obsessed with playing house, and who could blame him? I intend on doing just that with Laya.

"I've reached out to a contact in LA. I'm thinking we should be expanding and creating another branch there," Mase throws out, but I don't so much as blink.

My home is here.

And hers will be too.

"We should?" Shaw leans forward with eagerness in his eyes. "I mean, it sounds great. Perfect excuse to get away from Luca." His brother-in-law, Luca Varros of the Varros Mafia, would never let his little sister move away, but I don't voice my opinion. Poor guy needs some hope in his marriage.

"How's things on your end?" Tate scans my face.

None of my best friends have anything to do with my side of the business, and I choose to keep them and their questions at bay. It's not their expertise. I simply needed the backers to make the security business work. STORM Enterprises created the perfect cover for me. They know that as well as I do.

"Fine." I shrug.

"No news?" He's referring to Laya, and when I stare back at him, hope flickers in his eyes that I'm about to extinguish.

I swallow. "Not yet."

His shoulders sag, and I hate the defeat behind the action, but I don't have time to think on it because the door swings open and in strolls Reed, a beaming smile on his face that has our eyes darting to one another in question.

Our normally impassive, stoic-faced friend has been replaced with someone who looks like he swallowed a rainbow and shit out a unicorn.

His smile only grows wider when he lets out a heavy sigh as he takes his seat.

A gold unicorn, for sure.

"What the hell happened to you?" Tate studies him.

"The deal with Fanzio go well, then?" Mase asks with a grin rivaling Reed's.

George Fanzio, a billionaire property mogul, has been dangling the prospect of Reed signing off on some land in bumfuck nowhere for a while now, and Reed has been like a bitch in heat desperate to sign off on the deal that will have George handing over a portion of his empire.

I'm not entirely sure how it will work, but I know

Reed, being the best lawyer out there, will oversee it to perfection, as always.

Reed's eyes narrow. "Actually, it went to shit."

I sit forward.

Shaw's gaze ping-pongs between ours and Reed's. "Well, why didn't you start with that, and why are you so happy when you wanted this deal for so long?"

Reed swats his words away like he's hitting a bug, and I chuckle.

He sits back, crosses his arms over his chest with a huge smile on his well-put-together self, then opens his mouth and shocks the hell out of us all. "I'm in love."

"What the fuck?" Tate chokes on his coffee, and our mouths fall open as he spills the rest of his drink over his shirt.

I shake my head. Such a dumbass.

"Holy shit, that burns." Before I know what's happening, he's unbuttoning his shirt, and I laugh at his frantic state. "Fucking Jesus. Do I need the ER or something?" He points to his bare chest, which is slightly red.

I point toward Tate's vacated seat. "Sit the fuck down, you wuss, and grow up. I need to hear this."

He grumbles before taking his seat. "I need a cold compress."

I'm tempted to throw my cup of water at him to get him to shut the hell up.

"The deal went to shit. He's not in a position to move forward yet, yadda, yadda, yadda."

Reed rolls his eyes as he tells us about his meeting. "So I go to the bar to drown in my misery." I nod along. "Then this woman sits down at my table."

"Gold digger!" Shaw barks. "She has to be a gold digger. No woman sits down at your table without intent."

"Oh, she had intent, all right." Reed smirks as we all listen raptly. "Intent on riding my cock until it was raw."

Mase snorts and I chuckle.

"So you fucked a gold digger. What's new? Why are you in love?" Shaw lifts his shoulder.

Reed shakes his head. "She wasn't a gold digger. Trust me, I know. She was a businesswoman. Had the hot-as-hell business attire on and a briefcase. A lawyer, actually." He smiles as if proud he bagged a fellow lawyer, and I want to roll my eyes.

"So you fucked one woman?" Mase asks, as if confused.

"I did. One!" He holds his finger up. "Best night of my life."

Tate lifts his head from surveying his chest. "When are we meeting this woman that managed to break you?"

Reed throws his head back on a heavy groan before bringing it back to face me. "Here's the thing… I didn't get her name or number."

Tate gasps. "What?"

"I know." Reed rubs at his forehead. "I fucked up. She said no strings, and I was good with that. I didn't expect that"—he motions toward the door—"she'd blow my fucking mind, and I've no idea who she is." His eyes meet mine again as realization sets in. He wants me to find her.

"Oh, no you fucking don't. Owen has enough shit to deal with, like my sister. Oh, and he needs to do his fucking job. Not hunt down women that don't want a repeat of you," Tate snaps.

Reed's eyes narrow. "You don't think she wants a repeat of me?"

A scoff rumbles from Shaw. "She didn't leave her name or number. Pretty sure it's self-explanatory."

A pang of guilt hits me when Reed's face falls, then he clears his throat. "Not like there aren't a billion other women in the world falling at my feet." He shrugs and plasters on a fake smile.

When all this is over, I'll hunt down this woman. Then it's up to him to pursue her.

In my experience, if they don't want to be found, there's a good reason for it. They're hiding something.

FIVE

LAYA

Carlos slides his hand around to our baby bump. "You look beautiful, amor." I bite into my lip. The man never fails to tell me how beautiful I look, no matter how fat or uncomfortable I feel.

"I really wanted you to meet my parents before the baby arrives, Carlos." We've been in the Bahamas for over a month, all while Tate got married. At Carlos's request, I've been pushing back the date for him to meet my family, telling them we'd like to wait until we're settled in our new home before they visit.

He sighs heavily and steps back. "I know. But I've been busy, Laya." The dark circles under his eyes prove it. "When I meet your family, I want it to be perfect."

I soften on his words. I understand but, in my mind, everything is perfect. Besides, I don't even know where our new home will be, and the thought has me anxious. As caring and loving as Carlos is, he's also very closed off. He only allows me to see what he wants me to see, and I'm very aware of it. It's almost like he doesn't want me to see all of him, and the thought of that has sickness rolling in my stomach.

If he thinks I believe the armed guards, bulletproof cars, and undercover bodyguards who follow us in the shadows are because he's a successful nightclub owner, then he has another think coming. Each time I bring anything up, he shuts me down or becomes distant, and I hate it. It feels like I'm losing him, and I can't lose him, not when I've already lost Owen. So instead, I put up and shut up, and take each day as it comes.

"Who did you say we were going to meet for dinner?" I place the diamond earring in my ear and fluff my hair, allowing the waves to flow down my back.

Carlos steps forward, his chest hits my back, then he smooths the stray hairs from my neck before his lips touch my neck. "A colleague of mine."

I've only ever met one colleague of Carlos's, a childhood friend, Nico Garcia. "Nico?"

Carlos chuckles. "Not Nico, no. I'll rephrase it, a potential colleague of mine."

My mind is already whirling with what we will talk about. I know full well Carlos won't discuss business in front of me. "Does he have a plus one with him?"

Carlos's ghost of a smile sends goose bumps over my skin. "I don't think so. Apparently, he doesn't date."

A bubble of laughter snickers out of me. "My brother never dated, but always had a plus one."

His palm rubs over our bump. "Hmm, this one is mending a broken heart if what I hear is true."

"That's …" I try to think of the right word. "Sad."

"It is. But one man's loss is another man's treasure." He pulls back from me, and our eyes meet in the mirror. His gaze is intense and stormy; he gets like this when he has meetings, an edge to him I don't recognize. It unnerves me, especially being so far away from home.

His cell buzzes in his pants pocket, so he withdraws it but stuffs it back in. "Come, amor. It's time to leave."

My hand slips into his as we make our way outside, and the moment my eyes lock onto the six black SUV's each with a guard standing beside them, I know this will not be any ordinary dinner, and a ball of unease knots in my stomach.

OWEN

My leg bounces uncontrollably as I try to rein in my emotions. The table is set for three; does that mean he's bringing her with him? Surely not.

I told him this was to be a one-on-one business meeting. I was planning to use it to gauge the kind of man my girl is married to and chose to have a baby with. My mouth goes dry and nausea overwhelms me at the thought of them together, but I push past it, determined to block the image of them together out and remain professional. The man cannot know my feelings for her; he cannot know she's my weakness.

The sound of footsteps approaching has me snapping my gaze up. And there he is, the Mexican drug lord with business links to a notorious human trafficking Mafia family.

His eyes sear into mine with hatred, yet his face remains impassive. I rise from my seat to greet him, but my blood turns to ice and I still, my hand outstretched toward him when the clicking of heels invades me.

She's here.

The bastard brought her here.

"Carlos, there's a boutique across ..." He pulls out a chair for her, and her footing wavers as our eyes lock. Her chest rises rapidly and mine follows suit. A flush travels up her face, and her breath hitches.

"Mi amor, please." He motions to the chair, and she slides onto the seat, using his hand to help her while I scan her heavy bump. She must be due any day now.

She's filled out, healthily so, and I've missed it all.

Carlos watches our exchange with no expression, and if I didn't know better, I'd say he hadn't realized we were connected, but I know better. I know enough of him to know he's a calculating piece of shit who has orchestrated this whole meeting, even if it was me who reached out.

"You look beautiful, Laya," I say without thinking, and I almost want to castrate myself. So much for acting blasé.

Her cheeks pinken even more, and she glances around the room, refusing to look at me, and I'd be lying if I said it didn't hurt. I want her eyes on me, solely on me, like they once were.

Carlos sits beside Laya, and I flinch when he rests his arm across her shoulders. "My wife always looks beautiful, don't you think, Mr. Stevens?"

I stare back at him. His eyes dance with jest as he strokes over her exposed shoulder. No doubt her olive skin is smooth to the touch. My mind wanders with the way she felt beneath me, my inked skin pressed against her flawless tone, a contrast so stunning it made it even more difficult for me to contain myself.

My gaze trails over the softness of her neck, the one I

OWEN

left my marks on, and now there's not a blemish in sight. Just how she should remain, deserving better, just not him.

Then I stare at her necklace, the one I gifted her before I broke her heart. When I took what she gave me and then destroyed her, but she still has it hanging loosely around her neck like a trophy of my love. The emerald in it sparkles like a beacon of hope. She still loves me, I know it.

After way too long, I swallow thickly and respond, "She does."

His calculating eyes drill into me, and if I wasn't the man I am, my balls would have shriveled from the threat. Then, like a switch has been flipped, his lip twitches as if he realizes how difficult her presence is for me.

Laya clears her throat. "I thought you said this was a business meeting?" She turns her head to stare at Carlos, and I want to take hold of her delicate chin and force her attention on me. Jealousy unleashes into my bloodstream at the way he touches her so freely, the way her hand rests on his thigh when it should be on mine, the way his eyes slide over her body like she's his when she's fucking mine!

His lip curls into a smile. "Mr. Stevens asked for a meeting, and here we are." He waves his hand in my direction, and I take a sip of water, trying to tamp the raging storm of fury inside me.

Carlos lifts his hand toward the server and orders drinks while Laya glares at me with annoyance in her bright-green eyes. "What do you want, Owen?" The anger in her snipe is obvious.

I take aim at her heart, knowing how compassionate my girl is. "Your family misses you."

She rolls her eyes and, Jesus, if my cock didn't twitch with a need to spank her for it.

"As soon as we settle in our new home, Laya's family is welcome to come visit."

I narrow my eyes at the pompous prick. The amusement in his gaze causes me to clench my fists beneath the table while every cell inside me screams at me to slam his good-looking face on the woodwork and crush it with my thick palm.

"You're welcome too," he tacks on, then takes a slow sip of the scotch I hadn't realized had been delivered to the table. The curve of his lips as he does so sends fury through my bloodstream.

"You've been doing a lot of moving around. Why is that?" I raise an eyebrow toward Carlos, ignoring his digs, then his hand stops moving on her shoulder. His mouth clamps shut, and I swear I hear him grind his teeth.

Resolve settles over his face, and I will her to see what I see in him. The way he clearly changes to accommodate her. "I needed to find the perfect place for mi amor and my son." His free hand now rests on her swollen stomach, and I swear to Christ I want to rip it off and force it down his filthy throat. He's no place touching what's mine, impregnating what's mine, raising what's mine, and yet here we are. *A son.*

Laya shifts in her seat, and I cannot decide if it's my presence making her awkward or the prick's touch, so I tell myself it's the latter to make this exchange more bearable. "We're settling soon. Carlos has somewhere picked out, ready for the baby coming." The hope in her voice sends a pang of pain through my heart because my beautiful girl is so full of expectation for her and her baby, yet there is none with a man like him by her side.

Slowly, I lean forward and steeple my hands on the

table, ignoring the prick and speaking directly to Laya, giving her no choice but to give me her attention. "And where exactly are you moving to?" She darts her eyes down toward the bracelet on my wrist, the one she wove with her fingers and, more importantly, with her heart. I wear it like a medal, a part of something crafted for me. Only me.

Just as quickly, she darts her eyes away, a flush coating her innocent cheeks.

"It's a surprise." His smug face lights up, and I keep from pummeling it. But one day, motherfucker.

One day real soon.

My eyes once again latch onto her necklace, a reminder of her love for me. Even after I broke her heart. My girl has simply lost her way, that's all, but I'll guide her home.

Laya clears her throat again, and guilt hits me. She's uncomfortable, and rightly so. She's sitting between the man who holds her heart and the one who holds her captive. I stare at her, trying to convey my thoughts through my gaze. I'm her future, I always was, yet she refuses to give me her attention, and I swallow harshly at the realization that she's shut me out. My shadow is rejecting me, and while it's painful, I refuse to acknowledge the ache.

She's mine, she always has been.

Her cheeks heat, and I follow the flush down to her rapidly rising chest. It gives away how much my presence affects her. *Look at me, baby girl*, I plead.

She clears her throat and pushes back in her chair, and the scrape of it against the floor echoes around us. "If you'll excuse me, I'm just going to use the restroom." Then she rises from her chair, and I watch her ass sway as she turns and walks away. The way she's always been so ignorant as to how she draws attention in a room has always astonished me, and nothing has changed. She's still the sweet girl I fell for when I shouldn't have.

"That's my wife you're eye-fucking." My focus snaps toward Carlos, who sits with his legs parted and his arm over the vacated chair, a smug smile on his cocky face. "Tell me, Mr. Stevens, why is it you reached out to a colleague of mine?"

He drags a finger over his lip. "Nico was insistent on me meeting with you. Why is that?"

"Because I commanded it. Tell me, Mr. Andreas, did Nico insist on you bringing Laya too?"

His lip rises. "No, that was my doing."

"And why is that?"

"I need my wife to be assured I have no issues with your past, because it's just that. The past."

I throw my head back on a mocking laugh, then stare straight back at him. "If you believe that, then you're a fool."

He gives no reaction, and it irks me. The prick is a mask of indifference.

"I do believe that. My wife and I have a common interest. We want to raise our children as a family unit, unlike our own turbulent upbringings, and we'll both do everything in our power to achieve it."

The confidence behind his voice has me fighting to remain calm, and the way he talks about children as if they have a future together beyond this one child has me seeing red, but still, somehow, I remain seated. Something tells me Carlos would be happy for me to explode, to give Laya the perfect excuse to keep me away. I glance around the room. He's brought at least six men with him, and a sudden awareness comes over me. This is exactly what he wanted. He wanted me to lose my shit, to make a scene, to go to war for her. That way, he had a reason to keep her away from her family, to keep us at a distance.

With that knowledge in mind, I decide to push back. "That's right, you were brought up in the cartel, right?" His glare on me intensifies. Now he knows I'm just as aware of his background as he is mine. "Your father was killed alongside two of your brothers by a rival family, and you witnessed the whole thing. The Garcia family took you in, and now you intend to rebuild your father's empire, creating a legacy in blood just like him. Does Laya know her son will be heir to a ruthless drug lord and calculated killer?"

The man looks fit to combust, all premise has fallen, his true self revealed, and I revel in it. He sits forward, leaning over the table. "Our son." His eyes drill into mine. "Mine and Laya's."

I lean back in my chair, my stare not leaving his. "We'll see."

His eyes widen slightly, taken aback at my repute. "Is that a threat, Mr. Stevens?"

I lift an eyebrow, then lean forward. The stare-off between us feels catalytic. At any point, one of us could explode and the room would become a bloodbath, but not yet. "It's a promise. A storm is coming, Carlos, and when the dust settles, you'll be nothing but ash. But don't worry, I'll look after Laya and our son." Then I settle back into the chair as if I didn't just threaten to destroy him and take his family away in one fell swoop.

At the sound of Laya's approaching footsteps, he

pushes back on his chair and stands, then leans over the table.

"I promise you this, whatever you have planned, she *will* find out, and she will hate you for it. Ask yourself this, can you live with her hating you because of your jealousy, Mr. Stevens, my son's hate too? Because if you can, go ahead and bring your storm. Her heart will always remain mine, our son's too."

He throws down a wad of cash on the table, then turns toward Laya. Her eyes dart from mine to his while he pastes on a smile I can only assume is reserved solely for her, and fuck me if she doesn't smile back at him while he glides his arm around her waist and steers her out the door.

They get into the SUV, and though I feel her slipping away once again, I know the next time we meet will be our forever.

SIX

LAYA

The door to the SUV closes behind me, and Carlos walks around the other side. He slides inside casually, but the moment the door slams shut, the car becomes heated under his glare. "Did he give you the necklace?" His eyes dart toward the necklace, and there's hurt mixed with rage in his eyes, and I hate myself for it, but stupidly, my hand moves toward it. "Fucking answer me! Did you take me, your husband and father of your child, to dinner with your ex-lover's necklace around your neck?"

A whimper catches in my throat, not because he's scaring me, but because I hurt him. For years, I've kept it around my neck like a treasure. In Owen's eyes, it was probably a sign of my pathetic devotion, and in my husband's eyes, a sign of my betrayal. "Mi amorrrr." His voice has an unhinged edge to it, one that sends a shiver down my spine, one I've not heard until today, and the thought has a gnawing ball of anxiety throbbing inside me.

I know this looks like I'm not over Owen, that I'm holding onto the past when my future should lie with him.

"Yes," I breathe out, averting my eyes as guilt rolls in my stomach like acid.

His face twists in disgust, then in a flash, his hand snaps the chain from around my neck as my heart slams in my chest, making it difficult for me to breathe through the shock of his actions.

Satisfaction flashes behind his eyes as I stare at him with my mouth agape, and desperation to repair the betrayal of me taking the necklace off floods me.

My heart hammers precariously, and I feel the need to reassure him of where my loyalty lies—with the father of our unborn baby—no matter how much it pains me to sever the only connection I have with Owen.

I pull my shoulders back with a renewed vigor, then swallow harshly and clear my throat. "I don't need it anymore, Carlos. I only need you. You and our son." I nod at him, hoping my words appease him.

"Romero," he states, and I furrow my brow. "Our son, I want to name him Romero after my brother."

"Romero," I repeat with a nod while stroking over my bump. "You don't talk about them." I know Carlos has suffered the loss of his family, and I hate that for him. One night when he was drunk, he told me they were hurt, and as a small boy, he saw it happen. He divulged no more information than that, and as time moves on with him, I've come to the conclusion that he fears me knowing what happened, so he pretends they never existed.

He entwines our hands and kisses my fingers. "I have everything I need right here."

"Why did Owen ask to meet with you?"

His lips move over my hand. "Simple, he wants you."

My heart catches in my chest as I stare at him, then a strangled laugh escapes me while he narrows his gaze on me. "Owen does not want me."

His lip quirks, and he tilts his head. "Oh, I can assure you he does." His tone is serious, and the intensity behind his eyes is like something I've never seen before. It terrifies me. The man I've grown to love is about to go to war with the man I've always loved. "He can try to take you from me, but he'll soon learn how far I'm willing to go to keep you." My gaze flicks back and forth over his face. "You and Romero are my world, and I intend to keep it that way." He kisses my hand, as if trying to reassure me, but there's something about the way he speaks that unnerves me, an undercurrent that fills me with uncertainty.

I turn away and stare out the window, hoping he doesn't see the way trepidation is bleeding from my pores, then realize where we are. Turning to face him, I ask, "Why are we at an airfield?"

He lifts my hand once more. "We're moving to our forever home, mi amor. It's in Mexico."

Shock hits me and pain lances through me and into my stomach, and I cry out. We're moving even farther away from my family, making me even more lonely and isolated than ever before.

"It's okay, mi amor, everything is waiting for us at home." It's the last thing I remember as my vision turns hazy and blackness consumes me.

SEVEN

CARLOS

TWO MONTHS LATER

The sun beams down on us as Laya nurses Romero beneath a towel, and my heart swells with pride. She's an incredible mother. Everything I wish my own had been to me. Affection pours from her like second nature, and while I continue to cocoon my family in a bubble of security, the underlying simmer of my impending doom eats away at me.

Nico takes another sip of his drink, then glances over his shoulder toward Laya on the sunbed, and anger floods my veins. Despite knowing he's happily married and doesn't see Laya that way, I can't help but want to rip the skin from his body for even glancing in her direction. His focus comes back to me, and I take a drink of my scotch to remain calm. Lately, I've been unraveling. I thought bringing Laya and Romero to Mexico would provide me with the reassurance I desperately need to continue with my business plans, but the mere thought of those plans has me tetchy, yet I refuse to admit it.

"Laya, take Romero inside." Her eyes narrow on me, and when I think my wife will argue, she merely nods and walks away with our son, and I watch her ass sway as she steps inside the house.

Nico places his hand inside his jacket pocket, then throws a block of cocaine onto the table. His dark eyes meet mine, and his jaw clenches tight. "What the fuck are you playing at?" The Carrera family insignia is stamped on the foil packaging, and the familiar combination of guilt and anger floods me. It's deadly, fierce, and self-destructive.

Nico has been like a brother to me, and while I appreciate his concern, this is really none of his fucking business, but he's treating it as such.

When I make no move to justify my actions, he drags a hand over his face with a sigh, then leans over the table. "Fuck, Carlos. Are you for real?" He glares at me while I remain stoic. It's an expression I have mastered since the moment I witnessed my family being slaughtered. "Carlos. I love you like a brother, but I can't stand by and be dragged into this shit." He points toward the cocaine.

I take another sip of my drink. "Then don't." I shrug while my heart thunders away. The last thing I want is for Nico to leave my side. He's family. When his father took me in, my inheritance was tied up until I was twenty-one, then I moved out and set about creating my empire, one my family would have been proud of, no matter the consequences. I lost my way a few times, with drink, drugs, and women, but Nico has always been the one to help me find myself again, as I did him when he split with his ex, Carmen.

"You're risking too much, Carlos." He shakes his head. "These people do not play around."

I scoff at the notion. "And we do?" I lift an eyebrow in his direction.

He shakes his head. "They're scum," he spits out with a sneer. "Human fucking traffickers." His face contorts in disgust. "You know it. I know it, and I refuse to have anything to do with them, and I'm surprised you're willing to." He sits back in his chair, his arms crossed over his chest.

The way he looks like a petulant child makes me chuckle as I take another sip of the scotch. "I have it under control." My smirk tells him everything he needs to know; I have leverage on them.

"Carlos, this isn't a fucking game."

I sit forward, angered at his words. Does he think I don't know that? My family died because of a business deal gone wrong. "You don't think I fucking know that?" I jab my finger into my chest as I bellow, then grimace at the thought of Laya overhearing.

"They're just moving product within my club, nothing major."

He leans over the table, his eyes boring into mine. "Nothing. Fucking. Major?"

"You're getting into business with the devil himself. You really think he's going to leave it at drugs?" He motions toward the cocaine. "This is just the start, Carlos." I roll my eyes at his performance; he always was too much a fucking saint to be a Mafia heir. "Women will be next, then what? Are you okay with that?" For the first time since I agreed to this plan, guilt swims in my stomach. "We're not talking prostitution, Carlos." I know what he's talking about. Everyone knows the Carreras deal in kidnapping and selling of women. Hurt swims in Nico's eyes, and he closes them and turns his head away from me. When his gaze slides back to mine, the hurt has vanished. "I won't be a part of this."

Anxiety creeps up my spine at his words. He will walk away. Then what will I have?

I'll have her, always her, and our boy. "I have leverage," I repeat, my tone almost pleading.

He shakes his head. "And if you play that hand …" He turns to look at our home and a shiver washes over me as I take in what he sees: a beautiful Mexican mansion painted a bright-yellow with roses running up the side, a pool for my family, and manicured lawns for Romero as he grows, a home for my family. "They will come for them, Carlos." Sickness rises in my stomach, but anger burns my veins as I grind my teeth and bite my tongue, determined not to tell the only man I trust to go fuck himself.

He rises from the table, and I try to contain my unraveling, the way I feel like my lungs are being crushed as he walks away. The fury that he's walking away because he doesn't trust my judgment has a tsunami of aggression bubbling to the surface.

As he pulls open the door, he turns to face me, and a glimmer of hope rises in my chest when his focus locks with mine. He's going to back down and support me, after all. It's just the guilt of working with traffickers that had him running scared, that had those harsh words leaving his mouth, and I almost want to balk at his sudden change in beliefs.

"Who are you doing this for, Carlos?" My eyes narrow. "This"—he waves his hand toward the extensive grounds—"who are you creating your legacy for?"

I grind my jaw; he knows damn well who it's all for.

It's for my family.

He stares at me blankly, awaiting a response.

"My family," I spit out reluctantly.

He nods. "Are they going to be proud of the man you're about to become? Will Romero be proud of the heir he's expected to be, and when you lay beside your wife at night, will she be proud of her husband, the father of her children, creating a legacy on the back of trading humans? I won't stand by your side as you abuse women and use them as nothing more than unwilling participants in a fucked-up industry we both know isn't right." He slams his hand over his heart. "Your family's here today, Carlos. But they could be gone tomorrow." With his departing words ringing in my ears, he turns and walks away, taking a piece of our relationship with him.

"Your family's here today, Carlos. But they could be gone tomorrow."

Nobody will take my family from me, and with the Carreras by my side, nobody will stop me.

EIGHT

LAYA

ONE MONTH LATER ...

Chewing my lip, I hover my finger over the send button. I know I shouldn't, but every day, Carlos is becoming more and more agitated, and it unnerves me. He's out late every night, and when he finally crashes, he doesn't rise until midafternoon: sleep, eat, rinse, repeat.

We barely see him, and when I do, he's a shell of the man I fell in love with. His clubs have been plagued with trouble, and the staff are saying he's being watched; they don't realize I'm fluent in Spanish while they talk freely about raids at the clubs. They even said Carlos was arrested, yet he returned home as if nothing had happened with no mention of it. I walk on eggshells around his volatile temperament, and I hate it. If I ask questions, I risk the staff being punished, but I'm constantly being kept in the dark, and I'm not stupid enough to believe this isn't about control. My stomach twists as I consider my future with Carlos. What will that future hold for Romero? I hiccup away the cry that always bubbles up when I consider our life here. Carlos barely pays Romero attention, so there's not a doubt in my mind our son was a pawn in his game to keep me trapped, and I hate him for that. It's like he's chosen to detach himself, and all I want is the man I fell in love with, but I am realizing he never existed. He reined me in and now I'm trapped, and the thought terrifies me.

In Mexico, I'm isolated. I miss my family, my job, and my friends, causing loneliness to eat away at me. I'm a new mom with an occasional permitted FaceTime to ask my mom questions about motherhood. When all I wanted to do was beg for her comfort, but my calls were monitored, so I crafted the perfect smile to disperse any of my mom's concerns. I'm crumbling inside, hoping for someone to rescue me. I should be out with other young moms, discussing motherhood, attending baby play classes, and shopping for cute outfits, but I'm being isolated for safety, and feel anything but safe.

My parents have not been allowed to visit yet, and on days when I feel so trapped, I close my eyes and dream that Owen rescues us from this place, which is quickly becoming my prison.

"Carlos has eyes everywhere." Lenard, one of the gardeners, points toward my phone. He's an older gentleman with a fatherly nature I've become attached to. "You thinking too hard." He points toward the phone. "Don't send if thinking too hard." His eyes skim over the lawn where I sit with Romero on a blanket. "Carlos has eyes everywhere," he repeats, sending a shiver of awareness down my spine, and I nod before quickly fumbling with the message I was going to send Tate, asking him to visit as soon as possible. It's deleted far quicker than it was created.

My lip wobbles as I stare down at Romero. My son has a whole family he's yet to meet, and it breaks my heart they're missing out on the way he's growing.

"A storm is brewing, Laya, and when it comes, it's going to be savage." My heart skips a beat at his words. Surely, he doesn't know my association with STORM? His words are ominous as he walks away, while my blood pulses with excitement and hope.

"Lenard, how do you know?" I call across the lawn.

He turns his withered face over his shoulder and points toward the sky. My eyes follow, and when I see the darkened clouds hovering above the house, my heart free falls.

Nobody is coming for us.

Taking a deep breath, I place my fork down and lift my eyes toward Carlos's. His are already on me, and it unnerves me, but I'm determined to get through to him.

It's rare he's home for dinner, so tonight is the perfect opportunity to speak with him.

"Carlos?"

He sighs heavily and places his cutlery on his plate, then leans back in his chair. His nonchalant attitude riles me, but I know better than to go head-to-head with him.

He will only close off and do what he pleases while I have no choice but to go along for the ride.

"My mom—" He holds his hand up.

"No."

Anger surges through me, and my eyes blaze with fire. "I'm on my own every damn day, Carlos, and my family haven't even met Romero yet."

He rolls his eyes as if fed up with my outbursts. "I told you it isn't safe yet."

"Safe from what?" I spit out, knowing we practically have an army surrounding this fortress he calls home, but I've no clue why.

"It's business, Laya." He grabs the napkin from his lap and throws it onto his plate, and my shoulders deflate, knowing he's shutting me out. Then his eyes flick over me and rest on my chest. The hunger behind them has me shrinking back in my chair.

While Carlos has helped me enjoy sex, it's not something I crave from him, and I sense he can feel my reluctance.

"I want you to stop feeding Romero. I want my fucking wife back!" he spits with venom.

My breathing stutters, and a dull ache sits heavily in my stomach at the thought of not nurturing my son as I do. He can't be serious.

I sit forward, meeting his stare with equal fury. "And I want my fucking life back!"

The truth behind my words is startling, more to me than him, judging by the way his lips tip up into a cold smirk. His eyes darken, and I become frozen to the spot.

"Be careful what you wish for, Laya. I might just make

that happen, but mark my words, our son belongs here, with me."

His taunt is chilling and has every hair on my body standing to attention, a cruel blow only a monster could deliver, and as if sensing my thoughts, a mask of normalcy takes over his face, leaving me reeling.

He leans over the table and takes my face into the palm of his hand, stroking over my cheek with a tenderness which was absent only moments ago. "Be the good girl I know you to be, mi amor." Then he pushes back in his chair and stands, leaving me struggling to breathe as I try to regain control over my shell-shocked body. All the while, my mind is left repeating his cruel taunt. *"Mark my words, our son belongs here, with me."*

Only one thought flickers through my mind.

I want to go home.

NINE

LAYA

The wind howls as I tug the sheet around me tighter. Mexico is hot as hell, but when a storm hits, we feel it to our core. I squeeze my eyes shut in an attempt to encourage sleep I know won't come anytime soon.

A crashing sound has me startling and my heart pounding erratically, and my eyes flare open. I glance at Romero to find him sleeping soundly. He's like his father when he sleeps, nothing unsettles him. The bedroom door creaks open, and Carlos stumbles inside. His eyes latch onto mine, and the way they glare at me has my blood running cold. This man does not look like my husband. His shirt is wide open, and his hands are bloodied, and my chest hitches with the intense way he stares at me. It's like he doesn't recognize me. A lump forms in my throat, but I refuse to fear him, so I slip out of bed and make my way toward him. My body trembles as I approach while he remains so still it's as if he's frozen, his stare unwavering while my pulse rushes in my ears.

"Carlos?"

He doesn't so much as blink, and as I get closer to him, the light from the hallway lands perfectly on his face, showing his pupils blown, which causes my footing to waver. He's taken drugs.

Holy shit, he's taken drugs. My mouth goes dry.

Does he even realize where he is? Who I am?

A prickling awareness that we're in danger pumps through me, and I whimper with nervousness.

Romero makes a soft cooing noise, and panic hits me square in the chest when Carlos's attention is drawn toward him. Then I find my voice again, it's scratchy and full of nervousness and I hate the sound of it, so foreign to my normal confident, happy self.

"C-Carlos, are you okay?"

His focus remains locked on Romero's bassinet, and my mind races with what to do. With shaky hands, I place them on his cheeks, cupping them gently and guiding his head to face me. "What can I do?" Tears swim in my eyes. I want to help him, to take away the pain hidden behind the need to destroy himself and, in the process, destroy us too. I want nothing more than for him to be the man I wanted to fall in love with, yet I know that man never existed.

"Tell me what to do, Carlos, and I'll do it." My voice wobbles as a tear slides down my cheek. "I'll do anything for you," I whisper to the man I've been desperate to love to no avail, but as the father of my baby, I want him to be that man, the one who will give me the fairytale family. The man who never left me with a doubt in my mind that he loves me wholeheartedly above anyone else.

Owen's smile flashes into my mind, and I squeeze my eyes closed to rid myself of the image, and when I reopen them, Carlos's wide eyes slice through me. They look empty, despondent, so detached it terrifies me. It's as if he can see the man I want him to be, and he hates me for it. "Carlos, please tell me what to do." The crack of thunder makes my heart skip a beat as fear engulfs me at the way he glares back at me. "You've taken something, and it's scaring me, Carlos."

My words pull him from his daze, and he grips my wrists, pulling them away from his face, but he doesn't let go. "Don't fucking question me!" he bellows, causing Romero to cry out. Then he pushes me onto the bed and quickly moves around me toward Romero. Every cell in my body screams at me that he will hurt him, and I can think of nothing but to protect him. I push myself up to stand and grab hold of Carlos's shoulder, pulling him back to face me. "Ple-ea—" He punches my cheek, my head snaps to the side, and I fall to the floor, the impact of the solid marble brutal to my hip. I cry out in agony, then his eyes lock with mine, and it feels like hours slip between us as I stare back at him in shock. My heart hammers as hurt lances through me.

"Don't ever try to stop me from seeing my son, you bitch."

He hit me.

He scared me.

He's not the man I want him to be. He never will be. That man would never hurt me, he would do anything in his power to protect me and our son, and it's at this moment I realize what a monster he truly is. I will never love him, no matter how much his blood runs through my son's veins.

I'll never love him.

My lip trembles and my eyes fill with unshed tears, but I refuse to let them fall for him. I refuse to cry for a man so undeserving.

His lips part to speak, but nothing comes out, and when Romero cries out again, my spine straightens with a steely determination. I'd die to protect him, and in this moment, I know I might have to.

Carlos pauses, and my body freezes as I wait in anticipation of his next move, and my gaze latches onto his Adam's apple sliding down his throat, then he drops his head forward and tugs on his hair, and I'm lost at what to do. Do I reach out to him to comfort him? Or do I back away and comfort my son?

"Fuck!" he screams into his hands, then slides his palm down his face. He holds my heart in a vise, but then he walks straight past me, slamming the bedroom door behind him, and I don't breathe again until I hear his feet thundering down the stairs. I fight back the need to cry as I scramble to my feet. Grabbing the chair in the corner of the room, I wedge it beneath the door handle and turn the lock on the door. My entire body is shaking, I'm dizzy, and my heart is aching.

I glance around the room, my adrenaline spiked with a need to protect my son. I drag the dresser in front of the chair, determined to keep him out. Then I rush to Romero, pick him up, and cradle him to my chest. "Shhh, it's okay. Mommy's here. It's okay." I don't know who I'm trying to convince more, as my instinct to protect him outweighs my need to make this work. With that thought in mind, I pick up my phone, and it's not lost on me that the first person I want to call is Owen. My fingers tremble as I type in his number, only to find the storm has left me with no signal. My heart plummets at the thought of being here for any longer.

What if he comes back? What if he tries to change my mind?

I'm about to leave my husband, and he'll do anything to stop me. I know without a shadow of a doubt that he'd create a war, and those I hold dear will get hurt, but as I stare down at Romero, I know I've no choice. It's only a matter of time before Carlos goes even further, and I refuse to be his victim. My husband is unraveling. The man I desperately wanted to love is not the same man who hit me tonight.

"As soon as morning comes, Mommy is going to get us out of here," I whisper against his soft hair. "I'll do everything I can to protect you, Romero." I hold him against my chest. "I'm going to make sure you're safe and never doubt the love of your family, little man, because you deserve better. We both do."

I lift my head and stare at the door, knowing it's only a matter of time before we can make our escape, and when we do, there's no going back.

I'm deserving of the life I dreamed of as a young girl, and I will get it, for both of us.

TEN

LAYA

The clock beside me blinks, reading 4:42 a.m., only six minutes since I told myself not to check it again.

After placing Romero back in his bassinet, I climbed back on the bed and drew my knees up to my chest, constantly checking my phone for a signal that hasn't appeared.

My wedding ring shimmers on the nightstand beside me, taunting me. A stark reminder of our loss, the potential of a love that never flourished, not when someone else held my heart in their hands while the man I entrusted with it destroyed it. Destroyed us.

Now I watch the door like a hawk, and when there's commotion downstairs, panic courses through me, making my heart painfully stutter in my chest. *Oh shit, he's back.*

I struggle to regulate my breathing as terror cripples me and my mouth goes dry. Then I mentally chastise myself, and my eyes dart around the room in search of a weapon, anything I can use to defend me and my son.

Before I can even think, I jump up from the bed and grab one of the bedside lights, snapping the cable from it with ease.

I clutch the heavy brass stem to my chest and stand against the wall. Footsteps rush up the stairs and a sob catches in my throat, and when the door handle moves, I feel like the air is being forced from my lungs. "Laya?" Carlos's panicked voice filters through the door, and I sense the change in him. "Laya, open the door." I shake my head, then internally kick myself, knowing he can't see me. "Laya. This is serious. Open the fucking door." His voice is firmer this time and much more in control, like the Carlos I know. A soft thud hits the door, and I can only imagine it's his head. "Please, mi amor. I need you to open the door," he whispers, and my heart crumbles. If I open the door, he's going to apologize, try to convince me it was a one off, that he's sorry. That it will never happen again.

"Please, Laya. This is important. Please." The way he tenderly whispers my name sends a sliver of unease through me. "Mi amor. I-I don't have much time. Please, I need you to open the door; otherwise, I'm going to have to break it down." I'm sure I hear him sniffle, and my throat clogs with an urge to comfort him. But can I trust him?

A sob erupts in my chest as I glance toward Romero. Do I take the chance and open the door?

"I know you're scared, mi amor. But please trust me, we're in danger, and I need you to trust in me. I want to protect you and Romero, mi amor. Please, let me protect you."

His words make my legs wobble. I've always trusted

him when, clearly, I shouldn't have, but if he wanted to hurt us, he could have, and he could easily break into the room. The realization hits me at how vulnerable we are, and it also makes me more determined than ever to get the hell out of Mexico and back to my family, where I don't feel isolated and unsafe.

"Please." The pleading tone in his voice has me moving. Rightly or wrongly, I follow my heart and drag the dresser away from the door. Each action has my chest rising faster. Then I push the chair aside, blow out a deep breath, and unlock the door. My fingers tremble with each move, and I will myself to remain strong.

Before I have a chance to step back, Carlos is pushing through the door. His fraught eyes lock onto mine, his hair is disheveled and face pale, and his body shakes with what seems to be panic but could easily be withdrawals.

His face falls. "Mi amor." His lip quivers, and the broken tone of his voice has me choking on my emotion. I step in front of Romero's bassinet, and my fingers tighten on the lamp, and his brow furrows until he sets them on the soft mewling sound of our son. My chest constricts when his face morphs into horror, as if realizing the enormity of his actions and my stance at protecting our son from the last person he should need protecting from. When his shaky hands cup my bruised cheek, I step back and turn my head away from him, refusing to give him the comfort he's craving. He nods, and his Adam's apple slowly slides down his throat. "I messed up." Licking his lips, he shakes his head, and I want to tell him this is so much more than messing up. "I messed up bad, Laya." Tears fall freely down his face, and he drops his head, and I itch to pull him toward me, to tell him everything will be okay, that we will be okay. But I refuse to do so because after tonight, nothing will be the same. A war is coming, and I've already chosen where I stand, and that's by my son's side.

He inhales deeply, then with a heavy exhale, he steels his shoulders, raises his head, and stares at me with a renewed vigor.

"You're in danger, Laya. I need you to listen very carefully to me." The severity of his tone pulls my attention. Danger?

My eyes roam over him, wondering if he's having some sort of mental breakdown, but all I see is anxiety laced in sincerity that makes my heart skip a beat with a foreboding feeling.

His eyes flit around the room. "Where's Romero's diaper bag?"

I furrow my brow, searching for a sign of the drugs that took hold of him only a short while ago, but find none.

His gaze lands back on me. "I got the doctor to administer me with a shot to help me recover quickly, and it's a good thing too because we're in danger, mi amor. Real fucking danger." His sharp eyes sear into me. They speak the truth.

"What are you talking about?"

He moves around the room, pulling open the closet while I follow behind. "Grab Romero and his diaper bag." My feet are frozen to the floor, unable to comprehend what he's saying.

"What's happening? You're scaring me."

"Laya! Fucking listen to me. Romero, get him and everything he needs. They're coming!" he screams, and it snaps me out of my daze. The frantic look in his usually controlled eyes has panic surging through me. I almost trip over the bed to grab the diaper bag, then move to Romero, scooping him into my arms, hoping he can't sense the terror unraveling inside me.

"Who is coming, Carlos?" I ask again as I clutch my son tightly.

He shakes his head, unwilling to tell me more, and disappointment fills me. The secrets he holds are not good ones, I know that, but I'd hoped he could trust me enough to keep them. I touch my cheek and stare at my frantic husband moving around the room like a tornado, and all I want is to feel the safety and security of strong arms wrapped around me, to tell me everything will be okay, that he'd never hurt me, and I'd believe it.

But those arms are miles away from here, and that thought terrifies me even more.

I want to go home.

My phone lights up, and I move quickly to pick it up. "No. Not the phone!" Carlos snaps, and I glance over my shoulder to see he has a backpack in his hand. His tone softens. "Not the phone, Laya. I don't want them tracking you." I search his face for truth and find it shining back at me with teary eyes. What the hell is happening? And why does my normally well-put-together husband look like a train wreck?

Leaving the phone, I turn back to him, and his shoulders relax, then he reaches out, tugging me toward the bathroom.

Once inside, Carlos scans his hand above the mirrored wall. It opens, and my mouth falls agape. How the hell did I not know about this? He turns to face me. "It's a panic room. Nobody will know you're in here. They won't be able to see or hear you."

"What? Carlos, why the hell do we need a panic room? What's happening?" He pulls me inside and drops the bag to the floor while I make a quick assessment of the small room.

A cot sits in the corner, a small kitchenette, a safe, and a wall of guns that has me reeling back on my feet. Carlos catches me, and I spin to face him, then realize we're standing in front of the mirror in our bedroom. It's one-way glass.

"You can't see inside here," he attempts to reassure me.

This time, I let his cold hands cup my face as a lone tear trickles down my cheek. "I'm so sorry, mi amor."

My chin wobbles, and I blink away at the wetness pooling in my eyes.

"I need you to know I love you with all my heart, and I need you to tell Romero what a good papa I was going to be."

His words whirl around in my head. He's talking with such finality. And then it hits me. He's not staying with us.

"C-Carlos?"

"Shh." He places his finger over my lips. "Listen carefully, mi amor. Nico will collect you and take you both to safety. I'm going to fix this. I promise everything will be exactly how it always should have been." The solemn tone of his voice sends a shiver down my spine. It's like he's given up, and that scares me even more. "Trust no one but Nico. And Owen." My blood stills.

I shake my head as panic surges inside me. "I don't understand."

"Look at me, Laya." Our gazes collide, and love seeps

OWEN

from him, making my breath stutter. "Never doubt how I felt about you, never." He pulls something from his pocket, and I don't have a chance to see it before he's tying it around my neck. But when the familiar pendant falls onto my chest, a pang of guilt and regret fills my bloodstream at how much I missed it. How much I miss *him*. Then I shake my head to rid the thoughts. "I need you to promise me that you will be happy, Laya. That you move on and give our son the life he deserves." I stare back at him with wide eyes. What he's saying sounds so final. He isn't saying he will see us later; he's saying goodbye.

My legs give way, and he catches me, anchoring me to the floor while my mind becomes hazy.

Holy shit. What the hell is happening?

"I will always love you, mi amor."

His phone beeps and his eyes close. He swallows slowly, and when his eyes open, they fix on Romero. He bends his head and places a soft kiss on Romero's hair. "Be good, my son." Then he lifts his eyes to meet mine.

I shake my head again, refusing to accept whatever it is he's planning.

He nods. "I have to pay for my sins, mi amor. I'm sorry. This was never how it was meant to happen. But I'll make sure you're happy. I promise you that." His hand trails down my cheek, cupping my chin between his fingers. "You were the best thing to ever happen to me. I knew I'd never get to keep you." He places a kiss on my lips and takes a deep breath, breathing me in. Then he steps back, detaching himself from me, and I feel the loss instantly. My mind doesn't have time to digest his words and seek the answers I so desperately need. They're riddled with confusion that only he can clarify.

"Everything you need is in the bag. Only use the contact on the phone." Reaching into his jacket pocket, he pulls out a memory card. "Give this to Owen." He places it into the chest pocket of his dress shirt I'm wearing. "It's important, mi amor. Only Owen."

I can only nod like a dumb-struck idiot.

He clears his throat and raises his chin. Then, before I can say another word to him, he spins on his heel and strides toward the door.

Panic bubbles inside me. "Ca-Carlos. Carlos, where are you going?"

He slams the door behind him and a whirring noise that sounds like locks slipping into place has me pushing on the door frantically.

Romero cries, and I rush over to the cot, securing him in the sheets before rushing back over to the door, pounding on it with my fists. "Carlos. Carlos, open this fucking door!" Romero wails, and I glance over my shoulder, torn between comforting my son or trying to get out of here and find answers. "Carlos, please!"

Movement catches my eye, and I turn around to face the mirrored window. Two men in balaclavas have entered the room, and I reel back against the wall as I watch in horror when they drag Carlos to the floor. One punches him in the face, sending a flurry of blood splashing into the air while he kneels at their feet. Terror ceases my lungs, and I struggle to breathe through the trauma of witnessing my husband being assaulted.

One man stands behind him and yanks his head back, and I step forward when Carlos's mouth moves. Trying my hardest to read his lips, I swear he's repeating, "Don't look." Without realizing I had stepped so close, my hands touch the glass as desperation floods me. I hang on to the glass to keep me upright when my entire body feels like it will crumble.

The other man steps to the side and then, out of nowhere, he pulls out a thick blade.

Oh Jesus, no.

My fingers curl into fists, and without thinking, I slam them against the glass. "No!" My voice ricochets off the wall, and Romero's screams become like white noise as I watch on terror stricken as time slows. He brings the blade to Carlos's throat, and I will myself to close my eyes, but I can't.

I can't.

Nothing works.

I'm frozen.

Blood spews from my husband's neck, and a choked gasp catches in my throat at the sight while my stomach rolls, churning with bile, fear, and dread.

The wound isn't a small one, and when they release his hair, his head falls forward, but not before his eyes, normally so full of love and life, fall on me with emptiness.

He's gone.

They drop him on the floor as if he means nothing, as if he isn't a husband and father. As if he isn't cared for.

Suddenly, like I've been electrocuted, I jolt, then something spurs me into action. I race over to Romero, pick him up, and hold him tightly against my chest. Then I stroke over his hair, my eyes not leaving the masked men as they tear up the room, searching for something.

The memory card tucked into Carlos's shirt pocket has me scrambling to retrieve it, and I stare down at it. An overwhelming awareness prickles my skin.

Is whatever is on this card what my husband was killed for?

I snap my gaze up toward the glass, and when one of the men stalks toward the mirror, my heart stills. I plead with Carlos that he was telling the truth, that they can't see us. His crazed eyes dart around the room, and I wonder if they can sense our presence, my pulse skittering with the thought.

Without realizing it, I'm backed up against the wall, as far from their eyes as possible, and yet somehow, as if knowing I'm here, one of the men focuses on the mirror. He licks his lips and I swallow hard, desperately shushing Romero as he continues to fuss, and when he snaps his eyes away, I blow out the breath I had been holding and sag in relief.

Keeping my eyes trained on the glass, I don't dare take my attention away from them until they storm from the room, then I drop to the floor. Clinging to my son, I finally let the tears flow.

ELEVEN

LAYA

A familiar whirring noise sets the hairs on the back of my neck on edge, and I snap my head up from the bedpost, with Romero on my chest.

Terror grips me, and Romero lets out a low whimper. When the door opens, relief floods me to see a familiar face.

Nico stands in the doorway, his face pale and full of uncertainty. "Are you okay?"

I shake my head and hiccup on the sob bubbling inside me.

"You're safe now, Laya. You both are." He nods toward Romero. "Come on, sweetheart, I'm going to get you both out of here." As he holds out his hand, I attempt to stand, but my legs are wobbly and won't comply. "I've got you." He steps into the room, and I back away, attempting to make myself smaller. "Laya. You can trust me, sweetheart."

My chest hitches on the familiar words, and when I tilt my head up, he has devastation bleeding from his eyes, and it hits me. He lost Carlos too; he was like a brother to him.

"I-I'm sorry." My lip quivers as much as I try not to let it.

He strokes a hand over his head, and when he glances over his shoulder toward the glass, he briefly closes his eyes before turning back to face me. "I covered him up. We need to get you both out of here."

"Where will we go?" I whisper.

"You're going home."

Those three words lodge in my chest, and I choke on air. A sudden need to get there quicker has me standing on shaky legs.

Nico glances around the small room. "Do you need to take anything?"

Swallowing, I stare down at my bare feet. I'm still wearing Carlos's shirt that I slept in, my bra, and panties, and nothing else. "The rucksack." I point toward the bag Carlos bought in with him, and Nico picks it up. He unzips it, then hands me a pair of sneakers that Carlos had the foresight to pack on my behalf. The feeling of sickness that has been taunting me threatens to rear itself at the thought he considered my footwear while knowing he would die. Because there's not a doubt in my mind that he knew his fate, and that knowledge sits heavily in my stomach.

Almost robotically, without releasing Romero, I push my feet into the sneakers, then bend down and grab the bag, and Nico helps me drape the diaper bag over my shoulder.

"You ready?"

My mouth that is unbelievably dry doesn't seem to want to function, so I just nod.

"Try not to look."

His words send a shudder through me, but again, I agree, and when he places his hand in mine, I allow it, unsure of whether it's comforting me or him. It's not lost on me that my husband would have killed Nico for touching me, but the way he's protecting us has me following him blindly through the bathroom and into the bedroom.

The room smells like a combination of copper and Carlos's cologne, a cruel taunt, the air bathed in his life as well as his death. The sheets are pulled from our marital bed and draped over his body, and I squeeze Nico's hand tighter as a thank you.

He steers us through the room and toward the landing, and I finally get to see the destruction of what used to be our pristine family home now filled with only nightmares.

TWELVE

LAYA

My mind reels. Unable to comprehend the events of the day, I'm not sure how long it took to get to Nico's private jet. I was in a state of shock, and again, I'm unsure when we landed, at which point I was carried to a waiting car. Nico tried to explain that Owen was aware of the situation, but the conversation fell on deaf ears, as I was in such a state of trauma I could comprehend nothing other than the destruction of my life. After feeding Romero, I fell asleep, then he woke me to say we'd arrived at a secure location.

In a complete blur, he took me and Romero through a private elevator in a hotel, then up to the presidential floor before explaining nobody can access the floor. Sympathy oozed from him, and as much as I wanted nothing more than comfort, I couldn't bring myself to ask for it.

Then he turned, leaving me here and telling me Owen was on his way.

He left, and I struggled to remain standing. With his departure, he was taking a part of my life with him I can never get back.

Only the haunting memories of its existence will stay with me.

Rushing toward the door, I slide every lock in place, then fall to the floor. I'd not uttered a single word to him the entire time we spent together, but now I wish I'd have said a thousand things, but mainly, thank you. Thank you for swooping in and rescuing us, for bringing us to safety.

Thank you for being Carlos's friend, brother, and ally.

Once I feed and change Romero, I put on the television, hoping to divert my attention from the clock beside me. Still, I glance at it every few minutes, like a couple of nights ago, when it glared back at me, not giving me the time I so desperately wanted to see.

Why does time go so slowly when you want it to speed up? Yet when you wish you had all the time in the world, it's over in a flash.

A soft knock at the bedroom door stills me, and I mute the television, then glance toward my son sleeping beside me, tucked in between a pillow fortress.

The knock sounds again, and I chew on my bottom lip. It's only been just over an hour since Nico left, and we're at least two hours from home.

"Laya?"

Owen's deep voice has me springing up from the bed. I rush toward the door, slip the chains off the latch with shaky hands, pull the door open, then throw myself at him, giving him no choice but to hold me against his muscular chest while uncontrollable sobs rack through me.

"Shhh, it's okay, baby girl. I got you." He scoops me up

with ease, his thick arms cradling me to his chest. "Shhh." He presses kisses against my hair as he breathes me in, and I relish it, his touch, his proximity, the familiarity of it being him holding me. "You're safe." I hiccup on his words, finally knowing it to be true, believing it. "You're fucking safe, baby girl. I'm never letting you out of my sight again." His confession sends a flurry of warmth through my veins. This is what I need to hear, this is the comfort I need, no matter how uncertain it may be. The turn of events that brought us here plagues my mind, but I don't argue with his words. I give in to the feeling of security and clutch his T-shirt in my fist while my face floods with the wetness of my trauma. "Let it all out, Laya. I'm here. Nobody's going to hurt you, baby girl. Nobody is going to hurt either of you."

He walks us over to the bed, then freezes. I tilt my head to see his face, and his throat works as he stares toward Romero. "He has your hair," he mumbles, as if speaking to himself, and I want to correct him. I want to tell him his shading is the same as his father's, but I can't get the words out.

"He's perfect," he whispers, his words laced in awe. "Just perfect."

THIRTEEN

OWEN

My muscles are wrung tight as I stride down the corridor toward her room. The moment I got the call from Nico, I dropped everything to be exactly where I belong, by her side.

The pressure inside is combustible, and I know deep in my soul that I won't settle until she's in my arms. I need to see her, to hold her and know myself she's safe. That she's mine. Above all else, I need to reassure her. I don't want a sliver of doubt to be in that beautiful head of hers that she's anything but mine.

All. Fucking. Mine.

Sweat beads on my forehead as her room gets closer, and my blood pumps with a feral need to touch her to bring me solace.

It's been too long. The day in the restaurant was the last time I saw her, and it feels like an eternity, and an unusual nervousness bubbles inside me. The moment I arrive outside her door, I take a deep breath to steel myself. Nico explained she was in a state of shock from Carlos's demise, so I have to show her my support and compassion, but I will also make it known that both her and Romero are mine now, as they always should have been.

I swipe my sweaty palms down my jeans and take a deep breath before exhaling, then raise my hand and give the door a knock. My body vibrates with an urge to storm the room when nothing happens, so I mentally chastise myself before repeating the process. "Come fucking on, Laya," I grumble to myself.

"Laya?" I grit out in annoyance.

Then I hear movement and the sound of the locks disengaging.

The moment the door opens, she flings herself at me, and my arms automatically band around her petite waist. I nuzzle into her hair, relieved her scent hasn't changed, that she hasn't changed.

"Shhh, it's okay, baby girl. I got you." I scoop her up in my arms, desperate to hold her close to my heart, to soothe the heavy thud that penetrates my skin, and walk into the room.

She's here.

She's here with me, and I'm never letting her go. "Shhh." I press soft kisses to her hair, using it to reassure me as much as her. She's finally here. Finally in my fucking arms.

"You're safe." She hiccups at my words while she tangles her fingers in my shirt, fisting it. "You're fucking safe, baby girl. I'm never letting you out of my sight

OWEN

again." I hate hearing her cry like this; the low sobs break my heart. "Let it all out, Laya. I'm here."

I walk us over to the bed, then my feet come to a standstill. Staring down at the pillows, I set eyes on my son for the first time—Romero.

Emotion lodges in my throat like a thick ball, stealing my ability to swallow. With it comes a fierce determination.

He's mine now. They both are.

I take in his little features, the way his lips are pulled into a cute bow, like Laya's when she pouts. His small fists are bunched tight, and his mop of dark hair looks as silky as Laya's.

Somehow, I swallow and whisper to myself, "He has your hair."

My lips twitch at his little romper. "He's perfect." Love drips from me, a fierce need to claim them both officially as mine. "Just perfect," I whisper.

This moment, with the woman I love in my arms and the first time I set eyes on my son, will be forever carved into my memories, into my heart.

Today is the start of the rest of our lives.

We just have to weather the storm to secure it.

FOURTEEN

OWEN

With Laya cradled against my chest, I sit on the mattress with my back against the headboard while she continues to fall to pieces in my arms. I take comfort in knowing I can bring her the reassurance she needs while also providing the security she should have had. Nothing will hurt my girl again. She and our son are my priority, and nobody will come between us, especially not a dead man.

When her sobs become shallow snores, I relax, using my hand to stroke over her silky hair to remind myself I finally have her with me.

The entire night I spent flicking my attention between her and Romero. Each soft noise he made had me on full alert, but ultimately, the little man slept through. I don't know much about babies, but I've been trying to learn since hearing about her pregnancy. I intend on being the best father I can be and give them everything they deserve and so much more.

A few times during the night, Laya cried, and I'd hold her close, whispering to her I have her. She's mine, and I reveled in the fact that my words sent her back to sleep.

Laya rouses from her sleep, stretching in my arms, and finally, she lifts her head to stare into my eyes.

My heart skips a beat. Pure anger fills my bloodstream at the sight of her delicate face swollen and bruised. Every cell in my body becomes embroiled in flames of fury, as a sudden need to annihilate something has me vibrating uncontrollably.

"Owen?" Her sweet voice filters through the haze of red coating my senses.

And when I see the panic in her wide eyes, a need to soothe her overcomes me. "Who did that to you?" My thick thumb grazes over her swollen cheek, but she stares back at me with a furrowed brow. Does she not realize she's bruised? I press gently and she winces, then her face pales and those red-rimmed eyes fill with tears. "Who?" I repeat.

She licks her cracked lips, and I realize she needs some proper care, and possibly medical attention. Then her eyes move toward Romero, and my stomach plummets with a desperate need for answers. If someone touched them ...

Her gaze comes back to me, and the way she stares at me with uncertainty pisses me off. She can trust me. She should trust me, yet she's unsure.

"Laya. Right now. I'm hanging on by a thin thread, and I know you've been through so much, but I want answers pretty fucking soon." My teeth grind as she scans my face, as if searching for something. What? I've no fucking clue.

Then she shakes her head. "It doesn't matter now."

My eyes narrow. "Of course it fucking matters. Someone hurt you."

She fiddles with the shirt she's wearing, and my spine straightens, only now realizing it's something of his.

"It doesn't matter because he's not here anymore."

Her words send a torrent of pain lancing through my chest.

Holy fucking shit. The bastard hurt her.

He. Fucking. Hurt. Her.

My chest heaves uncontrollably as I unravel. The fact she's been suffering at his hands, and I could have acted, could have helped her, is like someone is brutally ripping my heart out with their bare hands, destroying me.

I slide her onto the mattress, trying not to wake Romero as I move.

Then I march over and rest my forearms against the wall and breathe with my back to my family, squeezing my eyes closed to rein in the compelling need to decimate something.

If I could dig the fucker back up and slaughter him myself, I would.

"Fuck!" I roar as I slam my fist into the plaster.

"Owen?" Her delicate hand grazes over my back, and my eyes snap open. The warmth of her touch seeps through the material and into my skin. "Are you okay?"

I choke on a sardonic laugh and shake my head. *Am I okay?*

She's the one who has been widowed, run from her

family home, and beaten, yet she's asking me if I'm okay? Typical Laya. "He only did it once," she mutters.

I jolt at her words, then spin to face her. Only?

Her head is down, and she fidgets from foot to foot, that fucking shirt of his hanging off her like it has a right to be there. Like it's deserving of covering her skin.

Using my finger, I lift her chin to face me, hating the uncertainty that flashes in her eyes. Her usual steely confidence is missing, replaced with a vulnerability that I want to stamp out. "Once is one time too many, Laya."

She lifts her chin higher, and that strong, ballsy woman I know her to be glares back at me. "I know that. Do you think I don't know that? I was going to leave him."

My heart thumps harder on her admission, and I lick my lips. "You were?"

"Yes. But then ..." She darts her eyes away before closing them as if it pains her to remember.

"Then he got himself killed." I finish for her.

She flinches on my words, and I tug her toward me. The moment she wraps her arms around my waist, a sense of calm washes over me. I breathe her in. "Nothing will ever hurt you again. You hear me?" I step back so I can lock eyes with her. "Nobody will ever hurt you again. That's my promise to you."

Tears well in her eyes, and I grit my teeth at the shirt she wears and tug the collar with my hand. "This his?"

She narrows her eyes on me, and I elaborate. "The shirt. Is it his?" The deepness of my voice tells her I'm pissed, and the way her confusion turns to annoyance would make me laugh if I wasn't so angry right now.

"My husband's, yes."

My temple throbs as I try to regain some sense of calm,

but I'm struggling. Boy, am I fucking struggling. Husband?

I want to tell her the fucker is dead, where he belongs. *He isn't your husband anymore*, but I bite my tongue, knowing how much she's been through.

"He isn't the one looking after you right now, baby girl."

Her jaw tics, and she crosses her arms over her chest. The fire in her eyes makes my cock hard with a need to punish her disobedience.

"Go take it off." I tilt my head toward the bathroom. "And while you're fucking at it, get in the tub. Please." I tack on the latter, hoping to soften the bite in my tone.

Her eyebrows shoot up. "The tub?"

"Yes. The fucking tub. Gonna wash him from you."

"Wash him from me?"

I nod, liking this plan the more I think about it. "Exactly. Make you mine."

"Yours?"

I nod again.

Then she releases a heavy sigh. "I really don't have it in me to argue." My lip twitches at her compliance, then she spins on the balls of her feet and marches toward the bathroom, leaving me to check the closet. We need a crib for Romero.

We won't stay here for long, but while we are, my boy needs to sleep in his own bed so his momma can sleep properly in mine.

Exactly where she belongs.

FIFTEEN

LAYA

The fight has left my body, and I feel drained, totally spent from the turmoil of the last few days. I ignore the words Owen demanded and the meaning behind them and walk into the bathroom, suddenly desperate to rid myself of the physical aspects of the trauma that occurred back in Mexico. The need to scrub my skin clean becomes desperate, so I squeeze some body wash into the tub, turn the water on, then use the toilet.

After flushing, I take a deep breath and wash my hands. Finally, I exhale and lift my head to assess the damage. A pang of hurt slices through me. How could he do this? How could he have allowed himself to put us in a position where he caused so much heartache? How could he ruin everything we could have been?

The red rims below my eyes are puffy. My lip is partially split, and I'm unsure if it's because of his assault or due to the lack of care and simply existing. My complexion is unusually pale, and my damaged cheek is swollen and mottled with bruising from the blunt force of his fist. I wince when I press against my cheek.

"It's okay, baby girl." My gaze snaps up to Owen's, his assessing eyes drilling into me as he stands, being my protector. "Nothing will hurt you again."

I nod, then panic rushes through me, and my focus snaps toward the door. "He's fine. I got him a crib. Little guy sleeps heavy." He chuckles, and I smile. He really does. "Come on. Let's get you cleaned up." Stepping back, he allows me to turn, but he makes no move to leave the bathroom.

"Owen?"

Then he shocks the hell out of me by lowering to his knees, and his thick fingers unbutton the shirt.

"Should just rip it from you, but I don't want to hurt you." His voice is soft and his fingers tremble as he unbuttons me steadily.

"Owen. You don't have to—"

His gaze snaps up to meet mine. His bright-blue eyes hold tenderness to them and a shimmer of vulnerability he's only ever shown me once before. "I want to take care of you," he whispers, sending a trail of goose bumps over my skin while his words repeat in my head. He wants to take care of me.

When he reaches up to push the shirt from my shoulders, the air is knocked from my lungs at the intensity behind his eyes. He licks his lips slowly, like he's calculating his next move.

Heat travels over me as his eyes trail down my body. The moment he notices the bruising, he flinches, then his entire body coils tight. When his rough hand gently strokes over the bruising on my hip, I can't help but melt into him. The tenderness of his touch after being exposed to such brutality has my heart clenching with longing.

"It's okay, baby girl. You're safe with me. Always safe with me." His palm glides over the area, warming me from the outside in, and the familiarity of him calling me *baby girl* has my toes curling into the tiles.

The moment he pulls his hand away from me, I feel the disconnection in my bones, like a part of me is missing, and I hate it. The usual tsunami of emotions I feel around Owen threatens to make a comeback, only this time I don't have the strength in me to fight it.

"I'm going to take such good care of you, baby girl." The sincerity pouring from his tone and eyes tells me everything I need to know. But for how long? And what does taking care of me look like to Owen?

When his fingers fumble to unclasp the front of my bra, I'm snapped out of my stupor and see the lust in his eyes and can't help the wetness that instantly pools between my legs.

Jesus, the man is on his knees in front of me like he worships me, his gaze transfixed on my heavy tits.

"Fuck," he grunts, and suddenly, I'm feeling a little self-conscious.

My body has changed a lot since he last saw me naked, yet he still looks at me as if I'm his everything.

He rolls his lip between his teeth. "Jesus, baby girl. I didn't think you could get any more beautiful." He lifts his eyes to meet mine. "You're so beautiful."

I move my arms to cover myself from his gaze, and his hand snaps out to keep me on display. "Don't ever cover up from me, Laya."

"I have stretch marks." My reply is monotone. I'm stupefied by how he can find me attractive, but then he places a kiss on my stomach, and a bolt of electricity courses through me, bringing life to every cell inside me that withered away in Mexico.

"So beautiful," he murmurs. "You're so fucking beautiful and you don't even see it. I'm going to spend every day of my life making you see, Laya." The honesty in his tone causes emotion to settle deep inside me. He's saying everything you wish a man would say to you and his eyes implore me to believe it.

Then his trembly hands move to my hips, holding me in place for a moment as our gazes remain locked on one another. The atmosphere between us is intense, and my pulse quickens to the point of boiling. His rough fingers slip beneath the lace of my panties, then he slides them down to my feet, our focus remaining on one another as he discards them to the floor.

Then his focus turns toward my center, and my heart skips a beat. When he licks those traitorous lips of his, I think he's going to move his face toward my pussy, so I step back, remembering I haven't washed in a few days, disconnecting us in an instant.

I turn away from his deep chuckle, and he stands and walks over to the tub, holding his hand out for me, then I slip mine into his and he helps me into the tub of bubbles.

The moment the water hits my skin, I sigh in relief; the stress drains from my body like a dam breaking.

Owen kneels beside the tub and lathers up a washcloth. Then he surprises me by gently washing my face, tilting my chin in each direction with his thick fingers while I watch him through hooded eyes.

He's as handsome as I remember, more so, if that's even possible, and I wonder if he has someone important in his life, someone meaningful to him, someone he would risk it all for. Jealousy swims in my stomach, yet I have no right to it; I know that, and I hate myself for it. Despite that, it's there, gnawing away at me as always.

For years, I watched him with women from a distance, then within touching distance when I felt brave enough. I've witnessed Owen in every position possible, sneaking peeks through his bedroom door at every opportunity. I've seen it all: the raw aggression he delivers when he fucks women into semiconsciousness, the way his handsome face twists in a battle of desire while he fights the urge to come, yet his release so euphoric the pure masculine beauty seeps from him with each muscle that relaxes. A perfect synchronization of unadulterated bliss.

I've seen it all, up close and personal now, and it's engrained in my mind forever. A scar burned so deep it's embedded, and as much as that scar burned, I would endure it all again.

He's the flame that burned me, but I walked into that fire willingly.

OWEN

The little moans of pleasure she makes as I massage her scalp go straight to my balls, forcing my cock to stand to attention, so fucking tall it rubs against the top of my jeans. Her eyes are closed, and it allows me to trail my gaze over her perfect little body.

If I thought Laya was beautiful before motherhood, now she's a goddess who deserves me worshipping at her feet, begging to taste her.

Her hips are fuller, more womanly. Enough for me to hold on to while I fuck her from behind, and her tits are heavy. A bead of milk drips from them, and my mouth waters to taste it. How warm would it be when it reaches my tongue? The idea of her being full of milk for my child has my cock leaking in need. I can't help but to imagine what she looked like pregnant, full of my son, and I hate myself for not being there, not working quicker to ensure it.

A burst of excitement at the thought of filling her with another baby rushes through me with such power, I gasp in surprise. I want that; I want that so fucking bad, and I will make it happen.

"You feel so good," she whispers, and her soft, seductive tone causes my cock to ache painfully.

Jesus, fuck.

How the hell am I going to get through washing her without some form of relief?

I rinse her hair, and she snaps her eyes open. Those beautiful green orbs that render me powerless lock onto my lips, and I have an overwhelming urge to grab her head and push my tongue into her mouth. "Owen?"

My heart hammers, willing me to take what I want.

"Hmm?"

"Romero, he's crying."

I jolt, and like I've been pulled from a daydream, Romero's cries fill my ears. Before I know what I'm doing, I drop the sponge and stand. "Finish up here. I'll go grab him."

"He's probably ready for a feeding," she calls as I rush toward the bedroom like my ass is on fire.

Ready for his feeding? A heavy sigh leaves me, and I shake my head. Great. Another form of torture coming right up.

The moment I set eyes on Romero, every bit of tension leaves my body. His startling green eyes make me fall in love with him instantly, and a pain slices through my chest as I realize this little guy staring back at me with excitable kicking legs may not be my son by blood, but he should have been, and nobody will tell me any different; they're mine, both of them.

"Come on, buddy. Are you ready for a feeding?" I scoop a hand under his head and the other under his little butt. Nobody needs to know I've been taking notes from Shaw these past few months, determined to be as hands on as possible. To be everything they need. I've read every goddamn book on babies I could get my hands on.

Securing him safely against my chest, I smile when his heart beats against mine, and when I press a kiss against his soft hair, I grin at how much he's like his momma.

"Is he okay?"

Laya leans against the doorframe, a towel wrapped around her, and her wet hair hangs loosely over her shoulders as if she rushed to check on us. She holds the hairbrush in her hand, and the familiar need to care for her and be everything she needs has me pointing toward the bed.

Her eyes narrow. "On the bed, Laya. You can feed him while I brush your hair."

She glances at the hairbrush, and my lips twitch to hold back the chuckle at how adorable she looks right now. "You're going to brush my hair?"

"I am, baby girl. Now, get your ass on the bed like a good girl and feed our boy."

She rears back on my words. Her lips pull into a fine line, but she remains silent and moves toward the bed, and I follow behind.

"You're going to watch me feed him?"

Her words come out breathless, and it sends a wave of want through me, but Romero fusses, and I clear my throat. "I am. Open the towel to feed him and give me the damn brush." I hold my hand out, and she pushes it into my palm while I somehow manage to maneuver Romero into her open arms. Then she slips the towel down, and I position myself to sit behind her. I grip her hips and pull her closer so her back is almost flush against my chest. Her gasp of surprise sends a flash of arousal through me, and I work my way through her tangled hair as delicately as possible while willing my cock to go down.

"Never done this before." I chuckle awkwardly.

"Me neither," she says, and I know she's referring to the prick, and it gives me more reason to want to care for her and give her everything she deserves but never had.

We sit in near silence as I stroke over her hair with the brush, the sight of a bead of milk sliding down her has my cock standing to full attention, and I know she can feel me, and the thought only adds to my heightened state of arousal.

Jesus Christ, I could come from brushing her hair.

"You fuck anyone else?" I can't help the words that spill from my lips, nor do I care to take them back. I need to know what I'm up against, and while the thought of her with someone else ate away at me, it was my deserved, all of it. A punishment for the way I treated her, another sign of how undeserving I am of such beauty, yet I refuse to miss out a second time.

This time, we will make it work at whatever cost.

When I think she isn't going to answer, she surprises me. "No. I've only slept with my husband and you. Does that make you happy?"

Her tone is flat, not her usual snarky self, but it's not how she says it that pisses me off, it's her words.

"No." I bend to whisper in her ear. "He isn't your husband anymore. Don't refer to him as such."

She freezes, and a trail of goose bumps spreads over her delicate body, then a choked sound leaves her lips, but I don't have it in me to take the words back. No matter how harsh they are, they're the truth. The sooner she realizes it, the better.

I turn my attention toward our son, peering over her shoulder to see him watching me with as much intrigue as I am him. His small mouth works against Laya while he feeds and witnessing the action has my heart racing. "You're fucking sensational, Laya."

She tilts her head to face me, and the air is knocked from my lungs. How could I have ever let her go?

SIXTEEN

LAYA

After Owen finished brushing my hair, we bathed Romero in the sink, and he discovered firsthand how difficult baby boys can be when bathing. It was a good thing he brought a stash of fresh T-shirts with him.

We've spent the day watching television, ordering from room service, and relaxing. Then Owen took a shower and gave me his T-shirt to wear for bed.

I settled Romero in his crib, and the moment Owen slipped under the sheets, my body heated. His muscles and tattoos on display and the obvious bulge in his boxer shorts have my thighs clenching with desire.

He lifts an arm for me to snuggle into his chest, and I relax on his pec, trailing my finger over the ridges of his abs.

"What happens next? When can I go home?"

"Tomorrow."

I lift my head to look at him. "You're going home tomorrow. With me. You're moving into my place."

My eyebrows shoot up while he continues. "You're mine. You and Romero."

"Owen—"

He puts a finger on my lips. "You're mine. I should have done this years ago." The regret swims in his eyes. It bleeds from his pores as the pain of his words hits me. "I didn't. I fucked up, and I've regretted it every minute since."

His words wrap around me, bringing me comfort and reassurance. They're the words I wished to hear but never heard. They're everything I ever wanted but never received, but now? Now I don't know what to believe.

"I can see you thinking about this, baby girl. But I'm going to save you the time. It's happening. We're going to be a family. I refuse to lose another moment being by your side."

My eyes fill with tears, and my heart pangs at his words, but I refuse to acknowledge any of it after years of wanting and needing it, but now when I'm at my most vulnerable—

"I hear ya," he says, then I realize I voiced my thoughts aloud. "Let me show you," he whispers. "Let me show you everything." His thick fingers play with the necklace around my neck. "You never took it off." The love seeping from his eyes has me stopping myself from telling him I only recently became reacquainted with it when my husband gave it to me as a parting gift. The guilt surrounding the thought thickens my blood like tar, making it difficult for me to function. He gave me the necklace as acknowledgment of my feelings toward Owen, giving me permission to move on with him, and as Owen stares at me with such hope in his eyes, I'm torn between doing what's right and wrong. I want what I should have had, but know there's too much standing in the way.

"You got engaged. What happened?" I ask the question I always wanted to, but never wanted to give him the satisfaction of reaching out.

He chuckles, but it lacks humor, then he drops his head against the pillow with a heavy sigh and stares at the ceiling. "I got caught up in the moment."

I scoff. "Caught up in the moment. You just fucked me and robbed me of my virginity, Owen."

His head snaps up, and his jaw sharpens. "And you've hated me every day since for it." The accusation in his tone pisses me off. He has no right being pissed after the way he treated me.

My mouth falls open, then I sit up to stare down at him. "You knew how I felt about you."

He clears his throat. "Felt?"

"Yes, felt." I cross my arms over my chest.

He grinds his jaw and glares back at me. "Think I need to remind you, then." His stare never wavers.

"Guess you do." I lift my chin.

His fingers tangle in the ends of my hair and he tugs me toward him, lifting on his elbow so we're flush. "Gonna spank that sass right out of your luscious ass, Laya." His minty breath whispers over me, shrouding me with an all-consuming growl that sends a bolt of arousal through me and causes my nipples to peak.

His gaze darts down to my nipples, then his pupils

dilate with want. "You can pretend you don't want me, baby girl, but you know you do. Always have, always will. I own a piece of you, just like you own a piece of me."

He releases my hair, leaving me breathless and begging for more of his possessiveness while he throws himself back on the pillow.

"She meant nothing to me. I broke it off the moment you left for Miami."

"Why?" I fiddle with my hands, unsure if I want the answer.

He shrugs, then clears his throat. The moment his blue eyes latch onto mine, I know I will not like his answer, and my heart thuds heavily, waiting for it.

"So many things, Laya. Tate. Your mom. She had me promise I wouldn't touch you until you were older and experienced life. I knew the moment I touched you, you'd be willing to throw it all away for me." He's right, I would have. "I wanted you to live, Laya. Enjoy yourself. Then I thought you'd come back to me. You've wanted me for as long as I can remember. I knew that, and I took advantage of it."

I swipe away the tears that fall. "You didn't take advantage of me."

His jaw locks tight, and his temple pulsates. "I didn't treat you right." And I can't put my finger on it, but there's more meaning behind it than the obvious issue of him leaving me.

"You left me and made me feel like shit. Then I walked out to a crowd of people celebrating your engagement." I swallow away the bile that threatens to spill over each time I replay it in my mind.

"I'm sorry, baby girl." He knocks my hands away and

wipes the tears from my cheeks with his thumbs. "So fucking sorry. I didn't feel like I had a choice, Laya. I wanted what was best for you, and in my mind, that wasn't me. The worst thing I ever did was allow you to believe I didn't want you. But I swear to you"—he cups my cheeks in the palms of his heavy hands—" I promise you, baby girl, I'll be your everything and so much fucking more. I'm going to spend every day of my fucking life devoted to you and my son, and you won't regret a second of it, I promise."

Part of me always knew my mom had stepped in and warned Owen to stay away, and out of respect, I knew he would listen, but that night, the night he took my virginity, I genuinely thought that changed everything for us. It did, but not in the way we both wanted.

Romero uses this moment to make a soft gurgling noise, and my attention is drawn toward him, a reminder of how the course of that night changed everything for me. And now, I wouldn't change a damn thing about it.

Owen sighs, as if hearing my thoughts. "I should have been his father, Laya." When I turn toward him, his focus is on Romero. "He should have been mine." Then he turns to face me. "But I swear to God, I'll be everything he deserves." The sincerity in his words has my heart skipping a beat. "I'll be the best father there is."

I don't doubt a word of it, not with the way his eyes drill into mine with power behind them. Owen is capable.

I just have to let him try.

Can I do that?

Do I even want it?

"Let me love you the way I should have, baby girl."

A sob ripples through me, and he pulls me against this

chest while my heart breaks all over again. He holds me tight into the night, until there's no fight left in me and only the memories of before he broke us consume me, like most nights. Only this time, it's different because he holds me when the nightmares come too.

SEVENTEEN

OWEN

"No. No. Stop it!"

I'm pulled from my sleep and fall straight into combat mode, like a light being flipped on. I'm alert and wide awake, but the girl beside me wrapped up in the bedsheets and tussling with them is far from awake. "Laya." I nudge her gently. She's so wrapped up in her nightmare that she doesn't hear me trying to soothe her. "Baby girl." Her skin is clammy, and with the illumination from the bathroom light, I can see her chest rising rapidly as she becomes more and more agitated.

"Laya!" I rock her harder this time, my voice deep enough to make her snap her eyes open. She whimpers, and I want to kick myself for the fear embedded in her eyes.

Just what the fuck did he do to her? I clench my teeth so hard they hurt, but I shake away the pain and lift her chin to face me.

"What the fuck did he do to you?" She stares at me with a furrowed brow. "Tell me."

She shakes her head, and anger floods me. Worse than that, I want to reassure her but don't know how.

"Shhh, baby girl. I got you. Let me take away your pain. Be a good girl and stop crying, baby."

"I—" She hiccups. "Can't."

"I know, baby girl. Shhh, I'm here for you." My heart skips a beat with her in my arms, soothing her. Nothing has ever felt as right as comforting her in this moment. "What do you need, baby girl?" My throat goes impossibly dry, not knowing how to make her feel better or make everything all right, other than promising to find those responsible for her pain and making them pay with every ounce of strength I have. I swear I'll tear them apart.

"I don't know," she whispers, and I hate her admission, hate I can't bring her the solace she desperately needs and deserves.

"Don't worry, baby girl. I'll figure it out," I promise her, stroking over her silky hair and vowing to do just that.

She nods against me as I will myself to relax while I lie there listening to her whimpers of pain that adds another layer of my anger toward the fuckers responsible for her nightmares.

I'll show them fucking torture.

Nobody messes with what's mine and gets away with it.

EIGHTEEN

LAYA

Owen ordered us breakfast, then we washed up and packed our few belongings. My entire body shook as we made our way to his SUV in the underground parking lot, and I finally relaxed into the passenger seat when he leaned over, strapped me in, and closed the door, securing us inside.

Romero drifted off to sleep when we hit the highway while I spent the first hour staring out of the window, doing my best to avoid any conversation about my nightmare last night and Owen talking about us having a future together. My cheeks heat thinking about it.

When my stomach cramps a little, I wince, hoping and praying I can make it home before I need to use the restroom. Wherever home will be.

"My place is just over half an hour away."

I snap out of my daze and glance around at our

surroundings, the area familiar, yet we're not heading toward the city center.

"It is?" I turn to face Owen, knowing he lives in an apartment in the city, or he used to.

"I bought us a house."

I blink. Then I blink again. Did he just say he bought us a house?

"Baby girl, you look adorable with your mouth open. Makes me want to stuff it with my thick cock until you choke." My mouth drops open wider, then I replay his words in my head and snap it shut. Then he throws his head back on a deep chuckle and his bright-blue eyes dance with mirth before he brings his eyes back on the road.

"Owen?"

"Hmm?"

Trepidation fills my tone, and he doesn't miss it, as his spine straightens and his hands tighten on the steering wheel. "About last night …"

His gaze slides to mine, and his jaw sharpens, then he stares ahead again. "Whatever you're planning on saying, save it. Ain't gonna like it, so don't bother. But just know I'm going to hunt those pieces of shit down and make them pay for putting you through that." My heart stills. There's no way I want him to get involved. I don't want him to get hurt. I need him; we both do.

"I don't want you to get hurt."

He takes hold of my hand and brings my fingers to his lips, and my eyes fill with tears. "I promise you I won't."

I try to pull my hand from his, but he refuses to let go, his sharp eyes drilling into me to comply, and I finally relax, allowing him the control he wants and needs. "Do as you're fucking told. Your ass is already begging to be spanked because of how much you keep sassing me." He winks at me, the confidence oozing from him as his gaze trails down my body, no doubt taking in the redness flushing up my cheeks and over my ears.

The next words tumble from my mouth before I can stop them. "Is that what you're into?"

He licks his lips, then darts his eyes back toward the road. The veins in his arms contract, and I wonder if he's irritated by my question or if he's feeling vulnerable. His Adam's apple works, then he glances toward me. "You know I've done spanking, Laya. Don't act dumb." He's referring to the times I've witnessed him with other women, the times jealousy flooded my veins like a disease. He clears his throat. "I just don't want to hurt you, like last time." The vulnerability in his tone has my heart clenching.

I nod, remembering the way he pulled away from me when he choked me. But it felt right, really fucking right. So right, my morals went out the window in a split second, because what I want is so much more than him saying it. I want to feel it deep inside, every spank and his hands around my throat, his cock buried to the hilt; I want it all.

"It felt right," I mutter, and his shoulders relax. When his eyes meet mine, they're full of lust, making my cheeks burn brighter, then his gaze wanders leisurely over my body to my exposed legs.

I'm only wearing his T-shirt, and he knows I'm without panties.

"So fucking right," he repeats with a feral gleam in his bright-blue eyes, as if liking my response.

He glances in the rearview mirror at Romero, looks back to me, then kisses my fingers again. "Gonna make everything all right, baby girl." His words are full of promise, but even more, they're full of intrigue, and as much as I want to delve deeper and ask those questions, I don't think I'm ready. I'm not sure I ever will be. So instead of pushing further, I sink back into my seat and close my eyes.

The last words he whispers make me wonder if I'm dreaming already.

"Gonna make you my wife."

NINETEEN

OWEN

I place the car into park and put the handbrake on, then take a deep breath and glance over my shoulder at Romero. The little dude is cute as hell, all tucked up in his blanket. My jaw twitches at it being something the bastard provided for them, but I'll soon erase every memory of him from their minds and bodies. His very existence will be nothing more than dust, like his ashes.

My body tightens with a fierce need to protect them, to ensure they're mine at whatever the cost.

I take in every inch of my girl, and my heart throbs. The empty ache she left behind is now full, so full it causes me a different kind of pain, one of completeness. She blinks, and when those green eyes meet mine, her pouty lips tip up into a smile that sends a flurry of warmth through my body, something only she has ever achieved, and I mirror her smile, granting her the same happiness she gifts me.

"Hey," she breathes out, and I want to smash my lips against hers, but I refrain myself and tilt my head toward the house.

"We're home."

She darts her gaze toward the house, and her throat works. "Home?" Her voice croaks with emotion.

"Home," I confirm, broadening my shoulders with confidence as she takes in the house before her.

I had it built based off her drawings and images she had attached to her pinboard at home and on her Pinterest account that was way too easy to hack.

The way the vines are entwined up the turret which holds a drawing room and reading nook for her, the white picket fence surrounded with red posies, all created from her vision and from my memory of that night together when I took in her photos.

"How …" Her question hangs in the air as she stares out the window.

"Every moment we ever shared not only created a canvas in your mind, but mine too." I kiss her fingers, loving the way her body responds with a tremor, the same way she's always reacted to me, the way that tells me she's mine. "I told you I want this, want you, Romero. This is our future." I tilt my head toward the house.

She swallows slowly, and I wait on a knife-edge for her response.

"Owen. This is all too soon." Tears fill her eyes while I try to knock the anger building inside me away.

My jaw sharpens, and I grind my teeth. "It's not soon enough, baby girl."

Her eyes close on my admission, and when they reopen, I see the difference, her agreement. She blinks away the tears, but one escapes and travels down her perfect cheek. I lean in and hold her head in place. My breath fans her face, and she shudders, then I drag my tongue up her cheek to her forehead and place a firm kiss there. "Let me lick away your pain, baby girl."

A gasp escapes her, and I revel in it. My cock stands to attention, begging for a piece of her. With only the memories of that night together, I punished myself further for letting her go. Never allowing myself the pleasure of another woman. I didn't want it, not when they could never compare to her. The only woman to steal my heart, my mind, and body too.

She stole it all.

And now I'm taking it back.

"Welcome to your new life, baby girl."

LAYA

My heart stutters, and I blink several times, trying to take in the property. It's everything I ever dreamed of coming to life. An image of the drawing I created as a teenager flashes before me.

"If you don't like it, we can change it." I turn to face Owen, and he scrubs a hand over his short, cropped hair. His white T-shirt is stretched to capacity, like it's about to tear under the pressure of his muscles bulging, and I can't help but stare at him in admiration. Jesus, he's hot.

Then it's replaced by shame washing through me at the way my body reacted to his touch, his words and promises of more. My damp cheek still feels scorched by his tongue, and I clench my legs at the thought of him licking more than my cheek.

Oh god, help me.

"Are you ready to check out our house?" His eyes search mine, and I can only mewl in response, making his lip quirk up. "Come on, baby girl, let's get you home."

He opens the car door and steps out, shutting the door

behind him. I stare at the house. A sense of warmth encompasses me, and I delight in it.

"Home," I whisper as he moves toward my door.

The house is incredible. Every thought I ever imagined, every passing comment I ever made, has been recreated.

My fingers graze over the banister as we move up the wrought iron spiral staircase and step onto a landing. Double doors lie ahead of us, and I know that's the master suite because I created it.

He stops outside another door. "Romeo's room." He licks his lips and fidgets from foot to foot, giving away his nervousness.

"Romeo?"

"Yeah. I like the shortened version of it. Don't you?" I do like it. A lot, and when I stare down at him in the carrier Owen holds, my heart constricts. It's like Owen's nickname for him is his way of naming him, and my heart swells at the thought.

"I do."

A smile spreads across Owen's face, and I find myself replicating it.

When he opens the door, my breath is stolen from my lungs. A beautifully painted blue-and-gray nursery with a Romeo name plaque above the crib in intricate writing with animals surrounding it greets us. I spin on my feet and note the soft toys, blankets, and diapers neatly tucked away. Then I walk toward a closet, and my eyebrows shoot up at the rails filled with clothes.

He clears his throat. "I chose them all myself."

I turn to face him, and he pulls me toward him, making me gasp in surprise. "Do you like?"

My chest swells with love at his words and the way he stares down at me with expectation in his eyes. I bite into my lip as our gazes remain locked, then he dips his head and takes my lips. A soft sensual kiss has me melting against his firm chest, and I ball my hand into a fist to cling to his T-shirt. My body comes alive under his touch, and when he pulls back, I'm breathless and desperate for more, but a shooting pain has me wincing.

His eyebrows furrow. "You okay? Did I hurt you?"

I realize he's concerned about my cut lip, and I'm quick to reassure him. "No. I think my period is due."

His pupils dilate, and his Adam's apple slowly slides down his throat. "Yeah?" His voice comes out choked.

I nod and dart my eyes away, a little embarrassed. "Yeah. I've been having cramps all day. It'll be my first period since having Romero."

He nods, as if taking in all the information.

"Do you need anything?" His gaze rakes over me, and my cheeks heat under the intensity. The way his eyes eat me up has me squirming on the spot.

"I have some tampons in my bag, but I'll probably need more."

He blows out a deep breath. "I have all that shit in our room for you. Come on." He holds out his hand, and I slip mine into his, then he lifts Romero and we leave the nursery and head down the corridor.

Why would he have tampons in our room? Does he bring other women here? A sliver of uncertainty ripples through me and I tense, then Owen stops walking.

"What's wrong?" His gaze searches mine. Always so in tune with my body, it's almost like he controls a part of it.

"You said you had tampons here." I turn away, annoyed that I'm jealous of other women, yet hurt he created this home for us and allowed them to stay here. He turns my chin to face him, and his eyebrows become narrowed.

I sigh. "Why would you have tampons here?"

His shoulders relax and his lip twitches. "Let me show you."

He throws open the double doors, and I follow him into the master bedroom. Soft grays and white adorn the walls, and the sheets covering the huge gray wooden bed are white. With one wall of the room mirrors and a crystal chandelier hanging from the ceiling, it's almost identical to the one I had in my parents' home while growing up.

Placing Romero down, he marches toward what I'm guessing is the bathroom, and I follow him.

The room once again is in white and gray, modern and sleek, and everything I would have chosen, and again, I'm reminded how well Owen knows me, maybe better than I know myself.

He opens a door, and when my eyes latch onto the shelves, I'm stunned.

Every product I've ever used, every item I had when I left home, is on the shelves, all the items new and unopened.

He's purchased everything.

"Owen, I ..."

He scrubs a hand over his head, then drags a finger over his lip. "I wanted you to have everything you would need. Everything you always wanted. I didn't want you to have any reason not to be here." The vulnerability in his tone forces emotion to grip my chest, the feeling so profound, so strong, it takes me a moment to recover. "I didn't want you to have any reason to leave me." His gaze meets mine, and his eyes gleam with heartache, and for the first time since being eighteen, I see the love in his eyes.

Owen Stevens loves me.

"Owen." I push up on my tiptoes and wrap my hands around his neck to pull him down. He lets me, of course he does, he always has.

Even when he shouldn't have.

TWENTY

LAYA

SEVENTEENTH BIRTHDAY

The party is booming, and I survey over the crowd once again. Jealousy courses through me when I see one of the senior girls from my high school flirting with Owen. He throws his head back on a laugh, and I want nothing more than to cover his open mouth with mine. Instead, I'm stuck staring at them, drilling holes into the back of her perfect head. As if sensing me, his gaze darts over toward me and his eyes narrow. He peruses my body and slowly licks his lips, then he jolts and sits up before moving to his feet. With one last glance over his shoulder toward me, he walks inside the house, and I know exactly where he's going. The games room.

His eyes tell me to follow him. My heart hammers painfully, knowing I'm about to be rejected, yet I don't listen. I never do. Because I want Owen more than anything else in the world.

More than school, more than my friends, more than the design scholarship I'm working so hard to gain. He's my air, and if I don't have him, then I simply can't breathe.

I swallow the fruity punch in my hand, and without another thought, I push past a group of drunken high schoolers and make my way toward the games room.

My heart hammers in my chest as I saunter through the empty house. When I reach the door, I take a deep breath to steel myself. Then I adjust the little red dress, pull my shoulders back, and slip into the room.

"You shouldn't be in here, Laya." His gravelly voice sends a tremor through me as he pushes off the wall from behind me. He downs the scotch in his hand, then walks toward the lone armchair, places the empty cup on the table, and throws himself down.

"It's a games room, Owen. Maybe I want to play games."

His loud chuckle fills me with happiness only he can achieve, yet it's mocking. His head tips back as he faces the ceiling. "You sure know how to play games, Laya." He drops his head to face me, the seriousness of his tone now written all over his handsome face.

I roll my eyes.

"You're one to talk." I cross my arms over my chest, and it pushes my tits up. His gaze quickly darts away from the action, and I smile inside at how uncomfortable my body makes him. Owen wants me. He just doesn't want to want me.

"I'm an adult." He speaks so low I almost don't hear him, almost like he's speaking to himself, reminding himself.

My feet move in his direction, like a magnet drawing me in until I'm standing in front of him. When his tattooed hand touches the hem of my dress, I wiggle from side to side as my panties dampen from the heat radiating from him.

"You've no idea how tempting you are, do you?" His eyes search mine. "You make me want to be a bad man, Laya, and that outcome is deadly for the both of us."

I tilt my head, trying to figure out what he's saying. "How so?"

"Because men like me shouldn't play with girls like you."

"I told you I like to play."

"Some games are dangerous, Laya."

I roll my eyes. Not quite sure what he's talking about, only that he's trying to warn me away. But there's no way I'm leaving here without getting something from him. It's my birthday, after all.

"I want a birthday gift from you."

A deep chuckle leaves his lips, then I know exactly what I want for my birthday, what I've wanted for as long as I can remember.

"I don't do gifts."

He stands, but I don't step back; the heat radiating from him only adding to the heightened atmosphere between us. It's electric and full of an intoxicating need. When his hand finds my hip, I fall against him as if his simple touch can melt me, mold me to be him. The power he wields over me should be terrifying, yet I find myself willing, desperate, even.

"What is it you want for your birthday?"

"You."

He bites into his cheek and shakes his head, unwilling to look at me, and the defeat in his shoulders is evident.

"Your lips," I whisper. "My first kiss," I plead, feeling like I'm losing him already.

His eyes bounce back to mine, and he searches my face as if looking for sincerity. His nostrils flare. "First?"

"I saved it for you."

His grip on me tightens, and his shoulders become tense. "Jesus, Laya."

"I only want a kiss. You've done it a thousand times," I protest with a hint of jealousy and anger.

His jaw tics, but I see the moment he gives in. His resolve buckles and lust is written all over his perfectly chiseled face as he slowly lowers his head, and not giving him a chance to back out, I raise up on my tiptoes to meet him.

I coax open his mouth with my tongue as I hold his jaw in place, and he allows it. He lets me take the lead, take what I want. I'm stealing my kiss, my birthday present, and I'm keeping it.

His soft tongue swipes at my mouth, and my body comes alive. Every cell inside of me screams to become his, to give myself over to him. Our kiss quickens, and my pulse races as he invades my mouth gently. He's holding back. I know this, and I love him even more for it.

He's allowing me to experience my first kiss the way any girl would want—with a loving tenderness only someone meaningful can bring.

In this moment, I know deep in my soul that Owen is mine. He just needs to realize it too.

He pulls back too soon, and my shoulders sag, but a thrill shoots through me when I realize his hard length presses between us. Then he jerks back, as if burned, and I try not to take his action to heart. I shocked him, the feelings between us something immense, and I know he felt it too.

"Fuck!" He drags a hand over his head, then threads his fingers behind his neck.

"Fuck, Laya." His eyes flit to mine, and I want nothing more than to make him feel better, to bring him the relief he brings me.

So I tell him what he wants to hear. "It was just a kiss. No worries." I shrug, as if it meant nothing, and his mouth falls open.

"Just a kiss?"

I nod, hoping above all hope I'm faking my feelings, because we both know that was more than just a kiss.

It was something profound, life changing.

He licks his traitorous lips as if savoring my taste, and when I whimper involuntarily, his gaze flares with a fire burning so bright, my heart stills for a moment.

"Leave!" he barks, his voice thick and commanding, and I know the moment between us has broken. His morals are back firmly in place, and as much as I want to beg, plead, and cry at his rejection, I step away from him, giving him the space he seeks, the control he demands.

Hurt swirls in my stomach as I open the door, and before I'm about to slip through, his voice stops me in my tracks. "Laya?" I look over my shoulder to face him. "I'm sorry. I don't know what hit me. But you'll be all right." My shoulders deflate. "Happy Birthday, baby girl."

A smile graces my lips. Those few words give me hope as I replay the sound of him saying baby girl on my own lips while I walk away with a smile.

Because those words, they're a promise of my future.

Our future.

"I need you," I whisper against his ear, and delight in the shudder that racks through him. The effect I still have on him as strong as his on me.

He rolls his lips, as if contemplating my words. "I want us to be married first."

I stumble back in shock, but he shoots his hands out and grips my arms to steady me.

"Married?" My mouth falls open. Even the taste of the word on my tongue feels like acid.

His jaw sharpens, and the vein on his neck pulsates, giving away he's pissed. "Yes, fucking married, Laya. I want to do shit right this time."

"I-I lost my husband a few days ago, Owen."

His nostrils flare. "You shouldn't have married him in the first fucking place!"

This time, it's me who gets angry because how fucking dare he. "You fucked me and got engaged on the same night. You took my virginity and stomped all over it like it was nothing. Don't try making me feel bad for picking up the pieces of what you broke because you were an ass. I moved on with my life just like you did, just not as soon!"

He swallows hard, his body practically vibrating on the spot. I want nothing more than to strip him of his T-shirt and expose them.

"It meant every. Fucking. Thing. Laya." He drops his head and shakes it, and when he raises his eyes to meet mine again, I'm stunned by the longing swimming in them. "Everything." Emotion clogs in his throat on the word, and I see it all for the first time. A tear slips down my face.

"You got engaged," I whisper brokenly.

"I explained that shit. I was trying to do what would give you the better future," he snipes out. "Stop fucking bringing it up. I'm here now. I'm standing before you as the man who loves you with his everything, with so many regrets when it comes to you that they make me feel like I'm drowning."

OWEN

His words hit me like a sledgehammer, and I startle. *Regrets?*

"Regrets?"

He sucks in a sharp breath. "Yes. Fucking regrets, Laya. I should have stepped up, been the man you deserved. I should have told Tate how I feel about you." He shakes his head. "The thought of losing him, my family, it crippled me, Laya. I felt like I was betraying him. Then your mom asked me to let you go so you could have a fucking life, one without me in it. It's like she could see the darkness within me, and she was pleading with me to not drag you into it, to keep you pure.

"I wish I'd never left your room that night, Laya. My biggest regret has been walking away from you when what I should have done was scoop you into my fucking arms and walk down those stairs, telling the world we're together, that we're spending the rest of our lives together. I've never wanted to marry anyone but you, Laya. Nobody ever came close. It's always been you. Always." He licks his lips. "And I did all that shit, I did it all, for everyone else. But right now, I'm doing this for me." His lips slam against mine and our tongues thrash as he fights for control over me, and as always, I melt into him, happy to oblige, to give him the control he craves. Then he pulls back and rests his forehead against mine. "I'm doing this for both of us."

"For both of us," I agree.

OWEN

"For both of us," she whispers, causing the possessive beast inside of me to swell. Nothing and nobody will take them from me ever again. I've worked damn hard to get them here, and I'll do everything in my power to keep them.

She winces again, and that's when I remember why we're in the bathroom. Reaching over her head, I snag the tampons off the shelf. "Come on, baby girl, let's get you sorted." My cock thickens at the thought of seeing her bare and pushing a tampon into her needy little pussy while it drips her blood on my fingers. Her eyes widen, but I ignore the question in them, take her hand, and lead her into the bedroom.

"Get on the bed and open your legs." Her cheeks heat, and she remains frozen beside the bed, making me chuckle. "Laya, do as I ask you. You know I like control." I raise an eyebrow, and her flush deepens, no doubt remembering all the times she would sneak around to watch me take someone roughly.

"Do you normally—" She stops herself from finishing the sentence, then waves her hand toward the tampons. Then she clears her throat and tries again. "Do you normally do this?"

My eyes latch onto the box in my hand, and I can't help the chuckle that escapes me. She thinks I've done this for every woman I fucked. "No, baby girl. But with you, I can't help myself. I want to take care of every part of you, Laya." I step forward and tuck a piece of her hair behind her ear. "And for the record, the only blood on my cock has been yours." Her breath hitches, and her eyes become hooded. "Get on the bed and open your legs. Let me see."

She shuffles onto the bed, with almost a nervousness about her, and it has me craving her even more. When she opens her legs, my pulse races and my cock leaks pre-cum, and I hiss at the way the head rubs against my waistband.

A streak of blood drips from her pussy hole, and my mouth waters to taste her. "Fuck, that's beautiful," I groan, and she sits up on her elbows to watch me.

The tension in my body is like no other. The control it's taking me to keep my cock out of her pussy is like torture. But when I finally sink into her, it will be with her as my wife and Romeo as my son, just as it always should have been.

"It's my period, Owen. Pretty sure there's nothing beautiful about it."

Shifting, I kneel on the bed between her legs. "Wrong, baby girl, this perfect little pussy is weeping for me." I can't help but reach out and stroke over her little clit and swipe my finger through her blood, swirling it until the tip is coated. Then I paint over her folds, relishing the warmth of her skin. The smoothness of her little pussy has my cock jumping to be released. "It tells me my baby girl is ready for me to put a baby in her." She gasps, but I ignore her and push my finger into her pussy, then withdraw and add another, pumping inside her slowly. "It tells me it's leaking, ready to be filled with my thick cock. Your body is crying out for me, Laya." Her whimpers only add to my heightened state of need, and I won't be able to leave this room without coming, not when she needs that as much as I do.

I want to mark her, make her mine, coat her with my arousal like she's coating me. "You're all warm and wet for me, Laya. Is this just blood, baby girl, or more? Is this little cunt dripping with your pussy juice too?"

"Ye-yes," she pants out as I continue pumping, picking up my pace as she clenches around me.

"Come for me, baby girl. Coat my fingers in your blood." I circle her swollen clit with my thumb, and my mouth waters when her pussy convulses.

"Holy shit. Owen. Don't stop. Please, don't stop." Her pleas are a match that ignites an inferno inside me.

Her back arches and her head falls back, and fuck me, it's beautiful.

"My perfect girl, all swollen and bloody for me."

Her pussy contracts around me, tightening to the point that I hiss in pleasure. "Owen…" I groan at my name spilling from her lips. The sound I've longed to hear, the sound that's haunted my dreams and also brought me solitude.

"Good girl," I praise and revel in the fact she pulsates on the endearment. "Such a good fucking girl."

She collapses against the mattress, and I withdraw my sticky-cum- and blood-coated fingers from her. When she lifts her head, I bring my fingers to my lips and suck them into my mouth. My eyes roll back in pleasure. The copper tang blended with her cum has my free hand fumbling to unbuckle my belt.

I need to mark her, cover her in my cum.

Mark her with my pleasure, like she's marked me.

LAYA

Owen scrambles to open his belt buckle, and with his fingers in his mouth and his eyes closed in pleasure, my pussy throbs. Not only was that orgasm mind-blowing, but it was filthy and all-consuming.

Owen knows no bounds, and I'm here for it.

He tugs down his jeans and boxers, and his cock springs out, hitting his abs, and I want nothing more than to drop to my knees and please him. Blood coats his upper lip, and I have an insane urge to lick it clean, but I remain frozen, too consumed with lust to do anything. He withdraws his fingers, and his gaze latches onto my pussy. "Fuck. I need to fuck this pussy so bad right now, Laya." The tendons in his neck are tight, and when he drags his T-shirt over his head, my mouth salivates at the sight.

How can his body have gotten any bigger? The artwork on him calls to my pussy like a beacon, and it drips in need. I want to tell him to fuck me as hard as he can, but I'm paralyzed, my throat clogged with awe and post-orgasmic shock. Then he wraps his thick, tattooed fingers around his cock, and my nipples begin to leak, but I don't have it in me to be embarrassed.

His eyes flick up to my face as if hearing my thoughts. "Open your shirt, Laya." He fists his cock faster, and I swear I feel the pre-cum drip onto my pussy. "Fuck, baby, you're bleeding on the sheets, just like the first time I took you."

My fingers pause on the buttons, and I dart my eyes up to face him. "I-I'm sorry."

He shakes his head. "Don't be sorry, baby girl. I like the thought of your mark. I like the thought of owning your blood."

Oh god.

The mattress moves under his thrusts, and when I open the shirt and slip it off my shoulders, he growls, sending a wave of exhilaration through me.

"Are your tits leaking, baby girl?"

"Yes." I arch my back, thrusting my pussy toward him.

"Fuck, yes. Your nipples are begging to be sucked, aren't they?"

His fist moves faster and faster.

"Yes. Oh god, Owen."

"Begging for my tongue to taste your milk." He grunts. "For you to feed me."

Every inch of his perfect muscles is coiled tight as he pumps his cock with vigor.

"Paint your tits for me, Laya. Paint your tits in your bloody cum."

His cock leaks onto my pussy, coating it in his pre-cum, and my fingers trail down, itching to touch him, but I do as he commands and gather my wetness. Then I move toward my nipple, painting it with my bloody cum and mixing it with my milk.

"That's it, baby girl, paint those tits." His chest rises rapidly as I tweak my nipple, encouraging the milk to bead. "Fuck. Fuck, Laya, I'm gonna …" He explodes and clenches his jaw shut as rope upon rope of warm cum coat my pussy. "Fuckkkk," he breathes out, his chest heaving as he stares down at the mess we created. "I seriously want to eat your pussy right now." When he chuckles, my eyes widen. Then he grabs onto my thigh as if to steady himself before he lifts his gaze toward mine. "Gonna plug you." He tilts his head toward the tampon on the bed, and I nod along while he picks up the box to examine it. His eyes flick over the box as if reading the instructions, and I bite into my lip and watch the way confusion creeps over his face.

"It's simple." I move to take the box from him, but he bats my hand away.

"I got it."

He rips into the packaging, pulls out the tampon, pushes my legs up to angle me better, then drags the tampon through his cum. "When I come inside you tomorrow, I'm plugging you. You're not wasting any of it."

My mind whirls with what he said. "Tomorrow?"

He snaps his gaze up toward me, and his eyes hold me captive. "We're getting married tomorrow, Laya." His words leave no room for argument, then he darts his eyes back down, unwilling to discussing it further.

When I feel the tampon being pushed inside me, I can't help but wish it was him, but something tells me tomorrow will have been worth the wait, no matter how unsure I am about it.

TWENTY-ONE

OWEN

After fucking my fist so hard I saw stars, I plugged her pussy with the tampon. Not gonna lie, I was jealous of the little cotton fiend. I want nothing more than to slide into her warm cunt and stretch it to capacity while fucking her so hard she has no doubts about who she belongs to. Who she's always belonged to. I will pump her so full of my cum that her body has no choice but to give us another baby. Seeing her nipples painted in her bloody cum mixed with her milk had me ravenous for more. I don't know how the fuck I managed to hold back.

But now, sitting in my office while watching on the computer screen as she and my son sleep, I finally try to relax. My mind still hasn't caught up with my body yet, still on a high alert that they're in danger. Something gnaws at the back of my mind and swirls in my stomach that I'm about to lose it all, and I refuse to let that happen, not when I've worked so hard to get it.

My phone beeps beside me, and I lift it, then scrub a hand through my cropped hair.

TATE: Any news?

Of course it's Tate. He's like a goddamn dog with a bone. Ever since finding out Laya was married and pregnant, the man has been persistent. But since his girl's, Ava, past came to light and the abuse she suffered, he's been like a pitbull snarling for blood.

I understand, really, I do. He knows the danger Laya and Romeo are in, and he wants to prevent anything like what happened to Ava from happening to them.

No matter how many times I tell him I have everything under control, he still wants more. I can't blame him, really; I wanted Laya safe more than anyone, but he didn't have to deal with the fact the girl he's in love with left and married someone else. Worse, created another life with them and forgot about her old one. A pain lances through me at the thought, and my thick fingers work the keys on the phone to give him the same generic reply I always give.

ME: She's safe.

TATE: Is she with you?

How the hell am I meant to win Laya over when her brother is acting like a cock block? I want to tell him to fuck off and leave us alone, but I appreciate his concern. Guilt ravishes my veins, but I push it aside.

Done feeling guilty.

Feeling guilty got me nowhere. It made me push her away.

ME: Yes. She's fine.

TATE: I want to speak with her. The kid, okay?

ME: She's sleeping and yes, Romeo is fine too.

I grind my jaw. Just leave us the fuck alone.

TATE: Thank fuck.

I feel the tension release from him with that message.

TATE: Thank you, brother.

I wince at his words. Knowing how pissed he will be when I make her my wife tomorrow.

ME: I'll get her to call you tomorrow. Just let them rest today.

TATE: Okay. Do you guys need anything?

A scoff escapes me, and I want to tell him we need him to leave us the fuck alone.

ME: No, we're good.

I switch my phone off and turn my attention back to the screen, and the familiar love at the sight of her surges through me. She's even more beautiful than I remember, and she's all fucking mine.

They both are.

"Tomorrow, baby girl. Just how it should have always been."

LAYA

After sleeping for what felt like hours, I woke up to Romeo feeding. I smiled up at Owen while he watched on at my son nursing.

Then Owen drew a bath for me, and Romeo and I bathed while he went back to work in his office after telling me he only had so much self-restraint.

When I get out of the bath, there is another one of his fresh T-shirts lying on the bed for me. I search the drawers for panties and quickly dress before putting a fresh diaper on Romeo and dressing him in a cute little romper with a dinosaur on the front.

Then I take a deep breath and decide I'm finally ready to stomach some food.

"Come on, little man, let's get Mommy fed."

I lift Romeo into my arms and inhale his soft baby scent. Then I head downstairs toward the sound of Owen's voice.

"We're coming to visit tomorrow, Steph. Yes, she's fine.

I promise." My pulse races at his use of my mother's name as I push open the office door.

His bright-blue eyes land on me and glimmer with love and security, then his eyes slowly roam down my body as he spins in his chair to face me fully. He's wearing joggers and a white T-shirt and no shoes or socks. He looks fucking edible, and I can't help but appreciate the way his thigh muscles pull his joggers to capacity. The man is a powerhouse, and I wish for nothing more but to feel him between my thighs.

He clears his throat, and it's only now I realize he's ended the call. A slow smirk spreads over his face as if hearing my wayward thoughts.

My cheeks heat, and I flick my eyes away.

"Don't be shy, baby girl. You can eye-fuck me all you want."

I roll my eyes and finally meet his gaze again. The humor behind them makes me shake my head. He always was cocky but never openly reacted to my flirting. Not like now. Now it's like everything is no longer off-limits. It's like the invisible force field he always had between us has come down and he's finally allowing him to be himself.

"Go put Romeo in his bouncer, then come here." His firm demand has my eyes flitting around the room until they land on a bouncer with stuffed animals hanging from above. Warmth fills me. The fact he has adjusted his office to accommodate Romeo only makes me love him more.

Walking over to the bouncer, I feel Owen's eyes on me. "You were talking to my mom?"

"Yeah, baby."

I strap Romeo into the bouncer and set a soft lullaby to play, and his eyes begin to flutter closed.

"When can I see her?"

"Pretty sure you heard me tell her tomorrow." He lifts an eyebrow at me, and I bite on my lip as anxiety ripples through my veins. Will they accept me and Owen?

"Come here." He pats his thigh, and I move toward him, always so eager to please him.

As soon as I'm in reach, he pulls me by his T-shirt and lifts me onto his lap. "Don't worry, I told you I have everything handled."

"Tate?"

Owen's chest rises, and his body becomes rigid beneath me. "Don't give a fuck what your brother says." He tucks a lock of hair behind my ear. "Besides, we'll be married. So, he can go fuck himself and so can anyone else who doesn't like it. They'll get used to it." He shrugs.

There's that word again. Married.

"I ..."

His thick hand clasps my thigh, and he adjusts me on his lap until I'm straddling him. Then he places his finger to my lips. "Don't wanna hear it. We're getting married today." My eyebrows shoot up. "Gonna solidify our future, Laya. We're getting married, and my baby will be growing in your belly, baby girl, just like how it always should have been. Then when all this shit is settled, I'll give you a big wedding, if that's what you want."

"A renewal?"

"Know all about your wedding, Pinterest thing." He smiles smugly.

"You do?"

His lip twitches. "I do." Then he leans forward and kisses my neck, sending goose bumps scattering over my skin. "Know that fucker didn't give it to you. Let me have this today, then we've got the rest of our lives to make it whatever you want."

His soft lips derail my thoughts as I stretch my neck to give him access while I rest my hands on his knees behind me.

"Why does it have to be so soon?"

"I want it cemented. Official. I want to go to your family and tell them it's done." I press down on his hardness as he nips at my skin. "Besides that, our marriage will bring you protection. Nobody will ever consider touching you when they know we're married."

My blood runs cold, and I still.

Slowly, I lift my head to face him.

"Am I in danger? Is Romeo in danger?"

He chuckles, and I want to smash him between the eyes at finding humor in this, given the circumstances. "No, baby girl."

"Those men …"

His face hardens. "Are done. They're fucking done." The determination in his voice leaves no room for argument. Then he grips my chin and holds my gaze. "Trust me."

The finality pours from him in waves, and I've no choice but to accept it and, like always, I do because it's Owen.

"Now grind that little pussy on my cock, baby girl." He glances at his watch. "You're going to be Mrs. Stevens in a few hours and need time to get ready." My mouth falls open at his words, and he throws his head back on a laugh, then takes my hips in his thick hands and encourages me to grind against him. When his eyes meet mine, they're full of lust. "Make us come, baby girl."

And I want nothing more than to do just that.

TWENTY-TWO

OWEN

The moment she stepped into my office wearing my T-shirt, I became ravenous for her.

But I want to save her body for tonight—our wedding night.

If I could have my time again, I'd have made her eighteenth birthday a double celebration—her birthday and our marriage.

But instead, we're having to do things unconventionally.

There's not a doubt in my mind that shit will hit the fan tomorrow when Tate finds out I not only married his little sister but defiled her too. So having her tied to me before he tries to encourage doubt to creep into her mind ensures I get what I want.

I wasn't lying when I said she can have her dream wedding later. Hell, I even secured the lodge resort on her Pinterest for this summer.

But I hate the way she eyes me with such uncertainty, the doubt where it has no place to be, so I give her what we both want.

"Make us come, baby girl." Her breath hitches, and I know I have her. She leans back so her hands are once again rested on my knees and her pussy is flush against my hard cock.

"I want your T-shirt off," she says, and rocks against me, and my cock jumps as I make quick work of throwing my T-shirt off. I lift her shirt enough to tear her panties from her, and she gasps, and I chuckle as I drop the fabric to the floor.

"I need you, Owen."

Fuck, do I love to hear that. "I'm here, baby girl. Take what you want from me." I groan as my fingers bite into her hips, encouraging her quickened pace, causing my balls to ache for release. "Fuck, baby girl, that's it."

Her tits bounce beneath the fabric, and I'm hungry to taste her milk, but not yet. I'm determined to wait. To finally take everything she offers as my wife.

The head of my cock peeks out above the waistband of my joggers, and I groan at the sensation of her dragging her pussy over my hard length. "Fuck, baby, I need to feel you," I grunt in awe at the pleasure she brings without so much as skin to skin.

She shuffles forward, and the warmth of her little pussy heats the tip of my cock. "Jesus fucking Christ, Laya."

She rocks back and forth. Back and forth. Quicker and quicker. "Yes. Oh god, yes."

"My little girl's pussy is plugged, isn't it, baby? Gonna feel you bleed all over my cock tonight."

"Oh god." She moves faster, and I know she's getting close; her body tightens, chasing her release.

The string of her tampon drags over the head of my cock, and I practically salivate to rip it from her cunt and stuff her with my cock. Hanging on by a thread and with every muscle in my body coiled tight, I grit my teeth to refrain from stealing back the control I crave.

"Owen. Oh Jesus, Owen."

I snap my hand up toward her throat, but the small bit of restraint I have left enables me to cling onto my control. I simply hold her in place by her throat, determined not to unravel into my darkness, no matter how difficult I find it.

Her mouth falls open and her body stills, but with a firm grip still on her hip, I'm able to use her lax body as a vessel for my need as we sail into the abyss. "Fuck!" I curse, then slam my teeth into my lip as ecstasy consumes me.

My cum lands on us both, but she's too in the throes of her orgasm to care, and honestly, I revel in saturating us in my obsession. "Such a good cum slut, baby girl." A tremor racks through her at my words, a blush heats her cheeks, and I couldn't be more elated. Laya has a thing for degradation, and I can't wait to expose it.

"Did you just call me a …"

I nod, and her eyes widen, so I chuckle, then pull her forward by her throat until her tits touch my chest. "Get used to it, baby girl. I'm going to own your ass in a few hours, and if I want to make you my cum slut, I will." The pinkness in her cheeks deepens, and she pulls her lip between her teeth as my cock hardens, which only causes her eyes to bug out further.

I drag a hand down my face.

"Baby, as much as I want to play with you right now, we need to get you fed. But first, I need to change you."

LAYA

"Baby, as much as I want to play with you. We need to get you fed. But first, I need to change you." My eyebrows furrow, then Owen slides me off his lap and onto his desk as if I weigh nothing. He opens my legs and maneuvers my feet onto the desk. Embarrassment floods me. This is even worse than when I had my obstetrician appointments.

"Owen?"

"Shh. Stay still. Let me take care of you." His gentle voice has me relaxing. Like the codependent I am, I submit to his words and watch on as he pulls open his desk drawer.

My eyes widen when he retrieves a tampon box, and I move to close my legs, but his hands clasp on my thighs, holding me open.

"I'm taking care of you." His firm eyes meet mine, and his sharp voice slices through me, then he caresses my skin, igniting a thousand flames deep inside me. It's a caring touch, gentle and full of protection. "Be a good girl and let me change you." Why the hell does that sound so hot? Wantonly, I ease open my legs and let him slide the bloodied tampon from me, and I can't help but watch on as his eyes flare with arousal, making me squirm on his wooden desk.

When I think he's going to put a fresh tampon in, I'm mistaken. Instead, his thick finger enters me, and I moan, but just as quickly, he withdraws, then slides the tip of his finger over my already swollen clit.

"Mmm, fuck, it feels good to be coated in your blood again, Laya." He licks his lips, his eyes heavy with a hunger I want to explore. "I could spend all day playing in your bloody cunt, taking my fill while you drip so beautifully for me." He chuckles to himself.

A heady pant leaves my lips, and I clamp my mouth closed to stop myself from begging for more of his touch. He circles my needy bud, his eyes trained on my pussy. "You're dripping on my desk, baby girl."

"I-I …" No coherent thought enters my head.

"That's it. Soak my desk, my bloody little cum slut."

He presses down hard on my clit, and a gush of arousal combined with blood flows from me, but I don't have it in me to care as I buck against his fingers, letting his filthy words wrap around me and bring me the comfort and euphoria I crave.

Stars flash in front of my eyes as my body tightens, and my orgasm hits me. "Such a good slut for me, Laya." His breath caresses my pussy when he places a tender kiss there, and I melt against the desk.

My body deflates when he removes his fingers. He clears his throat, grabs a pack of wet wipes, then cleans his hand, my stomach, the desk, and my pussy of his cum and mine.

He tears the packet, takes a deep breath that has me wanting to laugh at his seriousness, then slides the tampon inside me.

"How's it feel?" he chokes out as his gaze snaps from my pussy to my face.

"Fine."

"Fine?"

I chew on my lip. "Thank you."

He pulls me back onto his lap, and I squeal at the sudden movement. Instantly, his warmth comforts me. "Good girl. Now let's get you fed before Romeo wakes, huh?"

I can only nod while he stands, taking me with him, and when he places a delicate kiss on my neck, I moan.

"Keep making those little sounds, baby girl, and I'm going to stuff that throat with my cock. Don't think you're ready for what I have to give you."

He walks over to Romeo and picks up his bouncer with his free hand while I cling to him like a koala.

Oh, I'm ready.

So fucking ready.

TWENTY-THREE

LAYA

Owen feeds me another strawberry while I sit on his lap like a child. He refuses to let me leave his side and has taken his responsibility as caregiver to a whole new level, including brushing my teeth and hair and moisturizing my body. Not that I'm complaining about the attention he lavishes on me, because his love for me flows from him freely now, when he always had his feelings so locked down while I battled to break through his defenses.

His phone buzzes on the kitchen table, and I glance at the screen to see the name Rafael on there. Owen grimaces and picks the phone up, answering the call.

"You've some fucking nerve, Owen," Rafael bellows.

"I know. I apologize." Owen winces. "I had a family emergency." His arm tightens around me as dread lines my stomach. I'm the family emergency. A shudder rushes through me, and Owen doesn't miss it. He pulls me against him, his hand stroking gently over my arm.

"Emergency? What about my fucking emergency?"

He exhales heavily. "You're in good hands with Oscar, Rafael."

A scoff emits the angry man. "We had a fucking business deal, Owen. This is not how you conduct business." The venom oozes from him, and Owen's shoulders tense.

"I have the best men on the job, Rafael."

"You shirked your fucking responsibilities. For what, huh?"

"None of your fucking business," he snaps back, and my heart races at the anger pulsating from Owen in waves.

"I want fucking answers, Owen!"

"And you'll get them. From Oscar," Owen spits back before ending the call and throwing the phone onto the table, then he drags a hand over his head on a deep exhale. "Fuck!"

"I'm sorry," I whisper.

His body instantly relaxes. "Don't apologize, baby."

I pull back and meet his gaze. "It's true." I wring my T-shirt between my hands. "I've ruined so many things, and now I'm affecting your business too."

"No. You're worth everything and so much more. It's not your fault. The blame is solely on me, Laya. I've told you before, you're mine and I will do anything to protect you." He lifts my chin to face him, and the intensity behind his eyes causes something peculiar to slither through my veins. It's heated, predatory, and possessive, like a warning or a promise. I'm not quite sure, but it makes me uneasy. "Anything to keep you," he whispers, and I repress the sliver of doubt edging to get out.

"Where are we getting married?"

He tilts his head to the garden. "Out back. A small ceremony, then anything you want." He lifts my hand to his lips and kisses it.

"Anything?" I lift an eyebrow, and his lip quirks.

"Absolutely." He nips at my ear, and I giggle, pleased at the change in atmosphere when he chuckles back at me.

Romeo takes this moment to let out a loud cry, which I know to be a *Momma, I want my milk* cry. Owen lifts me, lets me slide down his front, then pats my ass. "Go feed Romeo. When you've finished, check out the spare room. Be ready at 1:00 p.m." He pats my ass in jest, and I roll my eyes, then bend and unstrap Romeo and head out of the kitchen.

"Love you, baby girl," he shouts as I leave, and I can't help but have a spring in my step as I head upstairs.

OWEN

"You're sure about this? Tate is going to flip his fucking shit when he finds out." Mase paces like the stress head he is, while Reed looks on in amusement.

"Is everything in there?" I nod toward the file Reed planted on my desk the moment they stepped into my office.

"Of course." He replies with confidence in his tone, as expected.

Reed is professional to the highest of standards and thorough; another reason I chose to bring one of my best friends in on today. As a lawyer, I wanted him to oversee the legalities behind everything.

The backhanded payments for rushing Carlos's death certificate and Romeo's adoption papers made me anxious to ensure all the documentation was official.

"And you're sure about this?" He eyes me with suspicion, and I balk. I've never been so sure about anything in my entire life.

I turn in my chair so he can see the sincerity bleeding

from my eyes, from my heart. "I've never wanted anyone but her." I swallow away the emotion clogging my throat. "It's only ever been her."

Something flashes in his eyes, understanding maybe? Then his firm nod lets me know I have my friend's support when I need it the most, and I couldn't be more grateful.

When I felt like I had nothing, I always had these guys. Tate will take some winning over, but Mase and Reed are a start. Shaw will understand too. I mean, the guy has had his suspicions for years; I just never had the balls to act on it.

"And how much does Laya know about Carlos, exactly?" Mase spins to face me, the worried expression on his face a telltale of his doubt about the whole situation, but I push his concerns aside and broaden my shoulders.

"She knows what I want her to know."

Reed leans forward and drags a finger over his lip before speaking. "Which is?"

"Nothing. She hasn't exactly fought me on the marriage." I shrug.

"The girl has been infatuated with you for as long as I can remember. I get it," Reed asserts.

Mase stops pacing, and his eyes drill into me. "She should know about him. He's the baby's dad."

My spine straightens and anger bubbles inside me. "I'm his fucking dad," I spit back, causing his eyes to widen as he reels back on his heels at the spite in my tone.

"You're a better man than me." Reed lazes back in his chair, unperturbed by the fury radiating from me. "I don't want kids of my own, let alone someone else's."

I roll my eyes; my friend is so wrapped up in himself,

he can never see the bigger picture. How creating your own family can create happiness. Blood doesn't make you family, it only makes you related. Trust, support, and eternal love are what make you family, and Romeo already has all of that in me.

He has my everything, like his momma.

Mase surveys Reed and shakes his head. "You'll change your mind if you meet the right person."

Reed lets out a loud scoff. "Like fuck I will." Then he scrunches his nose. "I don't need people entering my space when they feel like it." He shudders, and I chuckle at the seriousness in his words while he continues on. "And the germs. Jesus fucking Christ, the germs." He grimaces.

Mase shakes his head with a glare in Reed's direction while I watch on in amusement. "You have germs too, Reed. You think you're perfect, but you're not, dude. You're gonna crash hard."

"The only crashing Reed will do is the bed against the wall while he imagines fucking the woman that got away." I laugh.

He scrubs a hand through his hair. "I'm still in shock. I mean, can you guys believe it? How can anyone want to leave me?" His gaze flicks from mine to Mase's and back again, as if waiting for us to agree.

Yeah, he's deluded. My poor friend thinks every woman is desperate to bag him.

"She was different from the others," he murmurs.

I ball up a note from my desk and throw it at his head. "Yeah, for once it was the woman that wanted a quick fuck, not a permanent uptight prick that starts his night with '*I don't date, ever.*'" I make air quotes on the latter.

His eyes narrow on mine. "I might be willing to date, if I get a good fuck out of it."

Mase exhales loudly, and my smile widens at the way he becomes riled at Reed's words, "Jesus, you're such a prick."

My phone cuts through the conversation, alerting me to the fact it's time to head out into the garden.

I'm about to get married, and I couldn't be happier.

TWENTY-FOUR

LAYA

Having Mase walk me down the aisle was bittersweet. The man is like a brother to me, but it felt like a betrayal to Tate and my father for him and Reed to participate without their knowledge or, truth be told, without their consent.

More than anything, I want Tate's approval, and without it, I feel cheated out of the wedding we should have had, but Owen reassures me as soon as his business settles down and Tate is over the inevitable tantrum he will throw, then we can have the wedding I always envisaged.

When Owen said, "I do," and I saw the only man I have ever loved standing before me with love swimming in his eyes, it brought with it the reassurance of our love.

But an unwelcome anxiety is creeping to the forefront of my mind. Like I'm missing something and our world will come crumbling down around us, and I hate it.

Determined to shove it aside, I simply put it down to the circumstances and the trauma we've been through, in a hope to move forward and leave the past behind.

My fingers toy with the wedding ring on my finger, a symbol of trust and eternal love.

The soft click of the bedroom door has me turning, and standing there before me is the handsome man I've lusted after, loved from afar, who's broken my heart over, and ultimately, the man who has become my son's and my protector. The man who was once my everything and is now my husband.

"You look so fucking beautiful, baby girl."

His gravelly voice sends a rush of electricity through my body, warming me from the inside out.

The way his dress shirt is stretched over his shoulders and the way his trousers are fitted tightly around his thick thighs has my mouth watering, his powerful demeanor an aphrodisiac for my need to please him.

His gaze is wild, hungry, and full of want. "Fuck, I want to do so much to you. I don't know where to start."

His words consume me, and my cheeks heat under his lustful gaze as I squirm on the spot. His eyes track the movement, not missing a single reaction, as always.

I glance down at the white satin dress he chose; it was gifted to me in his spare room, along with the heels I ditched as soon as I entered the bedroom. It fits perfectly and is not dissimilar to the one on my Pinterest board.

My heart hammers as he strides toward me, and the size of his feet allows him to eat up the space between us in no time. Then he cocks my chin up with his hand, holding my gaze. "I'm going to fuck you in your wedding dress, Laya." I gasp at his words. "I'm going to shove my cock so far inside your bloody little cunt that you forget any man but me." I want to tell him I already have, but the words stick in my throat. "I'm going to pretend the blood that soaks my cock is your first time with me all over again." *Oh, sweet Jesus.*

"Do you remember the way you screamed as I tore through your little cunt, baby girl?" He nuzzles into my neck, delivering me soft kisses. "I do. When I fist my cock, it's you I see." My heart skips a beat on his admission. "When I come, it's your name on my lips that I speak." Flurries of unbridled love expand inside me, and I place my hand on his chest for support. The hard ridge of his pec pierces through the material, making my mouth water to explore him and finally taste every inch of his delectable body.

"I ..." I become speechless with intoxication. The smell of his masculine sandalwood scent and the heat of his touch become consuming as I sway on my bare feet.

"What, baby? Tell me what you want." His voice is laced in struggle, as if this is just as difficult for him as it is for me, and the thought fills me with the confidence I need.

"I want you to take your shirt off so I can touch you."

He pulls back to stare at me, his blue eyes darker than normal, and arousal floods them. Then he takes another step away and unbuttons his shirt while his focus remains locked on me.

"Fuck, your tits look amazing, Laya," he says as he tugs his shirt from his waistband.

I glance down at the swell of my breasts, and nervousness skitters through me about the milk building up. Romeo only had a small feeding before bed, which means he will be up during the night wanting more, leaving me swollen and potentially leaking in the meantime.

Not really an attractive feeling, if Carlos's reaction was anything to go by. He insisted on me covering up at all times, and sex between us had become non-existent. Even after the obstetrician gave us the go ahead, we didn't return to having sex. When he was out late at night, I often wondered if he was seeking it elsewhere.

Another thing I will never know.

"Whatever doubt flashed in your mind just then, knock it out, baby girl." I lift my head to find Owen glaring at me.

"My tits are probably going to leak." Embarrassment creeps over me at my rushed words.

Owen licks his lips, and he pulls his shirt off his shoulders and throws it to the floor, then strokes over the outline of his steely cock constricted by his tight pants, and I practically salivate watching him.

"Yeah, they are, baby." His thick hand wraps around his shaft, and he begins pumping. "I can't wait to wrap my lips around your nipples. Are you going to feed me too?"

Holy. Shit. He's serious.

My heart misfires as wetness seeps from me, and before I can stop myself, I walk toward him and push my hands over his thick, coiled shoulders, and he sucks in a sharp breath, taking mine with his.

"Owen," I whisper as his entire being encompasses me.

"I'm all yours, baby girl."

His words wrap around me, giving me the security and confidence I crave as I breathe in the meaning behind his words.

Owen Stevens is finally mine.

OWEN

Her soft lips find my jawline, and I stand firm, allowing her to explore me how I want to explore her. The need for control makes my skin itch, but her touch is like a balm to the cause, gifting me with the comfort I crave.

She works down my throat, and I want nothing more than to tear the flimsy dress from her body to allow me to feel her skin against mine, but I refrain from doing so, the urge to see her blood coating her wedding dress as if it's our first night together outweighs the bubble of excitement.

"I've waited so long to touch you," she whispers, sending a trail of goose bumps over me. Her admission makes my heart constrict, and I both loathe and love it.

I've never had to try to get Laya's attention. Her acceptance has always been there. Even if she doesn't know how dark my depraved mind goes, I'm willing to leave that part of me behind in order to keep her. Anything to keep her.

"You're perfect, Owen." I want to balk at her words, but I broaden my shoulders, remaining still while she works her way over my pecs, tracing every tattoo with her tongue, and with it, pre-cum spills out of my slit like a geyser.

"So perfect," she whispers as she lowers herself to her knees and her soft hands reach my belt.

I've never seen anything so beautiful as I do right now, an ethereal beauty.

"Oh fuck," I pant out with excitement.

Her hair shimmers in the low lighting, her pouty lips beg to be tasted, and the swell of her tits plead to be drained into my waiting mouth. My body feels like it will combust, and it takes everything in me to remain focused, to allow her to continue her tender exploration of me.

She hooks her fingers into the waistband of my boxers and grazes the tip of my cock with her finger, coating it in pre-cum. Beneath her thick lashes, her eyes lock with mine, her pupils blown wide, and my lip quirks at how desperately hungry my girl is for me.

"Are you going to taste me, baby girl?"

She licks her lips, then slowly, so fucking slowly, my lungs constrict when she brings the tip of her finger to her naughty little mouth and sucks the evidence of my arousal from it. I lean down toward her until my face is so close to hers our breaths mingle, and I revel in it.

"I'm going to fuck your little mouth, baby girl."

Her lips part and her head sways, as if dizzy on my words, and her reaction only encourages me further. "Do you remember what I told you I was going to do to you?"

I take a hold of the back of her head; my thick fingers dig into her wavy hair as I hold her in place.

"You said you'd make me your cum slut."

Exhilaration ripples through me like a hit of a drug ravishing an addict's veins. Using my thumb of the hand supporting her head, I stroke circles over her cheek, and she turns into my touch like a perfect submissive, which only heightens my need for her. I'm not sure how I will tamper the animal raging inside me, fighting to become unleashed, but I'll do it for her.

"Good girl, baby." She melts against my touch, and as her eyes flutter closed, the power that consumes me is like nothing before. Her trust becomes the fuel to the fire burning deep inside me. "Such a good girl for letting me use you."

"Now, take my cock out." Her eyes dart open, and she pushes my pants and boxers down my muscular legs until they fall to the floor. She sucks in a sharp breath, which I ignore and continue on with my need to command her. "Now, I want you to lick my balls, then all the way up my shaft." Her soft hands land on my legs, steadying herself, and she doesn't even flinch at my sharp demand. Flicking her tongue out, she coats my balls with her spittle, eager to please me. Her nails dig into my thighs, and I relish the bite as she languorously follows the vein that protrudes from my cock all the way to the swollen head. A low groan of hisses leave my mouth at finally feeling her at my feet and worshipping my cock.

My good girl pauses and flutters her eyelashes at me as she awaits further instruction. "Kiss it, baby girl. Lick that slit nice and clean. Worship my cock, little cum slut." My nostrils flare and I tip my head back as the image of her tongue darting out to do just that remains frozen in my brain. The tender way she glides it over the slit before shoving it further in, as if hungry for more of my taste, has my hand pinching her scalp to lock her in place. I can't help the way I thrust up into her mouth, eager to receive more of her greedy tongue.

Then I jerk her head back by her hair until our eyes meet, needing to instill some boundaries before we continue. "I'm going to fuck your throat now, baby girl." Her eyes widen, and she looks adorable. "If you want me to stop, slap my thighs *hard*." I emphasize the latter so she's aware it takes a lot for me to stop myself, to cage the beast once again.

She raises her chin and straightens her shoulders. "I don't want you to stop." A smile forms on my lips at my pouty girl, always so confident and equally stubborn.

She's seen me in some fucked-up positions with women when she was younger, but that was all before I had her. I've worked hard to get a leash on the control, for her sake and mine. Besides, I was sure to hide the worst of me from her, determined not to scare her away. She was the only thing I had in the world, the only person to look at me with an ocean of love in her eyes I felt like it was consuming me, and Jesus, did I want to throw myself in there and drown in her.

The same unadulterated love fills her eyes now, mixed with passion and longing, a look so full of awe my chest tightens and my cock aches.

The tip is still wet from her delicate lips, and I bask in the pleasure of it, knowing she was there only moments ago, my girl, my wife. My muscles coil tight as I take my thick cock in my hand, and when my wedding band glimmers, possession consumes me.

She's mine.

She's finally fucking mine.

I fist myself harder, faster and stare down at her waiting lips. I've waited for this moment for what feels like my entire life, to have her as my wife at my feet, eager to please me.

"My good girl," I croon. Then I take my cock and wipe the pre-cum gathering on the tip down her cheek. She licks her lips, and I smirk, knowing how much she wants me. Her eyes beg for me to feed her my cum, and on that thought, I tug faster.

When she swallows, I feel like I'm going to combust. I smack my cock against her cheek as punishment, and revel in the shock on her face. Tightening the grip in her hair, I yank her head back. "Open your mouth," I grit out through clenched teeth. She complies, and I hover the tip of the angry head over her mouth, then slowly feed her my length. She gags, but I push past it, and the way her eyes widen and her hands tighten on my thighs are a giveaway to her panicked state, but I'm too far gone in the pleasure of controlling her to care. Then I wrap my now free hand around her throat and delight in the sensation of feeling my cock situated deep inside her. My fingers tangle with her necklace, and I revel in the control of holding her in place.

"That's it. That's my good girl." Her tongue thrashes about as she struggles to take me, and dribble spills from her mouth, but I hold her steadfast, then slowly withdraw almost all the way out as she gasps for breath before I slide back in. She chokes, but I push past it, then pull out and repeat, letting her get used to the sensation of me filling her hole for my pleasure. "Good girl. You're taking me so well." My balls draw up at the way her eyelids become heavy on my words, and my control snaps.

She winces as I pinch her scalp as a result of the tight rein I have on her hair. Then I thrust forward, holding her in place.

My hips move faster and faster as I slam into her throat, and sweat beads on my forehead and down my spine.

"That's it, be my little slut. My beautiful wife," I spit out with possessiveness and equal pleasure. Her warmth and wetness floods me down to my balls as arousal zips through my body at lightning speed. I use her mouth faster and faster. "So fucking good." She gags as tears spill from her eyes, and her nails pierce my thighs as I move quicker and harder, delighting in using her. When my balls tighten, I withdraw and remove my hand from her throat, aiming the tip of my cock over her mouth and face as I come. Shaking myself over her, exhilaration and relief flow from me in uncontrollable waves of ecstasy. I cover her lips and chin, then splash onto her cheeks, over her lashes, and down onto her necklace. Then I squeeze the tip of my cock on her tongue, drawing out every drop of my desire onto her.

"That's a good wife. Jesus, it pains me to see you coated in my love for you," I admit in a gravelly tone.

The grip on her hair remains forceful while I come down from my orgasm, desperate to keep the connection as I survey her response to my use of her. She flutters her eyelids, and when her lips tip up into a gentle smile, my shoulders relax.

I stroke circles over her cheek and swipe away the cum with my thumb. "You can swallow now, baby girl."

She rolls her lips and swallows, and the sight has my cock twitching. Something tells me I will never get enough of Laya.

Ever.

TWENTY-FIVE

LAYA

He stands above me like an avenger, his strong, broad shoulders covered in tattoos that travel over his torso. His pecs twitch under my scrutiny, and his abs contract as he comes down from his orgasm.

I've given blowjobs before, but never one where I was used so roughly. But I crave more. I crave everything that Owen has to give, all of him.

His abrasiveness calls to me, and his heavy hand and domineering composure sends excitement and arousal rippling through me, and I want to beg him to allow me to please him.

This man has owned my heart, soul, and body for as long as I can remember, and now he has it. I want him to use it to its full capacity. I want to please him, and it pleases me knowing he needs me as much as I need him.

There's a darkness inside Owen he tries to mask. He becomes too domineering for some women and that's why he gave me the option of tapping out, but I want that, I want him, every part of him: the dark, the destructive, and the dominating. I simply want him, whatever that is.

Licking my lips, I savor his taste on my lips, and his nostrils flare. The grip in my hair slackens and a part of me misses the roughness of his touch after only just receiving it.

"Please," I whisper, and his hands ball into fists beside him as he stares down at me.

"Please what, little slut?" His gravelly voice has me wriggling from side to side.

"I need to feel you."

"Where?" His Adam's apple bobs. "Where do you need to feel me, baby girl?"

I blush, and he smooths the hair from my face, then tenderly rubs his essence into my skin, and every cell of my body takes it willingly.

"Do you need me to stretch your little cunt with my cock?" My chest expands at his filthy tongue as need builds inside me to feel just that. I squirm in response. "Use your fucking words for me, baby girl."

"Y-yes."

His thumb travels down my jawline. "Do you want me to fuck your bloody cunt like a good husband?"

Holy shit. Yes.

"Yesss," I whisper, barely able to construct the word.

"I'm going to come inside you, Laya. I'm going to put my baby deep inside you, give Romeo a little brother or sister. Would you like that, baby girl?" I close my eyes as his words wrap around me. I've waited so long to hear that; I've wished for a family with Owen since being a small girl, and now he's offering me everything I ever wanted, and the emotion it brings to the forefront of my mind is almost debilitating.

"Say yes, like a good girl."

I open my eyes and see the love flow from him in waves. He wants this as much as I do, our own family.

The way I always dreamed we'd be.

"Yes, please."

Before I can blink, he lifts me under my arms, then throws me onto the mattress, and I can't help the giggle that escapes me when I bounce.

"I've waited so fucking long to do this, Laya." He crawls onto the bed, his huge form dwarfing mine, and with it, a sliver of unease flashes through me.

The last time we had sex, it hurt, and I just took his monster cock in my throat and can still feel the rawness. I haven't had sex since before Romeo was born, and now he's about to destroy me.

"Don't worry, baby girl, I'm going to look after your bloody cunt."

He tears my panties from me like a rabid animal, then sits back on his heels, staring at my pussy.

"Fuck me, that's hot."

I lean up on my elbows, and he fists himself to full length while staring at my apex. Desire makes me clench, and I want to beg him to take me, but instead, I watch in fascination as he lowers his head to between my legs. "I'm going to tug your tampon out of your bloody hole with my mouth, Laya." He lifts his head, and his gaze latches onto mine. "Then I'm going to bury my cock so deep inside you, baby girl, you've no choice but to breed for me." A moan escapes me when his palms clasp my thighs, holding me in place. "Are you going to bleed on my cock, baby girl?" I thrust my hips toward him in encouragement, and he smirks.

"Yes," I pant out.

"Good girl. Now let me play."

He buries his face in my pussy, and I throw my head back as he flattens his tongue and delivers a smooth stroke over my pussy and clit. The taboo element of my period on his tongue only adds to the thrill of his touch. He nibbles at my clit, toying with it, and presses soft kisses to it, then glides his tongue over my pussy lips, soaking them. Then he lifts his head, and my eyes clash with his, and I watch on open-mouthed as he spits on my pussy, once, twice, three times before he dips back down. This time, he works me into a frenzy, eating at me like a ravenous beast, the grunts and groans from him mirroring my own pleasure.

Then I feel the soft tugging on the tampon, and my body freezes as I realize that he's actually doing it, that his words weren't just his filthy mouth running away with him. He's getting a better grip on it, using his teeth to pull the tampon from me, and I don't know whether to be disgusted or turned on, but my body reacts before my mind, flooding with approval. "Please." I buck up into his touch.

He slaps my pussy, and I almost come.

"Oh, shit!" I throw my head back.

Then a gush releases from me with the tampon as he pulls back and sits on his heels, the tampon hanging between his teeth jarring me.

A smug grin encompasses his handsome face, and I melt against the sheets at the sight, full of bloody triumph, and I want him all the more.

OWEN

Her mouth falls open, and I grin manically, then spit the tampon out onto the sheets, the taste of her blood on my lips an aphrodisiac to the darkness inside me, roaring to be released.

Blood drips from her pussy, soaking into the fabric of her wedding dress, and I breathe in the scent of her like a predator about to consume its prey.

"My beautiful, bloody wife, dripping for me." I stroke over her soft thigh and move closer to her pussy. It's swollen, begging for my tongue, but I'm desperate to fill her, torn between taste and touch.

Taking my cock in hand, I line it up to her hole and close my eyes. I've waited for this moment for what feels like an eternity, to finally fuck the girl I love as my wife.

I drop down onto my forearms, hovering my lips above hers, and when she smiles at me, it fills me with the solitude and warmth only she can bring to my frozen heart, finally basking in the warmth her absence stole.

"Love you, baby girl," I whisper against her lips.

Tears glisten in her eyes, the enormity of the moment taking its toll on her.

So many walls put in place, so many feelings considered but never our own, yet we're finally where we were always meant to be.

"I love you too," she whispers, and I slide deep inside her, willing it to last an eternity.

TWENTY-SIX

OWEN

Her warmth encompasses me as I wait for her body to relax against mine. She fits me so perfectly, like she was made for me, and I hiss through my teeth at the thought.

"Mine," I grit out, then crash my lips against hers.

Her hand holds my jaw in place as we become feral for one another, the pressure building inside me so strong I have little choice but to start thrusting deep inside my wife while she wraps her legs around me.

"Are you bleeding for me, wife?" I nip at her lip and follow it up with a lash of my tongue.

"Yes." She pants heavily against me. "I'm bleeding for you, Owen."

"Fuck yes." Her words send me wild, and I power into her, each thrust stronger than the last, determined to leave my mark, to have her warm pussy molded to my length.

"You take my cock so well, Laya. Your cunt is greedy for me, isn't it?"

She throws her head back, and I deliver kisses down the column of her throat, delighting in the moans that escape her precious lips.

I grind my hips, making sure to hit her clit, and revel in the impact of her pulsating walls clamping around me like a vise. "Fuck, you feel so damn good. I can feel you gushing on my cock, Laya. All bloody and ready for me."

"Oh god!" Her body tightens around me, and I slam inside her harder and harder. The headboard hits the wall, and I push up onto my knees, grasp the wood, and hold on, staring down at her in ecstasy as she combusts on my cock.

"That's it." *Slam.*

"Bleed on my cock." *Thrust.*

"Soak me, baby girl." I power inside her. "Make my cock a bloody mess, baby girl. Make us both a mess." *Slam.*

The firm hold she has around me dissipates, so I take her in. The way her hair is splayed out over the pillows and her cheeks flush with her pleasure adds to her beauty. My gaze roams over the swell of her tits, and the fact I haven't tasted my wife's milk yet sends annoyance through my veins like a poison. My nostrils flare, and I ball the straps of her dress in my hands, tearing through the fabric with ease. Her mouth falls open as she lifts her head, her eyes wide.

"Jesus," I breathe out in exhilaration. "So fucking beautiful, baby girl." She chews on her bottom lip, then the moment my lips wrap around her nipple, she drops her head back against the pillow while holding my head in place. Her warm milk floods into my mouth, and I groan at the taste.

Fuck, this is incredible.

Absolutely fucking incredible.

"Oh god, Owen," she moans as I become feral, moving from one nipple to the other in wonderment while pumping her tits with my thick palm, encouraging her release. "That's it, baby, give me more milk." *Mmm.* Fuck, incredible, every inch of her incredible.

I swallow down everything she has to give, and my hips continue their assault on her little pussy, stretching her to capacity.

"Oh, Owen. Don't stop." I thrust harder.

"Don't stop," she pants.

"Not gonna." I nip at her nipple and grin when a blast of milk sprays out over my chin and down my neck, causing my body to vibrate with untamed domination.

Fuck me, that's hot.

"Please," she begs so beautifully, and I swirl my hips, hitting the perfect spots on the inside and out, causing her pussy muscles to contract around me once again and forcing my balls to ache. My mouth falls slack as I bury myself as deep as possible. "That's it, baby girl. Make me come inside your warm cunt." Not letting up on the pumping of her luscious tits, I ravish her peaked nipples with my tongue, lapping up her milk like a starved animal while her bloody cunt milks my cock.

"Oh god, Owen!" she screams like a banshee, and I revel in it.

"That's it, baby, take my cum. Take my cum deep inside you."

"Yes. Yes. Yesssss."

My cock pulsates as rope after rope of cum unload inside her, and I close my eyes at the splendor, willing it to create another life, one born from the eternal love of its parents. Something nobody will ever take from me.

No matter what our future holds.

LAYA

I nuzzle his bare chest, naked after he tossed my tattered wedding dress onto the floor.

Breathing in his familiar scent, I relax into him. His thick arms band around me like he's scared I will leave him. How could I? How could I ever leave these arms again?

"What are you thinking, baby girl?"

He strokes over my hair, caressing my heart with his gentle touch. Such a contrast from his bulky exterior and hardened features.

"I'm wondering how I'm ever going to leave your arms again," I whisper, my voice still sore from his cock and my screams. He stills, so I lift my head to face him.

"Why the fuck would you want to leave me?" He lifts an eyebrow, and I giggle at the sincerity on his face.

I bite on my lip, contemplating my words before delivering them with the honesty he deserves. "I just meant, I don't know how I'm going to breathe without you by my side, Owen. I spent forever longing for you. When I had you, you didn't just break my heart, you broke every part of me, and I don't think I'm going to be able to survive that again."

His heated stare makes me swallow hard, and the vein on his temple pulsates.

"You're mine." He lifts my hand to his lips and kisses the wedding band on my finger. "My wife. You're not going anywhere without me, and I'm not going anywhere either." My heart swims like a love-struck teenager's.

"You work away a lot."

"Not anymore," he grinds out with confidence. "You really think after years of being without you, I'm going to let you leave my side again? Not a fucking prayer." He sighs. "I just need you to know, whatever you're feeling, Laya, I'm feeling too." He chuckles, but it lacks humor. "I'm feeling too." He repeats, and my heart skips at the thought of his past hurt. "To know you did everything without me the first time around. I have to live with that, Laya. But this time, baby girl, this time, it's for keeps. I won't break your heart again, I promise."

He leans forward and kisses my forehead, and I relax against him. My gaze roams over his thick arm as he positions it beneath the pillow his head rests on. "I hadn't had sex since our last time together." His eyes dart down toward mine, and my mouth falls open, then he laughs, his eyes crinkling.

"That's ..."

"Years. I know. Trust me, I know." He lifts an eyebrow, and I narrow my eyes.

"Why?"

"Because the only woman I wanted was you. If I couldn't have you, I didn't want anyone."

His words swim in my mind. "But you knew I was"—I grimace as I say it—"married."

He swallows thickly. "I did. But I told myself it was punishment for letting you go." When his eyes come back to mine, I see the hurt in them, and I hate it. I hate it and understand it. Both of us have been living a lie, pretending to live a life of happiness when our hearts belonged to the unattainable.

"I think you should shower, baby girl. Romeo will be due for a feeding soon, right?"

The fact he knows our son's routine already is a testament to his commitment. When I signed the adoption papers alongside our wedding certificate today, I was flooded with guilt, but knowing how Owen feels for Romeo leaves no question in my mind that he will forever be the father he should have had. I sit up and stare down at him. "Are you going to help me?"

The hunger in his eyes gives me the answer before he even says it, and I smile with confidence. "Damn fucking right, I am. Let's see how messy I can get you first."

TWENTY-SEVEN

OWEN

After fucking Laya against the tiled wall of the shower, I pushed her to the floor and had her suck my cock. As much as I want to fill her with my baby, there's something hypnotic about seeing her mouth stretched, struggling to take my cock while I plow into her like a man possessed. Knowing her throat would be raw from my assault only added fuel to the inferno raging inside me.

She fed Romeo soon after, and I watched. With her back against my chest and our son in her arms, a sense of calm washed over me in a way I've never felt before.

My wife and son in my arms, bringing with it a tranquil feeling of completeness.

A purpose in life, my own family.

Pained whimpers set every hair on my body on edge, startling me awake. Laya thrashes about, gripping my thigh with her sharp nails.

My hand hovers in the air, about to rouse her from her nightmare. "No. No. Stop," she whimpers, the sound scratchy from taking her so roughly, and my blood stills, sending my heart freefalling into the abyss.

Just what the hell has she endured?

I've let her down in more ways than I could ever imagine, so I squeeze my eyes closed, then snap them open when she crawls over my leg and between my thighs. Stroking her head, I hope my touch brings her some comfort, then her wails turn to low sobs. "Shh, baby girl," I croon. "Shh, I'm here. Nothing can hurt you."

Her lips encompass the tip of my soft cock, and I wince as I begin to harden at her touch.

I grit my teeth, willing myself not to become hard while she uses my cock for comfort, and eventually, her weeps become gentle whimpers as I glide my fingers through her hair. "Shhh. I'm here." I'm unsure of who I'm trying to reassure more, her or me. Knowing I can comfort her has me determined to give her what she needs, so instead of delighting in the vibrations of her suckle, I concentrate on the fact that once morning arrives, I will find out who hurt my girl and make them pay. The sickening feeling wedged deep in the pit of my stomach isn't going away; it's amplifying and bringing with it a venomous fury I need to expel on the culprit.

Nobody hurts my girl.

Nobody touches my wife and gets away with it.

LAYA

Drool wets my cheek, and when I lift my head, I realize I've been using Owen's cock to comfort me.

Heat rushes over me like a tidal wave, and I want nothing more than the world to eat me whole.

"It's okay, baby girl. I like it."

My gaze flicks up to him. "Pleased to be of service to you." He grins.

I swat at his chest and scoot away from him, but he leans forward and lifts me so I'm straddling his body.

Then he tucks my hair behind my ear. "Tell me what happened."

I dart my eyes away, unwilling to share my nightmare.

Owen turns my head to face him. "We're married, baby. I need to know everything there is to know about you."

"Like I know everything there is about you, you mean?" I snipe back, then I grimace at the hurt in his eyes. I know Owen keeps things from me. He always has; "to protect me," as he says. But now that we're married, things can't be one-sided. That's not how I want this relationship to work. I want every part of him, like he wants every part of me, including the darkness lingering behind his eyes.

He swallows slowly, and his eyes flash with vulnerability. "What do you want to know?"

I search his face for a sign of insincerity but find none, and like always, I want to pull him close and reassure him I'll be by his side no matter what, that I will always be there for him.

Curiosity takes over me. "Your father."

His face falls slack, and he tenses beneath me, but I remain headstrong. He's offering me a lifeline, a deeper insight into what makes him tick. He's finally letting me in when I've spent years on the edge, silently pleading for him to give in to me. I saw the signs he wanted me, but his mind was another story, protected by a barrier he never let anyone behind.

He licks his lips and rolls them between his teeth.

All I know about his father is he was not a good man; my brother and the guys spoke in hushed voices whenever discussing him. I also know he was the original owner of a security firm that Owen took over and merged with the guys to create STORM Enterprise. Whenever I asked questions about Owen's family, I was always shot down, made to feel like the young girl I was, like I had no business asking questions that clearly distressed Owen. Anger would roll off him in waves, then he'd drink himself into oblivion. Many mornings, I would slip into the spare room at our house that had become a second home to Owen and his best friends, and watch him sleep off his hangover while imagining creating a life for us together, away from the pain that caused him to spiral so epically. I'd leave him Tylenol and water beside his bed, take away his dirty clothes, hoping above all hope that I wouldn't smell cheap perfume on his clothes when I brought his shirt to my nose to breathe in his scent.

Yes, I deserve to know, as his wife, as the mother of his children, and hopefully, as his best friend. "I don't want secrets between us," I whisper with yearning.

"The necklace you're wearing was my mom's." He swallows thickly while my heart hammers from knowing there's more to come. "I took it from her when she died." He closes his eyes as he screws his face up as if pained. "He murdered my mom," he blurts, his chest rising rapidly, and my heart constricts at the agony he must have endured and still endures to this day.

My hands find my necklace, and his eyes watch on as I press it against me.

Knowing he gave me something of hers, something he treasured so dearly, instills the love I know he feels.

Taking a deep breath, I remove my hand and draw circles on his chest with the tips of my fingers, hoping my touch brings him comfort. His eyes narrow, so I tilt my head, wondering what he's thinking. "I'm sorry."

"You're not repulsed by me?"

I rear back. Repulsed? Never.

"I love you." It slips from my lips, and a whoosh of air escapes him. "Tell me," I coax gently. "Tell me all of it, Owen."

His eyes plead with me to show mercy, but in this moment where we share our truths, I want all of him. It's the only way I can give all of me.

As if hearing my thoughts, his lips move as my mind

whirls over what he's just said to try to make sense of it. "He throttled her during sex. I found her in bed with his marks around her neck, her eyes... Fuck, her eyes were wide, bloodshot. Fuck." He slams his fist on the mattress, bringing me back to the present to make sense of his words.

His dad killed his mom during rough sex.

Owen likes rough sex.

He panicked after we first had sex at the marks on my neck and pushed me away.

"He wasn't a good man, Laya. It wasn't some sex game gone wrong." He shakes his head. "He wasn't a good man, Laya. Neither am I."

My body coils tight. "That's not true." I glare at him. "You love me and Romeo, and I see how much the guys mean to you, my family too. You're a good man, Owen. I just wish you could see it too."

He chuckles, but it lacks jest. "You always did see the good in me."

"That's because I saw all of you."

He clears his throat, then fidgets, brushing his hand over his jaw as if contemplating his next words.

"There was more to my father than everyone thought."

I nod. After years of hearing rumors, I've often wondered what is true. "He made me do things as a child, things that would make your blood curdle. That's something I never want for Romeo." He holds my gaze. "I want him to have a normal childhood, one where his father protects him and loves him above anything else, above the power and the money. Above everything." His eyes hold something so much more than the words he speaks, they hold love. I replay his words, thinking about the meaning of them because they cause my heart to flutter. The way he describes protecting Romeo's future is beautiful and freeing. Knowing this man would do anything to protect my son instills my belief in him, and I want nothing more than to live it.

I take his chin in my hand. "I love you." I speak with firmness, leaving no room for doubt. "I love everything about you, Owen. All your imperfections. I see them all and want to own them like you own mine. I want you to give them to me so I can be your everything."

"You are my everything. You always were."

I connect our hands, then bring them up to my throat. My pulse races, our fingers linked over his mother's chain, and now that I know the connection, it only makes my heart beat stronger for him.

"You're the only person to ever see me, the real me," he whispers. "That's why I fell in love with you, Laya. You saw every part of me and never gave up on me. If anything, it only made you want me more."

His fingers twitch over mine, encouraging me to press harder.

"It's true. I crave your darkness. I want you. All of you."

Then I crawl down him, positioning myself over his hard cock, and wetness pools between my legs at the way his eyes flare with arousal as I slide my slick pussy over him.

"Your bloody cunt is dripping on my cock, Laya."

I grind over his hardness. "It is." I'm relieved the flow of my period has weakened, as Owen wanted our wedding night free of anything between us despite my insistence on still using a tampon, and I was happy to comply with his possessive demands.

"Laya," he grits out as his fingers flex beneath mine.

"Please, I want you to shove your cock inside me, Owen." I squeeze our hands harder, and the thick vein on his temple pulsates, and the cords on his neck coil tight. As I raise myself up, he removes a hand and fists his cock beneath me before swiping it through my wetness. Then he slams me down on his thick length, making me whine at the stretch and intrusion to my already tender pussy.

"Oh Jesus," I squeak out, and choke when he brings his hand back to my throat.

"Yeah. That's it." He grinds his teeth and hisses through his lips. "Take that thick cock, baby girl. Take it deep in your little cunt." He powers up into me while I tweak my nipples and watch in euphoria at the way every muscle on his torso contracts.

He uses my body with ease, surging up inside me while his hands guide my body up and down over his broad waist.

"Fuck, you look good riding me, baby. So fucking good."

"Yes. Yes."

"I'm going to fuck my babies into you, Laya." One of his thick palms lands on my stomach, and electricity zaps down my spine at the contact. A promise of our future. Something I want now more than ever. I swirl my hips in encouragement, determined to milk him of his seed.

"Please," I beg wantonly.

His thrusts become erratic as my pussy contracts. "Say you want it, say you want it as bad as me, Laya."

"I want it. I want your baby. Please Owen, I want you!"

I scream the latter while I shatter around him, clutching his cock so tightly he's no choice but to follow me over the edge, and when his cum shoots deep inside me, I close my eyes and will our future together.

The one that always should have been.

TWENTY-EIGHT

OWEN

Our hearts beat erratically but in time with one another's. It's amazing what a confession can do for you, the way it can pull you closer together or tear you apart.

A heavy feeling lingers in the pit of my stomach, knowing my secrets could destroy us, destroy her, and even though I promised honesty in our relationship, I know deep in my heart she wouldn't be prepared for this one.

Some secrets are best kept hidden in the dark where they belong, and my mind wanders back in time to when I was thirteen as the realization of my father's making haunts me.

My feet come to a standstill as I take in the scene around me.

I've only been home from boarding school an hour and already want to return. Sickness rolls in my stomach, and my breakfast threatens to make a return. I hate it when I'm summoned to my father's basement, but it's a necessity in our family business.

For as long as I can remember, I have been conditioned to take over his empire, yet not one part of me wants to.

Three men line the wall, each of them dressed head to toe in black suits and shirts. They stand with their hands behind their backs and their heads lowered as a mark of respect to my father.

My gaze hits the man chained to the wall. He's been beaten and is bloody, and I can only hope he has little fight left in him. Knowing he will scream less makes this whole situation easier.

"Owen, come here." My father points to the spot in front of him, and without hesitation, I move to the exact point he commands me.

"I'd like you to meet someone important. A friend of mine, an ally." I know that look. I'm to show respect. I'm to be the man I'm destined to be, no matter how much I don't want it.

At school, I'm free. I can be anything I want to be. My friends see me as Owen, the boy who loves sports, has a mean right hook, and can hold his own. But at home, I enter a cavern of darkness. A world surrounded by the deadliest, and my father in the center of it. His dealings within the underworld have become notorious, but only to those who seek it. To the outside world, he's a pillar of the community, a businessman who dabbles in the security network.

He fails to mention the forefront of his business is a façade which benefits him and his colleagues equally.

His connections are of benefit to both parties, full of wealth and knowledge while carefully entwining the worlds like only he has the ability to do.

"This is Lorenzo Varros." He holds out his palm toward his acquaintance, and without prompting, I step forward and hold out my hand.

Mr. Varros chuckles deeply but humors me by slipping his hand into mine and squeezing as he shakes it, tilting his head and assessing me. "Nice to meet you, Owen."

I deliver a nod but remain silent.

"Show Mr. Varros what we do to traitors, Owen." My father's steel gaze holds mine, testing me. His eyes say a thousand things while his lips say none. Don't fuck this up, boy. Be the man I created. Let the darkness consume you like it does me.

Pulling my shoulders back, I step past him and stride toward the table where my father keeps his interrogation instruments.

Knowing he's craving a performance, I select the scalpel, and like my father trained me to do, I fall into the depths of hell and move swiftly.

Using the man to pour out my anger over this fucked-up situation, I slice at his chest, stripping him bare of his skin while his howls of pain become background noise.

My mind becomes riddled with jealousy of my friends, their normalcy. I want to swim in Tate's pool and party to the beat of the music he blares out.

Slice.

My grip tightens as each contact becomes deeper, deadlier. The beast inside me unraveling at a terrifying pace, if the victim's pleads are anything to go by.

Slice.

To play tennis and celebrate the school holidays with a barbeque.

Slice.

My hand becomes slippery with the warmth of his blood, and I imagine it's from sweat while training Mase at the gym.

Slice.

Loud chuckles erupt in the room, but I ignore it. As a chill runs down my spine, I envisage Shaw shoving ice down my T-shirt as I give in to the scenarios playing out in my mind, each helping to make this task more bearable.

Losing myself to the demons beckoning me, more bearable.

Slice.

Booms of clapping echo off the concrete wall, and my father's firm grip pinches into my shoulder, then my shoulders sag.

"Well done, son." He spins me to face Lorenzo.

My skin itches to rid it of the blood coating me, and I swallow back the bile in my throat.

Lorenzo scans me from head to toe. It's calculating and forces me to gasp for breath. In that moment, I feel like he's staring directly into my soul. He knows this isn't me.

He knows I don't want to be the monster my father is training me to become.

I want to be free.

His eyes soften slightly. "I'll be seeing you, Owen."

His words hold a haunting promise, and I tell myself to never become the man my father wants me to be.

When I have a family, I will protect them at all costs.

Do whatever it takes.

Because you protect the ones you love from evil, not expose them to it.

I tangle my fingers in her hair, holding her tightly against my firm chest while my cock remains stuffed deep inside her. Then I breathe in her scent, letting it encompass me, bringing with it the solace I so fiercely desire. Her acceptance.

She's mine, I tell myself for the millionth time.

"Now tell me about your nightmare."

She lifts her head to face me, but my tattooed fingers remain on the back of her head.

OWEN

When she takes a deep breath, I feel it all the way into my balls, unable to help the way my cock throbs for her.

She swallows, and the way her eyes flicker with fear before she licks her lips and gives in to my command stirs the devil inside me, eager to get out.

"When I close my eyes, I see it all happen." The soft tremble in her voice sends my pulse racing with anxiety.

I nod toward her. "Go on."

"The men that came into the room and made him—" Her breath hitches as tears fill her eyes, and I want nothing more than to take away her pain, but her word sends my mind into overdrive. "Kneel. They made him kneel before they …" Tears spill from her eyes, and a shudder racks her body followed by a wake of goose bumps.

Awareness creeps up my spine like poison. She saw him die.

"Before they killed him." She gasps and sucks in a sharp breath, stealing mine in the process. "They killed him, and there was so much blood, Owen. And I shouted for them to stop, I shouted, and Romeo was crying, and his eyes, his eyes met mine, Owen." Her panicked words flow from her as she unravels while I remain steadfast, frozen beneath her with such volatile anger I'm too afraid to move, knowing the destruction I could cause.

They killed him in front of her.

My teeth draw blood from my lower lip as my girl breaks down, and when her sobs turn to wails, the hazy cloud of fury detonates, and I've no choice but to slide her off me and onto the mattress.

I jump up from the bed like a madman, and with a roar, I slam my fist into the wall again and a-fucking-gain until the plaster crumbles to the floor like my heart.

She saw her husband murdered.

The bastard didn't even protect her from that.

I should have been there. I should have stopped her from leaving, from marrying him.

"You couldn't have done anything." Her fingers graze over my back, disconnecting me from my descent into the abyss, and now I realize I voiced the words I was thinking.

"I should never have let you go, Laya," I whisper, brokenhearted at the terror she must have endured.

"I'm here now," she reassures me, smoothing her hand over my back. "I'm not going anywhere."

Turning to her, I swipe away the last of the tears streaking her face. I will not allow her to cry for him. "Promise?"

She smiles and toys with my mother's chain as she raises her chin with confidence. Her words are low but strong and passionate, not a flicker of doubt in her eyes. "I promise." And I relax against her words, knowing she believes them as much as I do, that we will weather a storm together. We will remain strong and unbroken; the way we were meant to be.

TWENTY-NINE

LAYA

After showering, feeding Romeo, and dressing, I leave the bedroom and head downstairs, smiling as Owen talks to my son in a gentle voice reserved solely for him.

"Daddy is going to build you the biggest fort, little buddy. Just like on Mommy's Pinterest." My heart floods with love for them both. There's something hot about a man holding a baby, especially barefoot in tight jeans and a white T-shirt stretched over his muscular frame.

Romeo stares back at him, and I swear it looks like he's taking it all in. When Owen grins down at him with love in his eyes, a sharp pang hits me square in the chest.

Carlos never looked at him like that.

He never spoke of a future with our son. He didn't discuss spending time with him, his dreams of a life together.

"You okay, baby? You look like you've seen a ghost. I

think we need to get you a therapist for trauma or something."

"You do?"

"Damn fucking right, I do." He steps closer, and heat radiates from my pores at his fresh, masculine scent I know so well. "You clearly have PTSD, although …" He grazes a hand over his head, another sign of his nervousness I know so well. He did it a lot around me when I was younger, as if I terrified him by being so close to him. Resting his lips beside my ear, the touch of his breath sends a shimmer of desire through me. "I like you suckling on my cock."

I rear back to search his eyes. "You do?"

"Absolutely, you can take me in your mouth whenever you like."

Oh, sweet Jesus, how I've longed to hear those words. "I can?"

"Yes, baby, you can." Then he steps back, and my body deflates. "Now. I made you breakfast. Sit." He points toward the table. "I need to change Daddy's buddy, then we're going over to your parents' for lunch."

Daddy's buddy? I practically melt on the spot.

"We are?" Excitement builds inside me at the thought of seeing my mom and dad, but it quickly diminishes at the thought of coming clean to them and, worse, to Tate.

"I'll handle Tate," Owen says with confidence.

An onslaught of panic ripples through me. "I don't want any trouble, Owen."

"There won't be any trouble, baby girl. I'm just telling him how it is."

I cock my eyebrow. "And how is it?"

"That we're married, we're going to spend the rest of

our lives together, and that you're the love of my life. I'm Romeo's father." The fact he included my son in his admission only makes my love for him shine brighter.

"I've got this, baby girl." He takes my hand and kisses it, and I can only hope he's right, that he does indeed have this.

My mom rushes me as soon as I step foot into the house. Her familiar warmth wraps around me, bringing me the comfort I've craved for what feels like a lifetime.

She peppers kisses over my cheek. "My girl. Oh, thank God you're home."

Steph Kavanagh is a saint, concealed in high heels and sophistication that rivals any runway model's. Beneath her exterior of a successful businesswoman and a fortune of wealth dating back decades, there lies a deeply passionate woman. Her drive and ambition to give others a better life, an opportunity to be better, and in doing so, she's surrounded by a series of charities gifting her time and money in helping the next generation succeed.

It's through one of those charities that my brother met his wife, Ava. She was a part of the charity in which my mom and dad host as summer guests and, in most circumstances, future education sponsors.

Ava was celebrating her birthday. Unbeknownst to my brother, her eighteenth birthday. The following morning, he found out, and they went their separate ways until a few years later when she interned at STORM Enterprises. They've been inseparable ever since, despite Ava's dark, traumatic background that resulted in a monster from her past attempting to break them up and kidnap Ava. They remain stronger than ever, and it's with the knowledge that my brother loves so deeply despite age or circumstance that I hope will win him over today.

"And let me see my boy!" My mom pulls back and beams in Owen's direction, who walks in with Romeo in his carrier. "Oh my word, he looks just like you!"

I don't know a lot about my birth parents other than they were addicts who passed away due to their misuse, but I do know that when I arrived here, I was a scared little girl used to eating out of garbage bags. My mom and dad showered me with the love every child deserves, and not once did I ever feel anything but family. So I know Owen looks at my son with such love and protection because it's exactly how my parents looked at me, like they want to wrap me in cotton wool and treasure me all the same.

My mom unclips and lifts Romeo out, and his little butt scrunches up, and I smile at his adorable, sleepy, pouty face. "Laya?" Tates voice cuts through my mom's soft coos toward Romeo.

Slowly, I spin to face my brother as he practically runs toward me. The panic engrained in his face makes guilt swim through me. He gasps, his mouth falls open. "What the hell happened to your face?" His eyes dart toward Owen.

I had thought my face was no longer bruised and the cut almost gone, but clearly, I was wrong. I wring my hands in front of him but decide to rip off the Band-Aid. "My husband did it." A deep growl emits from Owen, anger radiating from him, and I wince at the realization.

"He fucking hit you?"

Owen steps to the side. "Her husband didn't hit her." Tate's eyes narrow before he brings his gaze back to mine, as if searching for the answer. "The mistake hit her. That same mistake is dead, so he won't lay another finger on her ever." He laces his fingers with mine, and Tate's eyes follow the action. "I'm her husband now, and I'm going to worship the ground she walks on."

Tate jolts as if he's been electrocuted, then laughs, but it lacks mirth. "You're kidding?"

Owen broadens his shoulders, and my heart hammers in my chest. "I'm not kidding. I love Laya and she loves me. I should have done this a long time ago, but ..." He pauses and glances at my mom. "I made the mistake of giving her time." He clears his throat, as it becomes apparent he's getting emotional. "I refuse to give her any more time. I refuse to back down. She's my everything, and Romeo is my son. We're married, Tate. I adopted Romeo. Deal with it."

Tate's face morphs from shocked to pissed in the blink of an eye. "Deal with it?" he whispers while his focus remains locked on our joined hands. "Fucking deal with it!" he bellows, making me jump and causing Romeo to cry out. Owen grinds his jaw, and his grip on my hand tightens. I want to tell him it's painful, but I remain motionless.

My mom shushes Romeo as she slips from the foyer.

"Fucking deal with it?" he screams again, and his face grows redder by the second, making my throat become dry and filling me with tension. Owen feels it too, so in tune with my body, like I am his.

"Enough," he spits out while his free hand slices through the air. "Enough, Tate. Just calm the hell down."

If he thought that was going to ease the situation, he was wrong. Tate's eyes bulge, and before I know what's happening, he lunges toward Owen. His fist connects with Owen's jaw, and Owen releases my hand, pushing me to the side. I watch on in horror as Tate delivers blow after blow to my husband's stomach, but he continues to hold his hands up, allowing him to pummel him.

"Oh, shit!" Mase and Shaw come rushing into the foyer, followed by Reed, who leans against the wall with not a care in the world. I want to scream at him to help, but Mase wastes no time in dragging a flailing Tate off Owen, who stands unperturbed by my brother's outburst.

"You son of a bitch! You goddamn son of a bitch, Owen!" Spittle flies from his mouth, and I wrap my arms around myself, hating this, hating all of it.

Mase speaks lowly in Tate's ear, and his shoulders seem to ease, so Mase loosens his hold, but no sooner does he do that does Tate fly through the air, sending Owen crashing into the side table.

The sound of them hitting the marble floor and my mom's vase shattering sends a tsunami of memories through my head, and suddenly, my chest feels like it's being squeezed, my airways become restricted, and I can't breathe. Oh, sweet Jesus, I can't breathe. My vision becomes blurry as panic takes hold of me.

I close my eyes, trying to regain some form of control over my own body, to no avail.

Carlos's hand darts out and hits my face. The hateful glare in his eyes is terrifying. My head hits the floor with a crack, and all I feel is the terror of knowing our son is in the same room.

"He's going to kill me. He's going to kill us," I chant, feeling trapped inside my head.

Wetness coats my face, but I'm too detached to register what that is. "Please. Someone. Please." My body shakes uncontrollably as I beg for someone to rescue us.

"I want to go home," I murmur. "I want to go home."

OWEN

Tate's fist slams into my gut, and I accept it. I accept each of his hits, knowing I deserve it, each and every one of them.

The fucker catches me off guard, and I lose my balance while attempting to save Steph's vase, but fail.

"Fuck," I grunt when he lands one above my eye, and I have to grind my jaw to stop from retaliating.

"He's going to kill me. He's going to kill us." Her soft, terrified voice filters through my senses, and like that, a switch has been flipped as my stomach rolls at her broken tone.

I flip Tate onto his back and jump to my feet and stride toward Laya.

My poor girl is huddled into a corner of the room, her legs drawn up to her chest, and her arms banded tightly around her.

"Please. Someone. Please."

Jesus, my heart cracks right then, knowing she's having a panic attack brought on by the fight, and once again, I hate myself for it. I knew there was a possibility of Tate reacting this way, and I never considered removing her from the situation, thinking going in as a united front was the best way of winning him over. Of course, I was fucking wrong. I swipe the blood dripping from my eye away and kneel in front of her, ignoring the sharp bellows from Tate telling me to stay away from her—my fucking wife.

"I'm here, baby." I stroke her cheek, hating how despondent she is. The way her eyes are squeezed closed, and her body riddled with tension. "Open your eyes, baby."

"I want to go home." I rest my palm on her cheek. "I want to go home."

"You are home, Laya. I'm your home. Open your eyes for me, baby girl."

Her eyes snap open, and my heart fills with warmth. I could swim in the depths of the love she holds there. "That's it, I got you." I scoop her into my arms and cradle her against me, reveling in the way her arms band around my neck as her protector.

"I love you, Laya," I whisper as I place a tender kiss on her neck, and she shudders.

"Baby. Fucking. Girl?" I spin to face Tate. His face is red, every vein on his neck protrudes, and his fists clench beside him, making me want to roll my eyes at how he's overreacting.

Shaw steps forward, putting himself between us, and I want to high-five my friend for doing that when the atmosphere is so volatile. "Tate. Now's not the time," he grits out, clearly pissed at him too.

Tate scoffs like a petulant child.

"What the hell is going on here?" Ava storms through

the foyer and heads straight toward Tate, her eyes darting from my distressed girl in my arms to her husband. "Are you fucking kidding me right now?" Her mouth falls open. "Seriously, Tate?"

In a split second, my friend's balls shrivel as his body slackens and his fists uncurl. "That's your sister right there!" She points. "And you're acting like a thug, terrifying her in the process."

"I didn't mean—"

She holds her hand up, and he clamps his mouth shut. The action would be comical if I wasn't so infuriated. "I don't want to hear it." She turns to face me, putting her back to Tate, and plasters on a smile that makes my lip quirk. "Maybe take Laya into the family room?"

I nod and head out of the foyer, ignoring the jibes of contempt as we leave, knowing this will be a lot tougher than I first thought. Putting a ring on Laya's finger and adopting Romeo was supposed to help prove my commitment to them both, but it's only added fuel to Tate's wrath.

THIRTY

OWEN

"How long has this been going on, huh? How long have you been fucking my little sister, you backstabbing prick?"

My teeth ache from clenching them so hard.

Mark and Steph took me, Tate, Shaw, Reed, and Mase into the dining room. I know the guys are here in case Tate loses it again. From his death glare to his taught body seething with hate, his fury radiates toward me, and I get it. That's why I take it.

"How old was she when you fucked her?" he spits out.

"Jesus." Mase pinches the bridge of his nose and looks up toward the ceiling.

I cast my eyes around the room, uncomfortable at this question. Her parents are here too, and I have too much respect for them and her to discuss our private life.

Reed is swiping on his phone with not a care in the world. Lot of good he is. Mase looks two seconds away from leaving the room, as he starts pacing again, and Shaw's face is etched with concern, his focus switching between Tate and me.

"She was legal," I reply, hoping it dissipates any concerns that had no place arising.

Tate scoffs. "Legal? Like how fucking legal, Owen?"

I glare back at him. He's some nerve to talk when he fucked Ava at eighteen too.

"Enough." Steph slaps her palm down on the table.

"Owen won't be answering any more questions about his and Laya's private life. Show some respect. We've brought you up better than that, Tate."

His mouth falls open, and he scoffs.

Mark slides a drink into my hand, then squeezes my shoulder. Tate doesn't miss the action and looks seconds away from exploding.

"You're okay with this?" He waves his hand toward me with a sneer on his lips.

Steph raises her chin, and I couldn't be more grateful. "We are, and you should be too. Your sister is happy and safe and, more importantly, she's loved. Her and our grandson are loved. What more could I possibly want for them? What more would you want for them?" Tate's eyes don't leave mine, and I graze a hand over my head, uncomfortable with his scrutiny. "That man that took my daughter away, secluded her, whether she was aware of that or not, I don't know. But he had a control over her that broke my heart to witness, from a distance of course." Steph's voice wobbles, and Mark pulls her against him. Hurt stirs in my veins at the time Steph and Mark have missed out on with Laya and Romeo, but not anymore, not now that they're mine. "He clearly abused her, Tate." She holds Tate's gaze, and he swallows as his eyes fill with tears, and my heart thumps heavily at their pain.

"He lied to me," Tate whispers as his eyes meet mine again. The hurt evident in his tone and his eyes, and I suck in a sharp breath at the impact that has on me.

I hurt him.

My mouth becomes dry, and I lick my lips before responding. "I'm sorry. I never meant to hurt any of you, especially Laya."

"But you did anyway," Tate bites back, his anger returning, something I hope I can diminish with my next words.

"I love her, Tate. Her and that little boy. I love them so fucking much it hurts in here." I clasp my fist over my chest. "Every day she was with him, creating the life I wanted with her but never had the chance of experiencing. Waking up in the morning, wondering if she was thinking of me like I was thinking about her. Tormenting myself that he was touching her when it should have been me." Jealousy courses through me as I relay my life for the past few years without her. "I stopped myself so many times from stepping in. Too scared to hurt you." I nod toward him and then Steph and Mark, but ignore the tears on my mother-in-law's face as I continue on. "I didn't want to lose the only family I had at the risk of her having a crush." My eyes hold Steph's, and her lip wobbles.

"It was more than a crush, we all knew that," Shaw adds.

"You didn't even try; you were a fucking coward. I asked you if anything was happening and you said no." I wince at the hate in Tate's tone.

Steph clears her throat. "I asked him not to act on his feelings."

All attention is turned toward Steph. "I asked him to give her the opportunity to have a life outside of this one."

I bite the inside of my mouth, unable to stop the anger and hurt bubbling inside me as she recalls the moment she crushed me, making me feel inadequate for her daughter no matter how much I know she didn't mean it that way. Hell, if I was her, I'd have done the same thing.

"I just never expected her to meet someone … like him. I'm sorry, Owen. If I could take it back …"

I tilt my head toward her.

Part of me will never forgive her for asking that of me, for solidifying a decision I never wanted to make, but I love her like a mother, and I know she had Laya's best interests at heart.

I lean across the table and hold Tate's gaze, knowing he can see deep into my soul as I deliver my final words.

"I love her, Tate, and I'll do anything to keep her."

Anything.

THIRTY-ONE

LAYA

I glance over my shoulder at my sleeping son swaddled in the pastel-blue blanket my mom knitted for him.

"He asleep?" Owen's eyes flick into the rearview mirror for confirmation.

"Yes. He was out like a light after his last feeding."

He turns his gaze from the road to me, and heat blooms on my face. His eyes travel over me, then flick back toward the road too soon, leaving my body aching for more of his attention.

I lick my lips as uncertainty ripples through me. "Owen?"

His eyes snap to mine, and I instantly feel better. Something flashes in his eyes, some sort of understanding, and when he unbuckles his belt, my pulse races.

"Come on, baby girl, come and suck on this cock like the good girl I know you to be."

He pulls his semihard cock from his boxers, and I lean

over the center console, then bury my head into his groin. I breathe in his masculine scent as relaxation takes over me. He taps the head of his cock at my mouth. "Open, baby girl. I want you to suckle on me. Take what you need from me."

The moment his velvety cock slides into my mouth, I close my eyes and suckle, and when his thick palm tangles in my hair, I melt into him.

"Such a precious girl. You did good today, baby; everything is going to be okay now," he croons, and his security and love wrap around me, providing the comfort I desperately crave.

OWEN

Laya fell asleep suckling on my cock, and it brought a dominance I never knew existed; I did that. I created such comfort for her that she melted into my touch and allowed me to bring her solitude. Possession and love ran through my veins, such an intoxicating blend that rendered me powerless in that moment. She owned me, every part of me, and was the one with control, and I happily gave it to her.

When we arrived home, I alerted my security team to carry Romeo inside while I carried Laya, then I placed my son in his crib and undressed my wife. Now I sit watching her sleep, calculating every moment her heart beats, counting the small gasps of air leaving her pouty lips, being in awe of her very existence.

My wife.

She stirs from sleep, her eyes snap open, then she sits up with a startle. Her gaze flicks around the room as if confused, and when her eyes land on me, emotion lodges in my throat.

The swell of her bare tits and the way her nipples are pebbled have my mouth watering. Her wavy hair is messy, and I want nothing more than to add to the chaos of her untamed curls with my hand as I guide her over my aching cock.

The sheet pools to the mattress, giving me the perfect view of every inch of her, and I feast on it.

I touch my throbbing cock, opening my thighs wide to accommodate me. With her eyes on me, I move my hand down toward my heavy balls and tug before wrapping my fist around my thick girth, stroking to ease the dull pressure ebbing to be released.

She rolls her lip between her teeth as if contemplating her next move, and when she parts her legs, gifting me with a perfect view of her pussy, eagerness floods my bloodstream and I almost choke on my tongue, losing the ability to swallow or construct simple words to command her.

Fuck me, that's hot. She parts her pussy lips, allowing me to see her juice drip from her; her blood has stopped and only a clear stream of eagerness leaks from her small hole, one I can't wait to push my cock into.

"Crawl," I bite out, and point toward the floor beside my feet.

That gritty air of confidence I love about Laya comes back, and she throws her hair over her shoulder and complies. Sliding from the bed onto her knees, she crawls toward me, and my heart hammers against my ribcage.

"So fucking beautiful under my control, Laya."

Her heavy, milky tits hang as my girl takes measured movements toward me, and my cock leaks in approval.

I swipe the head of my cock with my thumb and hold it

out for my girl. "Come." My gravelly voice is choked under the sexual haze surrounding us, and when she rests on her heels at my feet, my cock spits out more pre-cum. I hold my thumb out for her, and when her small, wet tongue trails languorously slowly over my digit, I almost combust.

"You're a good girl, Laya."

My eyes roll when she moans around my thumb, suckling on it like she does my cock.

I continue pumping myself due to the persistent ache in my cock. "My good girl has earned this cock, haven't you, baby?"

She moans as I push my thumb farther inside her warm mouth, and I relish the choking sound she makes before I withdraw it again until her greedy mouth finds it and continues sucking. "My baby girl likes feasting on me, don't you, my perfect little slut?" My cock jumps at my filthy words and the way her eyes become hooded.

"Come on, baby girl, suck my cock into your greedy mouth. You earned this."

I pull my thumb from her mouth, and she scrambles between my legs, then I wrap her hair around my fist, leaving her no room to argue with who is in control here.

Every cell of my body is electrified under her lust-filled gaze, and every vein inside me pumps with a ruthless adrenaline begging to be controlled, and when she darts her tongue over her top lip as if savoring me, my command for her is vilified. She needs satisfied as much as I do.

"Lick." I nod toward my balls, and she complies by sticking her tongue out and flattening it, then slowly drags it over my balls, causing me to hiss through clenched teeth. My gaze wanders over to the mirror on the wall, and fuck me, what a sight. My girl's mouth working over my thick cock almost has me at the brink. She circles my balls with her tongue, and when her fingernails dig into my muscular thighs, every cord of my body is wrung tight with desire.

Tipping my head back, I close my eyes as I use my hold on her hair to guide her up and down my shaft, delighting in her breaths stroking over me like flames of passion.

Fuck, she's incredible.

Every swipe of her tongue and every whimper as I manhandle her urges me forward. "Fuck, you earned this, baby," I grunt as I force her to gag around me. "You earned this big cock in your little mouth." Her saliva hits my balls, and I bask in it. "So fucking greedy for me."

She swallows as I hit the back of her throat, causing her to choke, but I hold her head in place, not allowing her to detach from me. "Breathe through your nose, baby girl. Be a good girl and take this cock," I croon while massaging the back of her head. "Be a good girl, and I'll feed you." She settles and opens her throat, and I couldn't be more elated. "Fuckkk," I groan as my eyes roll. "So perfect. Let me feed you, my pretty girl."

Her moans of pleasure cause my balls to throb as I guide her up and down my length. "That's it. That's it, pretty girl." I praise with each thrust, gag, and splutter. "Such a good girl for me." I groan. "You earned this cock so well." *Thrust.* "You earned this cum." *Thrust.* Pleasure takes hold of me, and I surge inside her once more. "I'm coming for you, Laya. I'm coming in my baby girl's throat. I'm feeding you. Jesus, I'm feeding you." I hold her head in place as my cock pulsates inside her, bringing with it utter euphoria. "Such." *Thrust.* "A." My hips grind against her face. "Perfect hole for me." *Grunt.* "So fucking perfect." I groan as thick pumps of cum fill her. She gags, and my grip tightens. She's taking it, all of it. "That's it. Fuck, that's it. Choke on me." The last of my cum spills from me with an intense burst full of the power I feel inside, and my girl accepts it all.

Slowly, I slip from her mouth as my chest heaves in sync with my girl's, as if perfectly timed. Then I sit back in the chair, and my focus remains locked on hers. The seductive way a few wayward hairs stick to her cheeks gives away how hard she worked my cock. The flush coating her face like a second skin and the way her eyes are alight with hunger as they roam over my naked form has my body wrung tight, as if I hadn't just shot a load down her throat.

I brush the hair from her face.

"Did I do good?" I swipe the cum from the corner of her mouth, and she opens her lips to accept it.

Did she do fucking good? I scrub a hand over my face and chuckle.

"It was fucking incredible, Laya."

"Good." She stands, then stares down at me. "Now I want all of you. I earned it." She pouts, and I stare back at her as her words run through my mind.

My eyebrows furrow as I struggle to register what she's asking. "All of me?"

Does she not see that she has it all?

"All of you."

I clear my throat and sit forward as I contemplate what she means, and a heaviness pulls at my chest at the realization.

"You gave it to other women. You gave them a part of you I haven't had. I want it."

I shake my head. "You're wrong, Laya. I never gave them all of me." How could she possibly think that?

She rolls her eyes, and I want to spank her for it.

"I see you, Owen. I see you holding back." She points at her chest, and my eyes follow the bounce of her tits, causing my cock to stir at the motion. "Owen, I want every part of you, just like you said. I earned it." Her voice cracks, and I hate it, but I refuse to hurt her. I refuse to have her look at me with disgust like women before when they realized my depravity.

"No."

She scoffs. "No?"

I shake my head.

"You deserve better than that."

She laughs, but it's full of sarcasm. "You're wrong, Owen. I deserve all of you."

Her words hit me like a knife to the chest, but I remain undeterred despite the clawing feeling inside me, begging to get out, begging to be released and share my darkness with her. I'm scared to extinguish the light I hold in the palms of my hands.

I lower my head, ashamed to feel so weak.

But ultimately, I'm nothing without her, and I'm not prepared to risk it. I refuse to give her an excuse to leave me.

THIRTY-TWO

LAYA

Anger boils inside me at his refusal to give in to me. I'd spent years watching him give himself to other women. My body ached to be them. My core clenched as he hammered inside them with such intensity, he took my breath away. My soul broke as I came to terms with that person never being me. Always on the outside looking in.

But now I have him; he's my husband, and he still won't give me what he gave them.

He refuses to give me the same unadulterated passion he gave them, and I hate it. I hate them and the jealousy rushing through me so strongly I spit the words out to make him feel the same hurt he's caused me. "Carlos called me baby girl whenever we were in the bedroom. It got him so hard it drove me wild. He took the one thing from me you never did, and I gave it to him with a smile on my face, knowing you'd never own that part of me. You think I didn't recreate every scene I ever witnessed you do? You think I didn't recreate you?" I ignore the fury emanating from him and deliver him the same pain he caused me over the years. "You think I don't deserve that side of you? You're wrong, Owen. It's the only way I could get off, imagining he was rough like you, and he loved it!"

His head slowly raises, and the violence behind his eyes makes my heart skip a beat.

"What the fuck did you just say?" Each word is cold, calculated, and detached, and my blood freezes over at the way his muscles constrict, then with them, a coiling feeling weaves around my heart as each breath becomes ragged under his strained glare.

I shake off the vulnerable feeling that washes over me and pull my shoulders back, then throw my hair over my shoulder, feigning confidence.

"He fucked my ass so hard, Owen. Then he wrapped his hands around my throat as he whispered baby girl into my ear." I lick my lips. "It was his name I screamed when I came, my husband's."

His control snaps on my final word, and an almighty roar erupts from his chest as he jumps to his feet. He launches the chair across the room, then stalks toward me and grips me by my throat to walk me backward toward the mattress, making my pussy clench at his aggressive dominance.

Then he releases me, and I sag in disappointment.

"Crawl on the bed. I want that ass. Get it up in the fucking air, Laya. I'll show you how dark I fucking go." Before I climb onto the bed, he takes a hold of my hair and yanks me back against his chest. His thick cock is pushed up against me, and I moan when it twitches. "You asked for this, remember that," he grits out.

I want him to destroy me. I want him to take every memory with Carlos that never should have existed and obliterate them.

"Ruin me," I whisper, and his eyes blaze with a promise to do just that.

OWEN

"Ruin me," she whispers, and my body vibrates as my blood bubbles in my veins and an uncontrollable lust mixes with anger, a deadly concoction of dark passion.

I release her, and she crawls onto the center of the bed, and I follow, positioning myself behind her. My hand trails up her spine as I press onto her shoulders, encouraging her face to touch the mattress. "Open your ass cheeks," I growl as I stare down at her with fury.

Is it possible to love someone passionately, yet loathe their actions to the point of hate?

Baby girl was reserved solely for her. She knows this; she knew the love behind the name, and it's been tarnished by the bastard who dared to steal her from me.

She moves her hands to pull her ass cheeks apart, her small asshole now on full display, and my mouth waters at the thought of pushing inside her, making her realize once and for all who owns every inch of her body.

She may have given him her ass first, but I'm taking it back.

I raise my hand and smack her cheek hard once, twice, three times while she cries out. My cock leaks pre-cum onto my abs, so I swipe it up, then drag it over her asshole, causing her to flinch each time I do. Then I lean forward and spit into her hole, and she jolts.

"Owen?"

"Mmm?" I glide the tip of my cock down her ass cheeks and over her puckered hole.

"Are you going to use lube?"

She tries to raise her head, so I place my palm on her back, holding her in place. Then I spit at her ass again, watching with fixation as my saliva drips down the crook of her cheeks and over the tip of my cock.

"No. This is my lube, baby girl." I spit out the latter and she flinches at my spiteful tone.

Then, without warning her, I press the head of my cock into her ass. Her hands move to grip the sheets, but she needs to learn I'm in control here. I move quickly and pull her wrists behind her back, holding them together just above her ass. "This is my ass. Understand me?" I bellow, and push forward a little more, delighting in the way my cock stretches her small hole.

"Oh, shit. It hurts," she whimpers.

"Yeah? Good, I hope it fucking hurts you, Laya. I hope it hurts like you fucking hurt me. You want to be treated like a slut. You got it." I slam inside her, and her small body tightens as a scream tears from her lungs.

"Fuck, that feels good. So fucking tight." My eyes roll and my jaw clenches while my body stills, unable to move, trying to keep from orgasming so soon. Then I draw my cock out and slam back inside, ignoring her whimpers as I do. "You're my little slut, baby girl." I pull back and slam inside harder. "Mine!" I roar.

The mattress squeaks as I dig my knees firmly into it while I pummel her ass, giving her small body no choice but to take me. All of me, just how she wanted.

"You wanted my darkness? You fucking have it, Laya."

I release her hands, and before she can brace herself, I yank her up by her hair so her back is against my chest. Her face contorts in a perfect blend of pleasure and pain, yet all I feel is my need to possess her. I place my hands around her throat, rear back, and spit in her face, then follow it up by licking the saliva from her cheek. "You got all of me, baby." I drop her onto the mattress, and she falls face-first. Then I maneuver myself so I have one foot on the bed to give me the perfect angle to drive deeper inside her.

"Oh god," she cries out, and I feel like a fucking king conquering the world, knowing I'm pushing her limits.

I lean down on one side and wrap my fingers around her throat, loving the way she fits so perfectly beneath my tattooed fingers. "You belong to me. Say it!"

The pulse on her neck skitters, forcing my cock to swell with unbridled need. "Fucking say it!" I grit out as I press harder, loving the way her eyes flutter closed at the pressure behind my force. "That's it, fuck, that's it." Her ass clenches and her body tenses, and with that feeling of power over her, my cock unleashes inside her, flooding her stretched hole as I slowly ease the pressure around her throat. "Fuck, soooo good." I plunge inside again, hoping to drag out my orgasm as my warm cum fires from my cock, filling her to capacity.

"Fuck," I grunt as I fall forward, completely spent.

Sweat coats my body as I crash against her, my cock still lodged inside my wife's ass.

Silence fills the room; the only sound I hear is that of my heart beating rapidly against her.

"I lied." I still above her. "We never did that together. I wanted it rough, Owen," she murmurs as a tear slides down her cheek, and my lungs deflate on her words, all anger diminished, then I'm flooded with guilt.

"That was your first time?" I question, pissed I took her so roughly. That she allowed me to take her like that without saying a damn word.

"Yes," she whispers.

Horror swirls in my stomach. "Jesus, Laya."

"I wanted to feel the real you, Owen. All of you." Her confession makes my heart ache, but I understand it. I was holding back, and, in turn, it was hurting her.

"I'm here now, baby girl." I stroke the hair from her face. "You have all of me," I confirm as I tilt her head to face me.

"You have all of me. You always have."

Her smile turns sleepy as I stroke over her hair.

I place a kiss on the side of her face. "You stepped into my darkness, Laya, and now all I see is you, my light."

Then I spend the rest of the night lavishing my girl with the care she deserves, all while she remains in a post-sex stupor. I tend to her every need, gifting her with the love she yearns for as I cover her body in soothing lotion, brush her hair back into place, and follow each stroke of the brush up with a kiss to her forehead while she smiles back at me with contentment. Our love grows stronger with each reassuring touch, and I feel it deep in my soul.

"All I see is you," I whisper as she drifts off to sleep.

THIRTY-THREE

OWEN

It's been a week since I fucked my wife's ass and she rolled over to tell me she was sorry she lied. I narrowed my eyes, and she bit her lip with the innocent look she's come to perfect, only to tell me that she'd never done anal before but wanted to push me into giving her every part of me. Not gonna lie, I wanted to both spank her ass and ride her raw for letting me lose my shit on her like that for her first time.

She assured me she loved every minute, telling me she never orgasmed as hard as when my fingers wrapped around her neck until she saw stars.

My cock hardens, but I ignore it.

Not when I have a job to do.

Nico Garcia delivered the two men to the basement of my apartment block last night, and today, I will deal with them.

They terrorized my wife and have left her with PTSD.

They will pay for their sins, and I will love every second of extracting it from them.

I turn into the underground car park and switch off the engine, then climb out of the car, slamming the door behind me. I stride toward the elevator and step inside, then stab the button for the basement and descend.

My body vibrates with adrenaline as the doors slide open. Three of my security team turn in my direction as I take in the room.

The two men are hanging from their wrists by chains attached to the roof.

"Do you want us to leave you to it?" Dale asks, and I give him a firm nod. He tilts his head toward the other two men. They all nod in my direction as they enter the lift, and I wait for the doors to close behind them before I make a move.

They're stripped down to their boxers and gagged, their faces a little bruised. I step forward and push the gag down for the man to speak. "You killed Carlos?"

"I did the job," he replies with confidence in his eyes that has no place being there.

I shake my head. "There was a woman and child in the room, you sick fuck."

"No bitch there," he snipes back, and I close my eyes at the derogatory word used toward my wife.

"Liar!" I bellow, then grab his face between the palm of my hand. I squeeze and squeeze until his jaw cracks, and only then do I feel the hit of euphoria. Clenching the tips of my fingers harder, I'm determined to make this piece of shit crumble, to shatter beneath me.

His eyes bulge in horror, and he splutters around me,

his body thrashing while his friend fights against his own bindings, knowing what's going to happen to him as well.

When his jaw gives way, I tear through the flesh with ease, then I rip his lower face from him, throwing it to the floor. I swipe away the remnants of his spittle with my forearm, relieved I had the foresight to wear a black shirt today.

Then, while the fucker bleeds out onto the floor, I move toward the workbench and collect my tool of choice.

A screwdriver.

You can do many things with a screwdriver, including deliver pain. My father, the son of a bitch, taught me at a young age how vital this piece of the toolkit is. I felt the pain of his lesson in my thigh during a visit home from boarding school; that's something my children will never learn, not by me.

For me to become man enough to receive his wealth, my father delivered multiple lessons, not one of them compassion. At the end of each lesson, I would tell him I didn't care about money, and he would laugh in my face.

It's part of the reason I asked my best friends to go into business with me. I never received an inheritance, not deemed strong enough. All I got was a list of contacts when I used my IT skills to target his security firm and steal his data, then I liquidated the firm and used my newfound knowledge to help create the security side of STORM Enterprises.

My mother would be proud. I destroyed everything he loved, everything that mattered to him.

And I created my own family, my destiny, with Laya right there in the center.

My children will inherit my business by passion driven by love, not brutality.

I slam the screwdriver into his eye and quickly step back to let the surge of blood and fluid fly from him. Then I yank it out before delivering the same treatment to the next. I turn to his friend. "Are you watching? What should I do next, hmm?" The prick's face falls like he's about to pass out, and I know I will love every second of keeping him alive just to endure a sliver of the pain my wife had to witness.

Next, I flick open my penknife and slash through the scumbag's boxers. Then I close it and slide the knife back into my pocket. My grip on the screwdriver tightens as I deliver a sharp slam of it to his balls, relishing the squeal of terror behind his gagged friend.

"I'm going to enjoy slaughtering you, motherfucker." I grin sadistically as his bloodied body mingles with images of Carlos's face while trying to shake away the edge of insanity I feel.

My bloodstream becomes potent with a jealous poison reserved solely for Laya. Every touch he gave her that was meant to be mine.

I lift the sledgehammer off the floor and swing it with ease. The thud against his thigh has my blood pumping, and the sound of his femur cracking causes adrenaline to swell inside me.

Each moment they shared that was stolen from me.

The sledgehammer cracks against his kneecap, one after the other, as Carlos's face haunts me.

His screams play out like background noise to my internal hysteria.

The way she smiled toward him, when her smiles were once reserved purely for me.

How he slipped inside my girl, feeling her body raw against his.

Pulling back from the bloody scumbag, I swipe the sweat from my forehead, then draw my arms back, raise the sledgehammer one final time, and deliver a solid crack against his skull.

"Nobody takes what's mine."

LAYA

"I don't care who the fuck they are. They should have been dealt with before now." Owen's firm voice filters through the foyer as I finish washing the dishes from dinner. Romeo is soundly asleep in his bouncer, so I pick up the baby monitor and head toward his office.

The door is open, but I knock anyway.

"Come in, baby."

I step into the office, and like a magnet, his gaze pulls mine to his. Slowly, he licks his lips as his eyes roam over my body, causing heat to infiltrate my bloodstream and wetness to pool in my panties.

He spins his chair to face me, then widens his legs. "Kneel." His deep, gravelly voice sends a tremor of anticipation rushing through me.

Without a second thought, I lower myself to the floor, my eyes never leaving his.

"Lose the T-shirt."

My hands move quickly to comply, pulling his T-shirt

over my head, and I revel in the way his eyes devour me like a starved man craving his next meal.

"The bra. Lose the bra, baby," he chokes out. His tongue darts over his bottom lip, and he adjusts his cock in his pants as he watches me unclip my bra and drop it to the floor. Beads of milk adorn the peaks of my nipples, and I know it will drive him wild with fervor to taste me.

The air fills with a commanding haze of tension as we stare at one another, like an electrical current threatening to combust at any second. When the milk slips down my nipple, hunger flashes in his eyes and he pops open the top button of his pants, then drags his zipper down while I wait with bated breath for his next command.

Then he pulls his thick cock from his boxers, and excitement rushes through my body, spreading like a wildfire as every cell in my body burns under his scrutiny.

"Crawl."

One command makes my pussy pulsate and my clit throb with an unadulterated need to satisfy him. To give him the control his dark desires crave while letting me relish every second of it.

My heart thunders wildly against my rib cage as the room becomes fueled with a heady intoxication that leaves my mouth watering. I finally settle at his feet and peer up at him from beneath my thick lashes.

His whole demeanor is commanding, in control, and deadly. With every breath I take, his powerful stare strips me bare, taking all of my insecurities and doubt and squashing them with nothing more than a look.

He releases his cock, then he taps his desk with his pointer finger. "Up."

I rise to my feet, and before I have a chance to think,

Owen lifts me and places me on his desk. Then he grabs my ankle and places a gentle kiss on it before positioning my foot on the top of the desk and repeating the action with my other foot. The chill of the wood bites into my ass, but the heat of his stare warms me from the inside out, filling me with a burning need to release the arousal building inside me at an expeditious speed.

He sits back in his chair, slowly dragging his pointer finger over his lip, and for the first time since entering the room, I dart my eyes away from his scrutiny. Sitting on the desk so open and exposed makes my cheeks flush.

My eyes latch onto the gun resting on his paperwork, and the enormity of my current position hits me like a Mack truck, causing my body to jolt with a foreboding awareness.

Owen is a dangerous man, and I've been living in ignorant bliss.

"Hey." He turns my chin with his fingers. "I don't like that look." I lick my now dry lips while he scans over my face. "Is it the gun?"

A whimper leaves my throat, and I force myself to nod.

Hurt flashes in his baby-blue eyes, and I want to take back my admittance. "You know I'd never hurt you, right?"

He'd never hurt me. I know more than anything else in the world that this man would never harm me.

Softness coats his handsome face. "It's for protection, baby."

"Are we in danger?"

"Never. I'd never let a damn thing hurt you or my boy." He says the words with so much conviction my body sags in relief. "Now, let me show you."

I pull back from him with narrowed eyes, and when he dips his head and swipes his tongue over my slick folds, I melt into him, gripping his shoulders to steady myself while he feasts on me. Every stroke of his tongue is like ecstasy as I drop my head back and give in to this man, my protector.

OWEN

She melts against the wood of the desk; her whimpers of pleasure are like euphoria on my tongue.

Without her realizing, I slip the gun into my hand and double-check the safety is on, even though the gun isn't loaded. Then I use it to nudge at her entrance, and her body reacts instantly. My eyes roll with the intoxicating feeling of control I have over her.

Slowly, I feed the tip of the gun into her pussy hole, and she accepts it while my mouth works over her clit, sucking her swollen bud and bringing her to the brink of orgasm.

"Look down, baby girl. Look down at me fucking you."

She raises her head, her eyes heavy with lust, and I pull back so she can watch me slip the gun in and out of her pussy.

Watching my weapon slip inside her has my cock leaking desperately, and I wrap my fist around it, pumping it in time. "Touch yourself, Laya. Touch yourself. Get off on my weapon fucking you."

Her mouth falls open, a combination of startled and aroused marring her pretty features as her fingers move frantically over her clit. "Oh god," she pants. "Oh Jesus, Owen."

"Fuck yes," I grunt as the sound of our pleasure fills the room.

My gun slides out of her with ease, and I want nothing more than to fill her while using the only form of protection I will allow to enter her pussy.

I stand abruptly. "You're going to take us both, Laya. You're going to let me fuck you with our protection."

Her eyes widen.

"Be a good girl and do as you're told."

She nods, then rests her elbows on the desk, which allows her to watch as I slide the gun from her pretty, dripping cunt, leaving only the tip inside.

Then I line my cock up at her hole, the metal of the gun resting above me. With one hand on the handle of the gun, I push us both inside her. "Oh fuck, baby girl." She stretches to accommodate us both, and the sight has my balls drawing up as I bite into the side of my mouth to stop myself from coming. "Fuck, that's it."

"Owen, oh god."

I push the barrel of the gun in while her pussy muscles pull tightly around me. My body coils tight, my muscles ache with a need to expel my aggression. "Only me and our protection fuck this pussy, Laya."

"Yes."

"Say it!" I bite out.

"Only you and our protection fuck your pussy."

The ways she says it's my pussy sends me feral, and I withdraw before slamming back inside her, causing her to wince. My hips pick up pace as I thrust inside my girl.

"Slap your pussy," I demand. "Slap that fucking pussy while I fuck you."

Her hand rises, and the slick sound of her slapping herself fills the room while I let go, fucking her with my cock and the cold metal of my gun.

The warmth of her pussy and the way it contracts with each of her calculated hits has my cock eager to release.

"Oh fuck. Oh fuck, Owen. I'm—" She throws her head back, and her pussy convulses around us, and finally, I can fill her with my seed.

I erupt inside my girl, around the metal of my weapon, knowing deep in my soul that I hold all the power to keep her safe, but nothing can protect me from her.

THIRTY-FOUR

LAYA

The weeks pass by in a haze of happiness while spending time with my family and getting to know Ava. She's become the sister I never had but always wanted, and I look forward to the time we spend together at my parents' home.

Something tells me she could be a lot of fun.

The sun hits my face, and I smile at the sense of freedom blowing in the breeze. I cling tighter to Owen, then upon feeling the shift in him, I tilt my head up to face him. His eyes flit over my face, as if searching for a reason to my action, but when he realizes I'm gifting him with a genuine smile, the corners of his eyes crinkle. I step up on my tiptoes and trace over them with the tips of my fingers.

"Jesus," Tate balks from beside me. "You're so lovey fucking dovey." He grimaces and shakes his head, and the disapproving look on his face has me bursting out laughing.

When I first suggested meeting at the park, Ava bounced up and down with excitement so hard I was concerned she would trigger an early labor. Poor Tate didn't have a choice but to comply.

"Ugh, you make me want to vomit." He turns away from us to stare out toward the lake. "Ooof." Ava delivers a swift elbow into his chest. "What the fuck, baby?"

"I warned you not to be an ass."

My brother tugs her toward him and wraps his arm around her while nuzzling into her hair.

"He's sweet-talking her," Owen whispers, and I grin back at him.

"I'm sure he is."

Romeo takes this moment to stir in the baby carrier attached to Owen's chest. There's something incredibly hot about a giant of a man with a small baby attached to him who would destroy anything threatening the ones he loves but is also a gentle father all wrapped up in one mouthwatering package.

"You look like you want to eat me." He grins down at me as we follow behind Tate and Ava.

"Maybe I do."

In a split second, the playful look on his face is erased and replaced with a guarantee of filthy promises. Slowly, he licks his lips like a predator, causing my bloodstream to race with desperation.

Tate and Ava come to a stop, and I glance around to find Reed jogging toward us. Seeing Reed in his running clothes is new for me. It's the most casual I have ever seen him look, and for a moment, I see someone different from the work obsessed, perfected businessman he portrays himself to be.

The moment he realizes we're in front of him, he stumbles, causing Tate and Owen to laugh; he wraps his arm around Romeo to prevent him bouncing, and I sink into his side a little more, loving his natural reaction to protect our son.

Reed comes to a standstill. His eyebrows furrow as he scans us all over, as if searching for something. Then he pulls out his earbuds and tucks them into his pocket and swipes the sweat from his forehead. "Why are you out here?"

Tate scoffs. "Walking, dumbass." He waves his hand toward us. "Clearly."

Reed stares back at him. "Walking?"

"Yes, you know, you move your feet in front of you a bit like you were doing but slower, so when you see someone you know, you don't trip and look like an idiot." He grins back at Reed.

Reed's deadpan face has me smiling inside. He's without a doubt not the joker of the guys. I'd say he doesn't know how to have fun. Outside of the bedroom, of course, I've heard all about his antics over the years.

"Funny, you look"—his gaze roams over us, his lip curling in disgust—"kind of domesticated."

Owen scoffs. "That's kind of the point when you choose to have a family."

The fact he said, "Choose to have a family" has me swooning and, as if hearing my thoughts, he smiles down at me.

"Eww." Reed grimaces, with his hands on his hips. "You have to put up with that shit?" He waves his hand toward Owen and me while looking at Tate, who is now kissing Ava's neck and caressing her baby bump. "Never mind." He shakes his head. "But what the hell is that thing attached to you?"

He tilts his head from side to side, as if genuinely flummoxed.

Owen's shoulders broaden with pride. "It's my little buddy in here." He gently taps where Romeo's butt is situated.

"You have a baby attached to you?" His eyes widen.

Owen nods with a confident smile. "I do."

"Why wouldn't you just push him in a stroller or something?" Reed glances around the park as if searching for a stroller.

Owen's jaw sharpens. "Because, fuckwit, I like him close to me and he likes to feel my heartbeat. It reassures him."

He shakes his head. "Reassures him? Jesus, you're all insane."

Owen stares back at him. "When you have a family, you'll think differently. Trust me."

Reed chuckles. "That's never going to happen." He points toward Tate and Ava, then back at us. "This would be my idea of literal hell."

Tate shakes his head. "Na. Hell is when Ava can't have sex for a few weeks after birth."

"It's more than a few weeks, Tate," Ava reminds him.

"I don't mind a bit of blood." He shrugs.

Owen's arm tightens around me, and need flushes through him. He enjoys taking me while bleeding.

Reed rears back as if stung and his face pales, then he shakes his head. "I'm actually appalled with myself, wasting my time having this conversation." He glances at his watch. "You screwed up my entire morning routine. I hope you're satisfied."

"You're the one that can't run properly," Tate bites back.

Reed ignores his jibe and stares past us. "I'm going to have to forgo my stop at the organic store to make up for lost time."

"Oh, however will you fucking cope?" Tate rolls his eyes.

Reed narrows his eyes on my brother, but doesn't bite at his jibe. "I'll see you in the office tomorrow." He then nods in Owen's and my direction. "It was …" He seems lost for words for a split second. "Nice to see you." I smile because we all know how much it wasn't nice for Reed to bump into us, and that only amuses the men more. Their deep laughter rumbles through the park as Reed sets off on his run again.

"He's going to fall so fucking epically." Tate smirks.

OWEN

"I need to use the restroom," Laya announces, and I blow out a sigh of relief. About fucking time.

"Me too." I jump up from the blanket and brush off the grass. "Can you watch Romeo?"

My eyes flick from Tate to Ava. "Sure." She smiles coyly, as if knowing my intentions.

"Don't be fucking long. I'm starving," Tate grumbles, making me smirk. Yeah, I'm starving too, for a taste of your sister.

I take Laya's hand in mine and stride toward the restrooms. "Owen, is everything okay?"

Without replying, I march us into the women's bathroom and assess the stalls to ensure they're empty. *Thank fuck.* I flick the lock and spin to face her. The way her hair hangs in a ponytail has driven me crazy all day. The way her heavy tits have bounced as she took each step has had my cock as hard as stone, rubbing against the zipper with each step, and the way her ass was hidden beneath the white sundress she wears as if taunting me to expose it had me eager to drag her into the trees and fuck her ruthlessly like a rabid animal.

Instead, I was struggling inside to play it cool and bide my time for the perfect opportunity. "Turn and face the mirrors." Heat creeps up her cheeks and over her chest as awareness hits her.

She slowly turns and face the mirrors. Her small hands clutch the edge of the sink as I step up behind her. She looks so tiny compared to me, and I revel in it. Then my big hands find her heavy tits and I squeeze the weight of them in my palms while pushing my hard cock into her back. "Can you feel what you do to me, baby girl?"

She takes a moment to speak, and I delight in the effect I have on her. "Yes."

"Do you want my fingers in your pussy or my cock?"

She tilts her head back and lets out a heavy pant as I work one hand down her stomach and under her dress.

"Both," she moans as my fingers find the wet lace of her panties.

"You're a greedy little slut, aren't you?" I circle her clit over the fabric, earning a moan to slip from her delectable lips.

"Yes. Please, Owen." She pushes back into me, and that's all the confirmation I need.

"My wife needs fucked in a restroom like a needy whore, doesn't she?"

She nods, and I step back, going down to my knees behind her. I slip her dress up and hook my fingers into her panties. "I'm going to fill this pussy with my cum and then you're going to walk outside with me dripping out of you like a good little slut for me."

I bring her panties to my nose and sniff hungrily at her

musky scent, then my cock jumps in appreciation and drips with fervor.

"Please," she moans, and I use one palm to push down on the center of her back, giving me the perfect angle to see her dripping hole.

"Mmm, fuck, baby girl." I bury my face in her cunt, swiping my tongue over the delicious juice slipping from her. "Fuck, you taste good." I lap at her, and my eyes roll. "You taste different, baby girl." Hell, the taste of her will be forever embedded in my mind as if even my tastebuds are scarred from her pleasure.

"Diff ... different?"

"Mm." I swipe my tongue over her again, and she thrusts back, then I slide a finger into her tight little hole and pump. "Yes, different, baby girl. I wonder if I put a baby in here." I add another finger, brimming with excitement at the thought of her pregnant with my child. Curling my fingers, I pump them in and out of her slick channel.

"Oh god," she gushes.

"That's it, ride my face, my beautiful little slut."

Her cunt tightens around my fingers, and my cock leaks with need. A deluge of wetness hits me, flooding my face. "Oh, oh shit." My tongue works overtime as I attempt to drink her cum.

Before she comes down from her orgasm, I jump to my feet, pull down my zipper, and jerk out my dripping cock. I line myself up, push down on her back, and slam inside her. "Fuck yes." Her pussy is still contracting, tight and warm and perfect for my steel length as I drive myself balls deep into my wife.

With one hand on her hip, I wrap her hair around the

fist of my other, using it as a rein as I widen my stance and deliver her with a rapid surge of my thickness. "That's it. Take every fucking inch."

"Ahh," she moans, her mouth falls open against the sink counter as I fuck her ruthlessly.

My balls slap against her, my cock pummeling her cunt as I blast in and out of her like the hungry bastard I am, chasing my orgasm with vengeance.

Slowly, I slide the hand on her hip over her ass cheeks, then I stare down at my thumb and push it into her small, puckered hole. She tightens around me. "Owwwwen!"

Moving my hips quicker, I surge my thumb in and out in time with my cock; the euphoria hits me, but my pace doesn't stutter, not until the adrenaline rushing through my veins forces my slit to open, creating an intense orgasmic high I crave from my woman.

Only my woman.

My cum surges deep inside her, and I continue to pump my hips, determined to coat her womb with my seed. "That's a good girl. Such a good girl letting me use you."

As my orgasm recedes, I watch transfixed as I pull out of her ass and cunt. Divine pleasure escapes her, and I use my palms to spread it over her pussy like lotion.

"Owen, I think I peed a little."

I yank her up so she's flush against my chest. "You didn't pee, baby. You squirted on me." Her eyes widen, and the red on her cheeks deepens.

"I did?"

"Yeah, you did. Now lick it from my face." I tug on her ponytail in warning, and what do you know, my perfect little wife trails her tongue out over my jawline, and I groan in ecstasy at her compliance. "Fuck, you're such a good wife, Laya."

A smile lights up her face. "Thank you. I taste good on you."

My lip quirks. "You do, baby girl. So fucking good."

Realizing our absence won't go unnoticed, I reluctantly step back. "Come on, we best go. But later, I want to taste my cum from your mouth."

I grin at the way her pupils are now blown and the eager way she swallows, and I can't think of anything more satisfying than having my wife clean me up after I cleaned her up.

LAYA

"Can I have a phone?"

I lift my head from my meal to face Owen, but cutlery clattering to the table forces me to turn toward Tate.

"You don't have a phone?" His eyes narrow on Owen.

Owen tenses, and I squeeze his thigh beneath the table.

Then I clear my throat and shake my head toward Tate. "No, Carlos only allowed me one with him as a contact. He said it wasn't safe."

Owen growls, and the threat of violence vibrates off him.

Tate scoffs. "Damn fucking right it wasn't safe. Fucking prick."

Ava elbows him in the chest, and I bite into my lip to stifle a smile. This eases Owen's tension, and when he entwines my fingers with his, my heart soars. "You can have anything you want, baby. I'll make sure all your old contacts are in there too."

"You can have anything you want, baby," Tate mimics childishly while screwing his face up.

When Ava proposed a meal for the four of us, I jumped at the chance of bringing the guys closer together again.

"Don't be a dick, Tate," Ava snaps, taking the words right out of my mouth.

Owen curls his freehand around the back of my neck and tugs me toward him, then his breath touches my ear. "I'm so fucking hungry for your pussy right now. Are you still wet, baby girl? Or do you need filled again?" My cheeks flame with heat.

"Jesus fucking Christ, now he's whispering sweet things to her, right in front of my face."

Ava rolls her eyes, then I watch with a pang of longing as she rubs her stomach.

"Ain't nothing sweet about what I just whispered," Owen says, and I wince at his words. Then he takes a drink of his beer with a smug grin on his face that even I want to wipe off him.

Ava lets out a loud huff, then shakes her head before leaning over the table, done with their pettiness. "Did you manage to leave Mexico with anything, Laya?" The concern in her voice has me fidgeting.

"No."

She nods in understanding.

"I wish I had photos of Romeo when he was first born." My eyes drift down toward my son sleeping in his buggy. "Carlos shoved a bag at me. I actually need to sort through it, the documentation, passport, that sort of thing." I wave my hand around nonchalantly, trying to ward off the imposing fear I have at the thought of opening that bag up.

I don't want to see anything from it. It's why I shoved it up onto the top shelf of the closet, as far away from me as possible. Maybe it's something I could ask Owen to help me deal with instead of avoiding.

Tate relaxes into his chair, and I'm once again grateful for Ava's interruption. My brother rests his hand on Ava's protruding tummy, and I can't help the feeling of envy that washes over me.

Romeo fidgets, and I move to unclip him. "You want me to go change him?" Owen leans forward and grabs his diaper bag.

"No. I'm good. Just hand me the wipes and diaper, please."

Owen digs around in his bag, and his eyes swim in confusion as he pulls his hand back out of the bag.

Time stands still as he uncurls his fingers to reveal a memory card, and my breath stutters as a memory of the night Carlos gave it to me assaults me.

"Give this to Owen." He pushes it into my hands. *"It's important, mi amor. Only Owen."*

I snap my eyes open, not even realizing I'd closed them. "Carlos asked me to give it to you." His lips part to speak, but I shake my head, determined to get my words out. "I forgot all about it." Annoyance with myself ripples through me. "How the hell could I forget about it?"

"You had other things to think about. Like rushing into a marriage," Tate spits out, pointing his fork toward my wedding ring.

"Do you know what's on this?" Owen scans my face.

The intensity behind his stare makes it difficult to swallow, and I blow out a shaky breath before answering. "No." My eyes implore his. "I've no idea."

His shoulders relax, and he pulls me toward him,

placing a soft kiss on my head as I bury my face against his chest. "Okay, baby girl."

For the first time in my life, Owen's touch has anxiety creeping up my spine, consuming me and banding around my heart like a viper. "What do you think is on there?" I whisper.

"Nothing good, if it's to do with that prick," Tate snipes out, and Owen glares fire in his direction.

Then his attention is pulled back to me, and he strokes comforting circles over my back. "I don't know. But I don't want you to worry about it. I'll deal with it; do you understand me? I'll protect you." He lifts my chin so our gazes clash. "You can trust me to protect you both, Laya."

I nod, believing every word.

"Let's get Romeo changed and go home. I want to know what I'm dealing with."

A ball of dread lines my stomach, knowing deep in my heart nothing good will come off that memory card. Not a single thing, and I can't help but feel this is all so much bigger than what Owen can deal with, no matter how much he proclaims to protect us.

This is bigger than him, and he might not be able to protect us as much as he'd love to, and I refuse to let him get hurt trying.

He deserves more than that. We all do.

THIRTY-FIVE

OWEN

As soon as we arrived home, Laya fed Romeo, then I bathed my little buddy, allowing her the time to shower. My skin was itching to lock myself away in my office, but my girl needed me. No sooner than she wrapped her soft lips around my cock and began suckling, did her eyes close and her breathing even out.

Slowly, I slipped from her mouth and covered her with the bedsheet, ignoring my semihard cock as I zipped up the fly of my jeans and grabbed one of the baby monitors to take into my office.

I called Tate, and he and Mase were at my house within twenty minutes.

Blowing out a deep breath, I survey my friends. "I'm not sure what we're going to see on here." I point toward the computer screen while keeping my attention on Tate, knowing this could affect him deeply, especially after discovering his wife was kept a prisoner in a cage that provided entertainment to some sick, twisted fucks. My best friend had to witness her misery, and I want to know if he's strong enough to endure it again.

He clamps his jaw shut, his teeth grind, and his nostrils flare, then he gives me a firm nod toward the computer.

I press play, and watch as crackling appears on the screen, then it slowly clears, and I take in the scene. Carlos is in a warehouse, and the sight of him has my hands tightening into fists, wishing I could band them around his throat and rip him apart. This man married my girl and gave me the greatest gift in my son, but he's a wolf in sheep's clothing. He's dealing with shady characters that could have used Laya and Romeo as leverage, and not for the first time, I wish he was alive, just to personally extinguish him how he deserved.

A truck appears, followed by a black car, and out steps a man I know to be the don of a Mafia family on the West Coast. Benito Carrera, a man known to be a monster and a human trafficker for his own sick amusement. My stomach clenches at the thought and anger burns through me like poison.

My eyes scan the screen as I wait to see if his heir, Azrael, emerges from the car like his usual shadow, but he doesn't, and while that seems odd, I've no time to consider it because another man appears from the office behind Carlos.

I zoom into the image.

"Who is that?" Mase leans over me.

"Looks like Harrison Davis, the police commissioner." I lick my dry lips, knowing why the memory card holds such value. Carlos entrusted me with this for multiple reasons, and I can imagine one of those reasons is to keep this as leverage to protect Laya and Romeo.

The truck door opens, and Carlos steps forward. Bile clogs in my throat at the way he pulls a woman out of the vehicle by her hair, and I close my eyes, knowing how he's handled Laya.

Did he give her the same cruel treatment?

"Fucker," Tate spits out, and I open my eyes to witness Carlos drag the girl across the floor. Then he delivers a swift kick to her stomach, causing her to cry out in agony.

"What the hell are we going to do with this?" Mase waves frantically toward the screen.

Tate turns to face him. "We need to keep a copy, whatever we do."

"No." I shake my head.

"No?" Tate's eyes flit over my face.

"No. It has software embedded in it that will show that we have a copy."

"The police commissioner, Owen. That's the fucking police commissioner." Mase's voice becomes higher as he paces. "This is bigger than us. So much fucking bigger. We're meant to deal with advertising and shit, not traffickers."

I roll my eyes as he unravels.

"I know people that can help," I try to reassure him.

Tate scoffs, and I turn my attention back to him. "You know people. Just what the fuck kind of security does our company provide, Owen?" He crosses his arms over his chest as he glares at me. "We never signed up for this shit when we invested."

Anger boils my veins. "So, let me get this straight. You're okay with me handling the security aspect of the business when it suits. When your girl needs rescuing"—I point toward Tate with fury—"I can use my contacts then, and not to mention, when your sister needs help. But now you've decided this is all too much and you're questioning me?"

Tate lowers his head and shakes it, his shoulders deflate. "You're right." Then he tips his head up toward the ceiling. "Fuck. You're right." He scrubs a hand down his face. "It makes me wish I could have killed him myself, ya know?" He nods toward the screen, and the emotion in his tone has my anger diminishing, and I agree.

"I know. Trust me, I know." Then I scrub a hand over my head. "When I ordered him to die, I should have made it more brutal." Regret floods me, knowing how I could have done things differently and could have slaughtered the piece of shit who hurt Laya with the most brutal form of torture, yet I let him die so easily. It was Nico Garcia who assured me he deserved a quick death, that he treated Laya and Romeo well. The man practically pleaded with me to grant it.

Death was a privilege for a monster.

LAYA

A chill washes over me, and I tug the bed sheet tighter around me as I roll my lip between my teeth, missing the feel of his soft skin. Rolling over, I move to snuggle against him, but the bed is cold, and the feel of his loss makes me sit up in awareness and search the room for a sign that he slept here. Not once since being home has he ever not fallen asleep next to me, and I hate whatever pulled him away.

Maybe he's with Romeo?

I turn to face the baby monitor and flick the switch up to hear the soft snooze of our son, and a smile creeps over my face as warmth fills my body at how blessed I am to have such a good little sleeper. My hand finds my stomach as longing fills me. To have a pregnancy with the support of my husband and being surrounded by my family and friends feels like a dream, one that could actually happen.

Reaching over again, I flick the switch on the monitor, but like an idiot with sleepy eyes, I misjudge it, sending it crashing to the floor. "Shit."

With a heavy breath, I swipe the sleep from my eyes and roll out of bed. Bending down, I shove the batteries back into the monitor and static fills the monitor. "You're an idiot, Laya." I give it a sharp tap, and when voices come over the monitor, I listen in.

Tate's voice fills the room. "You're right." He sighs. "Fuck. You're right." There's a pause, and I narrow my eyes while my mind whirls at what they could be discussing. "It makes me wish I could have killed him myself, ya know?" His words make my blood run cold, and my body freezes.

"I know. Trust me, I know." Owen's voice is thick with aggression. "When I ordered him to die, I should have made it more brutal."

And like that, my world crumbles into a million pieces.

My heart shatters on the spot as I kneel.

He ordered him to die.

Please, no.

My lungs feel like they're collapsing as my airways tighten to the point of pain.

Please. He couldn't have.

I gasp for air, dazed by the tears landing on my knees.

It feels like I'm becoming detached from myself, like I'm unable to function.

He wouldn't do this to me.

To Romeo.

Then his words come back to haunt me. *"Anything to keep you."* I rush toward the bathroom in time for my stomach to expel the contents of our dinner.

He did this.

My husband killed a man to take what he wanted, and he's not even sorry about it.

Tears stream down my face as my love for him shatters to the floor with every promise, every loving touch, and every dream of a future.

A pain in my chest unleashes so powerful I fall onto all fours as I choke on the onslaught of my realization.

While I thought I knew Owen and every part of him, realizing I never knew him at all is devastating beyond anything I've ever felt before.

The man I love killed my baby's father to take what he wanted.

To take us.

THIRTY-SIX

LAYA

My feet move of their own accord, and with the baby monitor in one hand, I head downstairs toward the hushed voices of my husband, brother, and their best friend.

The coldness of the wood against my bare feet is nothing compared to the shudder racking through my body. As if I'm having an out-of-body experience, I float down each step, struggling to find the strength to hold on to the here and now.

The brutal betrayal by the one man I ever truly loved left my heart in ribbons, shredding it so it barely functioned enough for it to beat.

A loud chuckle jolts me.

They're laughing. They're laughing when my heart is breaking so mercilessly. I push open the door to Owen's office and step inside, then they cease laughter as the air thickens and my eyes lock onto my husband. His gaze flits down toward the baby monitor, then his face pales. My knees buckle, but I grip the doorframe for support, dropping the monitor, and it shatters against the wooden floor.

"Laya, I ..."

"You killed him." My words are broken, like me, like my heart, and when he moves to stand, I hold my hand out to stop him.

"I don't want you anywhere near me. Anywhere near my son." I ignore the way his face falls, unwilling to accept the hurt etched in his beauty, because all I see is his betrayal.

"Laya, you need to listen." Tate steps forward and my anger heightens.

"You knew. You knew he did this." I point my finger toward my brother, and when a thought occurs to me, I suck in a sharp gasp. "Oh, my God. Did you arrange it too? Were you a part of it?" My gaze ping-pongs over his face, searching for a sign of deceit.

"No. Fuck no, Laya. I just wanted you safe."

"So did fucking I!" Owen roars, getting to his feet, and I stumble back, grateful when he remains where he is.

"Everyone needs to calm down." Mase steps between Tate and me. "Maybe you both should give Laya a bit of space."

"No," Owen snaps out. "There's no way I'm leaving." The finality in his voice has my stomach somersaulting.

"Then I'll go. I'm taking Romeo."

"Laya. Please, you need to listen to me, baby."

I grind my teeth. *How dare he?* "You're wrong. I don't need to do a damn thing. If you won't leave, then I will."

"Laya, please," he implores again, his voice cracking.

My heart hammers, and I don't know how it's still

functioning. "I hate you. You know that? I hate you so fucking much, you bastard!" I rush toward him with clenched fists and hit him over and over and over. Tears fall down my cheeks as each moment we've spent together becomes obliterated with each hit.

He remains unmoving, and it only angers me more. He lets me mistreat him, and I hate him for that. Everything about him I hate in this moment.

How could he do this to me? How could he do this to us?

"We were supposed to be together. I was supposed to be your everything!" I scream against his chest, but he doesn't so much as flinch.

"You are my everything, Laya. That's why I did it," he whispers, and I fall to the floor, never feeling so low and broken as I do right now.

Never feeling so destroyed.

OWEN

The haunted look of complete devastation etched on her beautiful face will be engrained in my mind for the rest of my life. When she falls to the floor, I move to scoop her into my arms, but she flinches, and that reaction alone hurts like a knife slicing through my chest.

Mase shakes his head, and I want to argue. I want to tell my best friend to leave us the fuck alone, but in this moment, as panic consumes me, I can barely think straight.

Silence fills the room as cries echo around us. Each sniffle taking a piece of my heart, ripping it bare and leaving it exposed, and each tear crushing it hopelessly.

The clock in the corner of the room taunts me, each tick taking a second of my life, yet I remain frozen, staring at my girl I broke so epically.

After what feels like a lifetime, she clears her throat, then stands, and when she slips her wedding ring from her finger, I feel like the devil himself is torturing my body and tearing every organ from within me.

"La ... Lay." I can barely speak her name. "Laya. Please, baby." Wetness floods my cheeks. "Laya, look at me."

She turns her head like I no longer exist and places the ring on the corner of my desk. "You're not the man I thought you were, Owen. You're not my son's father." Her words cut me deep, so deep I rear back on my heels and cling to the desk for support. He's my boy. He's my fucking boy. No man could love him like I do. They're both mine.

"You promised me love and support. You promised me trust!" she bellows, and I wince at the heartbreak behind her voice.

"We're done." She draws her eyes up to meet mine, and the finality in them almost brings me to my knees.

I swipe at the snot and tears dripping from the end of my nose. "We can't be done, Laya. We only just fucking started!"

She shakes her head, and a humorless laugh leaves her. "We never should have started."

I grab her hands and pull her against me. "Don't fucking say that. Don't you dare fucking say that," I grind out as a storm of anger takes over me.

I've waited for years; my heart has been torn to shreds, and after she finally pieced me back together again, she's now tearing me apart.

She yanks her hands away, and I hate the feeling of her loss, of losing her. My ribs ache as my chest constricts.

"Laya, there's shit you don't know." Tate tries to reason with her, and the thought of her suffering more hurt has my pulse skyrocketing.

"Don't you fucking dare," I sneer in his direction.

She jolts at the poison in my tone, then turns to face her brother. "Tell me."

"No," I snap.

She doesn't so much as face me. "Tell me right now, Tate."

He scrubs a hand over his jaw. "Fuck!"

"Tate, if you don't tell me right now, I swear to God, we're done. You're my brother." Her voice hitches with emotion. "I need someone to be honest with me, please."

I want to step forward and swipe away the tears trailing down her cheeks; I want to pull her toward me and hold her in my arms, but I know she wouldn't allow it.

"He was trafficking women. Owen found out he was trafficking women, Laya. Selling them."

Her face becomes even paler, and her body shudders as I drop my head in defeat.

"I wanted to protect you," I whisper.

She turns to face me, and I almost wish she hadn't. The hatred in her eyes is palpable through the room, and it stops my heart from beating momentarily.

My throat is dry with the way she stares at me with malice. "I know you're hurt, Laya, but you have to know I never wanted to hurt you. I love you, baby."

Her lip curls. "Hurt is having the man who took my virginity walk out the door and down the stairs to announce his engagement on my birthday."

The tension in the room thickens.

"What did you just say?" Tate's head snaps up, and he steps forward, but she ignores his outburst.

"Hurt is watching your husband slaughtered in front of you while you beg for mercy. Hurt is knowing you'd rather hurt me than come clean to my brother. Hurt is learning my mom helped push away the man I love. Learning that the man I love, my husband, my baby's protector, caused all of that. It is more than hurt, Owen. It's destruction." She rests her hand on her heart. "You hurt me far more than Carlos ever could, because you owned my heart, and you knew it. You destroyed me, you've destroyed us, and I never want to see you again." Her eyes blaze with fire. "You're the one who's dead to me."

She turns to walk toward the door. "Laya, I can't do this without you." I rush past her to block her exit. "You're it for me, baby. You're my everything," I whisper through blurred vision as my arms block the only way out of the room.

"Let her go, man," Mase whispers beside me, but I shake my head in denial.

"I can't." Why can't he see? Why can't they all see? All I ever wanted was her. "She's my everything."

He takes my face in the palms of his hands, and our eyes lock. "You're going to step away from the door and let her leave the room." I move my lips to argue, but he speaks firmer than before. "You're going to do that because it's the right thing to do for her right now. Then you're going to leave with me and let her have a bit of space."

"I don't want to sleep without her in my arms," I mutter, needing him to know the fear I have at not being able to hold her at night when I've waited so long for that. Not being able to bring her the comfort she brings me.

His eyes flash with sympathy. "Just tonight, brother," he says, but swallows hard, and I know without a shadow of a doubt that he's lying and only telling me what I want to hear.

My legs give way with defeat, and I drop to the floor with a heavy thud. Holding the back of my neck with both hands, I pull my head between my legs as uncontrollable sobs strike me, knowing I could have had it all, and now I have nothing. My fingers tangle with the bracelet on my wrist, a stark reminder of her.

"Please," I cry, hoping she gifts me with mercy.

I'm nothing without them.

THIRTY-SEVEN

LAYA

"You need to get out. Get some fresh air." I cast my gaze over to Ava, then my eyes track down to her swollen stomach. Her future.

Jealousy grips me, and my hands tighten on my mug as I reply in the same monotone voice I've had for the past few days since Owen's sobs filled the house before Tate and Mase finally encouraged him to give me space.

"Not today."

She strokes over her bump, and I turn away.

"Laya, come on. I'm sure Romeo would love to go for a walk. Right, buddy." My son gurgles back in her direction and, as always, I react with a smile. His hair is spiky, adorably cute as he blows out a bubble toward Ava. "See. Romeo wants to go to the park, don't you, little man?" She pulls on his socks, and he blows a stream of bubbles back at her, making her laugh.

"Not the park," I clip back, knowing the memories it holds there for us.

My phone beeps beside me, and I glance at it, knowing it's more than likely Owen, and I contemplate turning it off completely, but when I see Brynn's name flash on the screen, I unlock the phone.

Brynn: I'm in your town this weekend. Wanna catch up?

I grimace, knowing what a shitty friend I've been.

"Is that him?" Ava wafts her hand toward the phone.

"No." I clear my throat. "It's actually my friend Brynn. We went to college together and I haven't seen her since the night I met Carlos."

Ava's eyes widen. "Oh, shit."

I nod, knowing how much has happened since I last saw her. "She wants to meet up."

"You should go," she encourages with a smile.

"I'm not leaving Romeo."

She shrugs. "Then take him with you."

"I will if you come with me." I raise an eyebrow with a smile tugging at my lips, the thought of leaving the house now exciting me a little.

My gaze goes over her shoulder to the guard standing on the patio. Ever since she was kidnapped, Tate insists on him tailing her. "Ignore him. He can blend in." She waves her hand nonchalantly, and I scoff a laugh.

"What do you say, Romeo? Drinks and cake?" Then she walks toward my son and lifts his hand against hers, giving one another a high-five, and just like that, the poor mood I was in dissipates.

"Wow. I can't believe you have a baby." Brynn flicks her hair over her shoulder. "He's ..." She winces. "Sweet, I guess."

"He's gorgeous," Ava snaps.

We've spent the last hour listening to Brynn tell us how amazing her new business venture is going to be, thanks to a windfall she's received by her own handsome stranger. I don't like to judge my friend, but that's probably code for she's fucking a rich guy for cash.

I love my friend, really, I do, but sitting here today, I realize how far we've grown apart, or were we never really close to begin with?

"So, you're expecting too." She points toward Ava's stomach. "Jeez, I swear I would die if someone told me I was pregnant. I can't imagine having to push something so big out of my vajayjay."

Ava chokes on her mocktail, then grimaces, something she's been doing on and off all day. She's six months pregnant, so it's way too early for the baby, but when she touches her stomach, I know she's concerned.

"Everything okay?"

"Probably gas." She frowns.

"Well, I plan on taking my bestie and her boy shopping." Brynn takes my hands in hers, and her eyes light up in excitement.

"Maybe another time. I want to get Ava home."

Brynn's face falls.

"Oh, no you don't. You've been cooped up for too long. I'm going to get a lift home, and you're going to enjoy your day." Her eyes implore mine, and I know she's referring to the security that will take her home.

I bite into my lip. "Are you sure?"

"Yes. I'm sure." Then she pushes back in her chair and takes a hold of her purse. "I'll be waiting for you at your place, okay?"

Getting to my feet, I round the table and give her a hug. "Thank you."

Brynn pushes out of her chair and claps her hands. "Oh goody, now we can really shop. Seriously, Laya, your style has gone down the drain. The Laya I know would not be seen dead in mom clothes." I roll my eyes and want to tell her I am a mom, a proud one at that, but instead I glance toward Ava, who fights back a laugh before she walks toward the door with a smirk and a backward wave.

I turn and face Brynn while she continues to eye me up and down with a sneer on her lips.

"We've got some serious work to do, and you've no idea how long I've waited to do it."

Her words seem a little cryptic, but I ignore them and plaster on the fake smile I learned to perfect around Carlos, only now realizing I haven't worn it in months because the only smile I've had has been a genuine one.

Until he destroyed everything.

THIRTY-EIGHT

OWEN

I drum my fingers on the counter again and glance around the kitchen. My lungs feel like they're crushing under the enormity of me being here. Everywhere I turn, I see her and my boy too. The way his elephant blanket is perfectly folded on his bouncer, and the toy octopus with the lights he loves so much is taking a time-out on the kitchen table, probably needing another batch of batteries added to. All the memories have my soul crushing. I need them and refuse to leave her today. No matter what I told Tate for him to agree I come over with him.

Tate told me to give her time. Not three fucking days. Each time I picked up my keys to come over here, he stood in front of me and told me I would lose them all if I barged my way into our home. He said Laya wasn't ready. No matter how much talking she has done with Ava and her mom.

Today, I've had enough. As grateful as I am for her getting out and enjoying herself, I couldn't fight the overwhelming sense she was forgetting about me, that she would have such a good time that she would realize she never needed me.

The only reason my heart is still beating is because of the way Tate has reassured me that everything will be okay. He believes his sister loves me with passion, and he can see I love her equally. He's wrong. I refuse to accept that Laya could love me the same, but I wasn't going to argue with him, not when he's finally on my side.

"Ava said she's on her way back here," Tate states, as if reassuring me. I nod, then glance at my watch.

When the door finally opens, breath whooshes from me in relief. My palms feel sweaty, and I drag them down my jeans as nervousness swims in my stomach before bubbling up my throat, making it difficult for me to swallow.

Ava walks into the kitchen with her security detail, and my eyes search behind her.

"Oh. Hi, Owen. I didn't know you were going to be here." She looks toward Tate, who grimaces.

I ignore her pleasantries. "Where's Laya?"

She rests her hand on her stomach. "I was having Braxton-Hicks contractions. She's gone shopping with Brynn."

"Brynn?"

She nods. "Her friend from college."

"I know who Brynn is," I snap back. Brynn is the little shit who was forever leading my girl astray. When Laya first left for college, I spent a lot of time watching her from a distance, until Mase warned me off the idea. He told me he was worried about me and if it continued, he'd have no choice but to tell Tate. I know he had my best interests at heart, but I hated him for that at the time. Brynn is also the girl who was out with her the night she met Carlos. Nope, I don't like Brynn.

"She stayed with Brynn to go shopping."

"Without security?" Tate airs my thoughts as I bring her tracker up on my phone, suddenly grateful that she has it, no matter how much I loathed her not responding to my messages.

Anxiety hits me like a Mack truck at the thought of her and Romeo out without protection, and my blood thickens, making it difficult for me to breathe.

"Is she in danger?" Ava's panicked voice becomes background noise as I scroll through my app searching for her latest location, which appears to be fucking difficult for some reason.

I grind my jaw while Tate and Ava's bickering plays out like background noise as I try and fail to regain control of the way my pulse races, causing my head to swim in anxiety.

"We're fucking billionaires, Ava. She's always in danger," Tate snaps while my blood bubbles at her stupidity. Mine too. They should both have their own security details, and I hate myself for not organizing it sooner.

"Oh, my God. I'm sorr—"

My phone rings, and Laya's name flashes up on my screen, taking away the stress at not locating her instantly.

"Baby." Relief washes over me at the fact she finally called me, and my heart rate begins to settle.

A dark, maniacal laugh echoes through the phone, sending my blood cold with fear I've never felt before.

Somehow, I speak, my voice deadly. "Who the hell is this?"

Tate's and Ava's voices stop as their attention is drawn toward me.

"My name is Azrael Carrera." A silent choke lodges in my throat. Please, God, no. "Now I suggest you listen very carefully, Owen." I nod like an idiot as fear grips me. My chest rises, and I drag my hand over my head over and over as I wait for him to speak, while inside, I'm unraveling at an epic speed. They're in danger, not just danger, it's worse than that. So much fucking worse.

"Put it on speaker," Tate spits out, nodding toward my phone, but I glance in Ava's direction, and knowing what she's already been through at the hands of monsters, I'm unwilling to let her witness this one's request. I shake my head, and Tate's face pales, then he nods as if understanding.

"You have something I want, Owen." My mind goes to the memory card locked inside my safe. "You're to come to this phone's location. Alone. No weapons. If I find out you so much as alerted your little friends, I will personally skin your woman alive, then sell her baby to the highest bidder." Romeo chooses that moment to cry out, and the weight of Azrael's words force me to my knees as a strangled scream lodges painfully in my chest.

"You have one hour."

I close my eyes while Tate shouts in my direction and Ava cries hysterically, yet the shrill cry of my son rings out in my ears, pleading for me and his mommy.

If they so much as hurt one hair on my family's head, I will rain down a new level of hell on each and every one of them.

Azrael Carrera may think he's untouchable, but when a man has everything to lose, he would destroy the world with a smile on his face to protect the ones he loves.

He may just start a war, but I will be the one to end it.

THIRTY-NINE

LAYA

My vision blurs again as my mind tries to make sense of what is happening. I was shopping with Brynn; we went into the baby store, and I took Romeo to change his diaper, then I felt a sharp pinch at the back of my neck. Oh my God... Romeo.

I snap my eyes open, only for complete terror to rip through me.

My mouth is gagged, and I glance down to see I'm tied to a chair by my ankles and my wrists are bound behind my back. I shuffle, hoping to loosen the ties, to no avail. I'm in some warehouse. It's dark, but the daylight from the windows offers enough light for me to see the silhouette of men lined against the large doors. Each holds a machine gun, adding to my panic.

Then I turn my head to the side, hoping to locate my son, but my heart stops when a man drags Brynn across the floor by her hair. She's lifeless, and he's treating her like he's taking the trash out. A wail erupts inside me, battling to escape against the limits of my restraints.

"I wouldn't cry over her if I were you," a dark voice drones out lazily, and my eyes locate the man in the shadows.

He sits with his legs spread out, watching me, scrutinizing me, and I feel his gaze deep inside my soul, chilling me to my bones. It's calculated, cruel, and unjust. Every part of me screams that this man is the devil himself, and I know deep in my heart that Carlos has something to do with him. For the first time since his cruel death, I wished him dead all over again.

"She wanted more money to bring the baby with her." He tilts his head toward Brynn, and I mewl at the betrayal. Surely, she wouldn't, not my friend. Sickness rolls inside me. What the hell did she do?

"She learned you're not the penniless friend you claimed to be. Jealousy can make you do just about anything. Even sell your friend and her baby out," he asserts, and I hate myself for not telling her my truth sooner, but I hate the person she must truly be more.

My eyes flick around the room in utter devastation as tears surge from my eyes while I search desperately for Romeo, silently begging him to cry for me so I know he's okay.

"She negotiated well, and I told her what she wanted to hear." He flicks his finger toward the man holding Brynn, and he drops her to the floor with a thud. Her head lolls toward me, and I wretch against my gag as blood pools around her.

Oh shit, they slit her throat.
They. Slit. Her. Throat.
Someone please help me.

OWEN

Tate gave me an ultimatum. If he didn't hear from me within an hour of my arrival, he would call for reinforcements.

Knowing the reach of the Carrera family left me no choice but to meet his demands. There's no way I'm putting my wife and son in danger to save my ass. Azrael needs the memory card from me, and I can only imagine it's for leverage. The fact he wants no one else involved confirms it. He wants a swift exchange, and I'm willing to give it to him. I'd give him anything, and he knows it.

I press harder on the accelerator as I make my way toward the abandoned warehouse complex just outside of the city center, and I can only assume he chose this location for the fact it's home to numerous buildings, all deserted. All more than likely hiding his men.

When my SUV approaches the metal gates, trepidation sweeps through me. There's a good chance I won't come back from this, but I refuse to go down without a fight. This is essentially suicide, yet I don't have it in me to care.

All I can think about is my girl being scared and needing me to comfort her, and hoping with all hope that she has Romeo in her arms.

My phone beeps, alerting me to the fact I'm within proximity to Laya's phone, so I pull up outside one of the buildings, not missing the snipers on the roof who aren't even trying to hide. I brush a hand over my jaw as I contemplate tucking a gun into my boot, but the thought of them discovering it and harming Laya as punishment makes the decision easy, and I decide against it.

Instead, I slip out of the SUV unarmed.

The door to one of the warehouses on my right opens, and a man armed with a machine gun steps out.

I feign confidence and pull my shoulders back, giving him the perfect view of my full height and power as I stride toward him.

"Where are they?" I spit out, eyeing the piece of shit with disgust.

He nods, and an onslaught of bullets whizz through the air.

"Son of a bitch!" I clamp my jaw shut as pain slices through my thigh, one then the other, my shoulder too, and as quick as the bullets started, they stop.

It was a test.

To disarm me if necessary and check if backup would arrive.

Of course, I pass with flying fucking colors. I did exactly what the prick asked. Now he needs to follow through too.

"Bring him in," the guy grunts, and men appear from nowhere behind me.

Just how many of these fuckers are there? I don't know

whether to be concerned about their presence or proud that he felt the need to gather an army against me. Maybe my reputation has proceeded me too. With that knowledge, I raise my head and ignore the way my legs feel like collapsing under the damage of the bullets.

The man at the door steps aside, allowing me to walk past him, and when my eyes lock on the scene before me, it takes everything inside me to remain standing.

FORTY

OWEN

Laya is gagged and tied to a chair, and my instant reaction is to lash out and run to free her, pull her into my arms, and smother her with my protection, but the way her pretty green eyes implore mine has awareness creeping up my spine. She tilts her head toward the darkness encompassing the room, and when my gaze follows hers, dread hits me like a searing knife, slicing through my core and stealing the half of my heart that beats solely for him.

Azrael pushes off the bare concrete wall, his entire demonic being unperturbed by the grenade my son clasps in his small hands as he cradles him.

"Az ..." My mouth moves, but I'm speechless.

After all, what is there to say?

He holds my world in the palm of his hands, and I'm rendered powerless.

"Take your shirt off." He nods at me, and I narrow my

eyes, trying to understand his thought process. Then he glances at Romeo, and I make quick work of pulling my T-shirt over my head with a wince of pain before depositing it to the floor.

Laya releases a low sob muffled by the gag, and my jaw clenches at her ill treatment. No doubt my girl can see the blood flowing down my chest, but its warmth is a reminder of my battle for them. If I have to be drained of every ounce of my blood to fight for them, I will.

One armed man circles me with a scanner, then nods in Azrael's direction, and it's only now I realize they were checking me for a wire.

"I'm impressed." Azrael chuckles. "Or should I be concerned?"

I stare back at him.

"You came unarmed. Or did you?" He raises an eyebrow.

"I did as you asked, Azrael. Now let them go."

I try to ignore Laya's frantic state. Her heavy breathing and choking noises tell me she's losing faith. That shouldn't hurt, but it does.

Didn't I tell her I'd do anything for her?

"The card." He waves his hand toward one of his men, and I take it from my back pocket, handing it over to him without a second thought.

"Follow me." He turns, and for a moment, I'm frozen until some prick with a death wish pushes my shoulder, so I shoulder-check him with such force he drops to the floor.

Azrael spins to face me.

"He tripped." I shrug.

He shakes his head and opens a door leading to an office, and I step inside. One man behind me closes the door and leans against it, and I contemplate my next move.

Could I take them?

"My men have full instruction to blow her brains out if you try anything. Sit." He points toward the chair opposite him, and my eyes track Romeo and the way he's dribbling on the damn grenade.

Then my gaze meets the man they call the devil himself. His hair is slicked back, his eyes so black you're unable to see his pupils. The scar on his cheek is ominous, and the rumor is, his father delivered it after hearing one of the girls call Azrael handsome. It only adds to his sinister stare, so deadly I swear my balls shrivel up.

This man has committed atrocities. He traffics women and sells them. His family owns sex slave auctions, and not a single one of those girls is willing.

He's evil beyond belief, and I'm paralyzed to protect my world, my loved ones, against him.

The enormity of being in his proximity has my chest seizing as my skin crawls to get out of there, yet I try to appease him and relax into the chair while every cell in my body fights against the action.

"I gave you the card, Azrael."

"You did," he confirms in a monotone voice that leads me to believe he barely cares about the memory card. This piques my interest, and I sit forward.

"What is it you want? You never asked me if I made a copy of the files on there."

He appears completely unperturbed. "Did you?"
"No."
"Okay."

Annoyance rumbles in my chest at the game he's playing. "Okay? You don't care about the fucking memory card, so why are we here?"

He sits back lazily in his chair and diverts his gaze toward the desk, no longer looking at me. "I need you to deliver a package."

My head rears back. "A package?"

"That's what I fucking said," he snaps, and it startles Romeo, causing him to whimper, and I ball my hands into fists while gritting my teeth.

My nostrils flare as I struggle to rein in my temper, yet Azrael appears completely stoic.

"I need you to deliver a package for me," he repeats, slower this time.

"You caused all this for a fucking package?" I keep my tone measured and wave my hand toward my son as irritation coats my skin.

Azrael's eyes hold mine, and realization hits me.

He's into the skin trade.

"A person. You want me to traffic a human?" Nausea creeps up my throat, and I stroke over my jaw to push away the discomforting feeling of wanting to vomit.

"Not traffic a human. I said deliver a package." The vein on his neck pulsates, and his arm tightens around my son. In that moment, I realize Azrael Carrera has a weakness.

"A girl?"

Awareness flashes in his eyes, and I know I hit the nail on the head.

"I need you to keep her secure." His dark eyes remain latched on mine as he allows me to see beyond the mask he portrays to the world. "I need you to use your contacts."

He knows I have links within the Mafia world, and he wants me to keep her safe using those links.

"Okay." I relent with ease.

"Okay? Just like that?" He tilts his head, as if analyzing me.

A humorless laugh leaves me. "You hold my son's life in your arms, Azrael, and my girl's. I'd do anything for them." I lean forward. "One day you might do the same." He cocks his head, and I go on. "A deal with the devil for a chance of happiness."

He swallows. "I just did." His words are barley a whisper, but I didn't miss them, nor do I have a chance to analyze them because he pushes back in his chair and stands. Then he holds my son out toward me, and I've never felt anything like it when I lift him into my arms.

I bury my head into his soft hair and breathe him in. "You're safe, buddy." His little heart beats against mine, and the comfort from that has me wanting to break down and cry, but instead, I clear my throat and just hold him tighter. "Daddy's here."

Azrael's right-hand man opens the door, and I step out into the warehouse, only now noticing the lifeless body of Brynn lying in a pool of blood.

"Oh, my God!" Laya screeches, and I lift my head to face my girl rushing toward me, and when her arms wrap around my waist, I embrace it with the knowledge that the Carrera family have a war on their hands, and not one involving me.

I'm about to do a deal with the devil himself, but I do so willingly, prepared to do anything for my family.

FORTY-ONE

OWEN

My girl curled up in a ball and shuddered all the way home, and I wanted to slice some fucker up for putting her through this trauma. She'd already been through enough, and from now on, I don't care how overkill it may seem, she and Romeo will have an entire security team to themselves.

Tate greeted us in the driveway and took Romeo so I could carry her through the house. The man looked how I felt, emotionally and physically exhausted.

Ava and Tate bathed Romeo and decided they were staying the night to watch over him, which I was grateful for. Laya burst into tears when they told her that, and you could see the anxiety fall from her.

A medic was on hand to dig out the bullets lodged in my leg and shoulder, and Laya never left my lap as I withstood the pain without medication. She's my fucking salvation and cure. After feeling my heart broken, nothing compares to that, and I refused to let her leave my side, no matter how much concern she had for me.

Behind our bedroom door, I tended to Laya. I filled the bathtub with bubbles and washed every inch of my girl, then wrapped her in warm towels and laid her on the bed.

I stare down at her beauty, the crushing feeling in my chest not easing as I expected it to. Instead, it amplifies with each gentle caress of drying her with the towel. Knowing I came so close to losing her is something I never want to endure again. Sure, I lost her to that fucker six feet under, but nothing compares to the realization of possibly never seeing her again.

"Are you sure they didn't hurt you?" My eyes sweep over her face as I ask the same question I've asked multiple times.

She shakes her head. "I'm okay. Romeo is okay?" Her soft hand glides over my jawline, and a shudder ripples through me as I press her hand against me, eager to feel the warmth of her touch seep into my soul.

"How do you know they won't come after us again?" she whispers, and alarm flashes in her eyes. I hate it. No woman should ever feel that, least of all mine, with me being the owner of a fucking security firm that failed her epically.

"He won't, I have assurances."

Her eyes flicker over my face, and her body freezes. "Like what?" Concern laces her tone, and I can't help the chuckle that escapes me.

"Nothing illegal, Laya. I promise." Then I lift her hand and kiss it gently before placing it on the steady thrum of my heart. "I have an important package in my hands that gives me all the reassurance I need."

Her eyebrows shoot up. "What does that mean?"

I lick my lips, unsure of how much to tell my wife. But after everything she's endured, she deserves the peace of mind of knowing her and Romeo's welfare are nothing to be concerned about. "His everything."

Understanding flashes in her eyes, and her shoulders relax, allowing the towel to slip from around her.

My eyes instantly latch onto her heavy tits, and I close them to avoid the way my cock hardens at the sight.

"Owen?" Her gentle tone has my eyes opening. "No more secrets."

I shuffle closer toward her on the mattress and cup the back of her head as I stare down at the most beautiful woman I've ever laid eyes on. My pulse races for her, my cock stiffens, and my heart hammers. "No more secrets. I promise I only ever did it to protect you," I whisper, then coax her lips open with mine. She allows me the privilege of tasting her after thinking I lost her for good. Her taste is somehow sweeter, as I once again allow myself to drown in her possession.

She unbuttons my jeans, and I pull back to stand and lower them along with my boxers. Then I toe off my boots and socks and kick them to the side with my clothes following, all while ignoring the pain radiating through me. I can withstand anything if it means I get to keep her, and more importantly, show her how much I love her.

Laya lies naked in the center of the bed, her hair splayed out over the pillows like a halo, and when she opens her legs, my cock jumps at the sight of her glistening pussy.

I climb between her legs and rest on my forearms above her, and her eyes shine with an uncertainty I hate.

She's giving herself over to me, exposed, raw from her trauma, and vulnerable in my hands, yet she's giving me her all.

And she deserves my everything too.

Slowly, I lower my lips to hers and breathe her in. Her proximity and the way her arms band around my neck, as if never wanting to let me go, give me the confidence for my words.

"I'm sorry I ever let you go, but I'm not sorry for protecting you from him."

Her heart skips a beat against mine.

"I always thought you'd come back to me when you were ready, Laya. I never expected you to end up with a monster. You were meant to be mine."

Her eyes fill with tears as she shakes her head. "I thought you'd moved on."

"How could I have to moved on from this, baby girl?" I push inside her slick pussy, and I revel in her stretching around me to accommodate my thickness.

"How could I ever move on from you?"

Her breathing stutters as I slowly pump my hips, delivering each gentle thrust with an admittance of my truth.

"My heart shattered into a thousand pieces, and I hated him, Laya. I hated him so much for taking what was mine."

"I never loved him like I love you. He just made me feel secure." He made her feel all the things I never did. He gave her all the things I wanted but never took, and I understand that, but the sting is still there. Her using those words toward him, the same words only ever meant to be mine, has an unadulterated rage coursing through me, yet somehow, I lock it down.

"You were always mine." I circle my hips and groan at the gasp that escapes her edible lips.

"Yes," she pants. "Always, Owen."

"I researched him. Contacted every Mafia member I had access to for information. But I swear to you, Laya, if I thought you would be happy"—my hips move faster as I admit my worst fears—"if I thought that man was right for you, I'd have let you go. I'd have lived my miserable existence without you, to give you what you deserve."

Her lips meet mine, but I only allow the touch for a split second, desperate to get it all out, needing her to hear all my truths. It flows freely from me, like the poison that ravished my veins and left me so brutally torn.

"It killed me knowing he gave you my son, Laya." A tear slips down her cheek as I continue the steady pumping of my hips. "That he watched my baby girl's body stretch, he held your tummy, he watched the life he created with the woman I love be brought into this world. I loathed him."

I lick the tear on her cheek away and her hold on my tightens. Her pussy clenches around me, and I know she's close, but I need her to hear it all.

"When I discovered the man he was, I knew he wasn't worthy, and it sickened me that someone like that was receiving your trust, your love, when it should have been mine. I would have held those feelings so close to me, Laya. I never would have risked destroying you. I'd do anything to protect you, baby." I thrust again, and her lips crash against mine, and this time I allow her to take the access she so beautifully demands.

"Anything," I whisper, needing her to know I did just that.

"Thank you." Her hips rise off the bed, meeting mine as I swallow her moans of pleasure, and when I grind myself against her clit, she clenches tightly around me.

"I love you," she whispers, and I squeeze my eyes closed at the intense pressure those words create. "Oh god, I love you!" she whisper-yells as her pussy grips my cock and her back arches off the bed. Her orgasm hits her so beautifully my cock willingly surrenders to her command, delivering her with a torrent of short sharp thrusts while I will my cum to give me the greatest gift of all.

"You have all of me, Laya. I love you, baby girl. Always."

LAYA

My body falls against the mattress. My orgasm hit me so spectacularly the air was stolen from my lungs.

Owen's admission was heart wrenching and everything I knew it to be.

I don't need the specifics of what occurred with Carlos, because I know deep in my heart that he did what was best for us.

My son was created as heir to one day take Carlos's place in his world, and that knowledge would tear me apart day by day. I can't even begin to comprehend the atrocities that he committed. That was not the man I knew or wanted, yet it was slipping over into our everyday life. He was becoming unrecognizable, and worse, I wasn't allowed to be me either.

Owen loves me for who I am. He knows the importance of family and values. He knows real love, and there's not a glimmer of doubt in my mind that he already loves Romeo as his own.

He's everything I want him to be, and so much more.

"You have all of me" echoes in my mind as exhilaration pumps through my veins.

Our labored breaths fan one another as a smile forms on my lips, and Owen's lips twitch as we stare at one another triumphantly.

Everything is out in the open, all our secrets laid bare with our souls. I accept each and every one of them.

I accept him.

My nails dig into his shoulders as I buck beneath him, wanting more for anything he's prepared to give.

His eyes flash with a seductive darkness I crave. "I'm going to fuck you like a good slut now, wife." His gravelly promise sets the hairs on my body on edge, eager for his pleasurable punishment.

In a flash, he rolls us over, so I straddle his hips. "Push your tits together and squirt me some milk. I want you to drown me in it while I show you who owns this body." He slaps my ass hard, making me yelp.

His gaze roams over my legs and freezes on where we're joined. "Do you see how much I fill you, baby girl? How my cock stretches your little cunt." His hand slides up my stomach and over my chest, then his thick fingers splay out over the column of my throat.

"Yes," I pant as I rock against him. The tips of his fingers dig into my skin, bringing with it a sense of command. Ownership.

"That's it. Rub that greedy little clit on me. Rub yourself off, you filthy little slut." He smacks my ass again, and the sting behind it burns through me. "You take me so beautifully. All stretched and eager to please me."

"Yes, please." I moan, then caress my tits, and I revel in the swell of his cock deep inside me.

"That's it. Touch those big tits for me. Play with your nipples, baby girl. Let me see your milk." I gently pump myself until milk bubbles down the swell of my tits. "Fuckkkk, that's it." He rolls his hips, then powers up into me. "Such a good girl." Each surge encourages a stream of warm milk to flow from my nipples.

Then he leans forward, and I push my nipples into his greedy mouth without direction. He groans around me as I tip my head back and become a doll for him to use. He feeds from me, holding me tightly in place as his cock works against the bounce of my ass, pounding in and out of me with each beat.

I grip onto his shoulders for support, knowing I'm leaving marks on him sends me wild with need. He's mine. My beautiful savage, a handsome manipulator, my savior.

Ecstasy sparks inside me when the milk pours from his mouth. He eats like a feral beast. His hungry mouth devours me while his cock punishes me.

Pleasure strikes, and I can't hold back.

"Yes. Oh god, yes. Owen!" I scream into the night as he grips me harder, causing sparks of light to dance in my vision, and I float in a sea of tranquility, never feeling so secure yet so owned.

"Fuckkkk," he grunts against me as his teeth tug on my flesh, and when I open my hooded eyes, he raises his head to face me. His mouth falls open, releasing a deluge of warm milk, the most intoxicating sight I've ever witnessed.

His cock spurts deep inside me, and I float into the abyss with a smile on my face when he whispers, "I love you" into the night.

Finally, feeling complete.

I finally have it all.

FORTY-TWO

LAYA

Slowly, I roll over with a groan. My body feels heavy and achy from yesterday, no doubt from our night too. During the early hours of the morning, I fed Romeo, then Owen put him back to sleep in his nursery under Tate's and Ava's watchful eyes. They said they wanted practice ready for their little one, but ultimately, I know it was so I could rest during the night, knowing he was being watched.

I throw the sheets off and go into the bathroom. After using the toilet, I wash my hands and brush my teeth, then track the marks on my neck and flick open my makeup bag to cover up his fingerprints. The last thing I want is for my brother to see them.

The necklace hanging around my neck glimmers in the mirror, and I stroke over the emerald, entwining my fingers in the chain with the same steely determination I had only a few short months ago.

A fresh start.

Choosing to be the strong woman I want my children to look up to, I pull my shoulders back and throw open the bedroom door, heading straight toward the closet. I decide to hit my past head on. I want Owen to deal with whatever is in the backpack Carlos gave me. If there's more evidence of his crimes, I trust the only man to ever truly love me to deal with it. Raising up on my tiptoes, I lift the backpack off the top shelf, but misjudge my step and stumble backward. The bag slips to the floor and out spills the contents.

I lift the paperwork and wince. I'm pretty sure it's legal work, much of it jargon to me. Then I get to an envelope with my name on the front in Carlos's handwriting. My heart thunders as I stare at it. Equal worry and intrigue slice through me. Sitting on my ass, I take a deep breath and open it.

Mi amor,

I wince at my nickname, hating the way it pains me to hear his voice ringing through my ears, as if calling me from the grave.

I'm writing this letter because I know my life is ending, and I deserve it, amor, fuck, do I deserve it all. I screwed up and I'm sorry. Sorry for so many things that I hope you never hear of.

I've always tried to protect you, mi amor, from the real me. You see, I'm not a good man, however much I want to be in order to keep you, I'm simply not.

From the moment I set eyes on you, I wanted you and so desperately wanted to be the man that you deserve, but how can I be when my whole existence has been so corrupt. You became my light, my small beacon of hope, the woman that would love the man I wanted to be, not the man I was.

I want you to tell our son how much love I had for you both. How we spent the evenings on the veranda with you between my legs while the stars shone above us, our son cradled in your lap, and I looked down on you both with warmth in my heart, having never felt so complete.

I trust in you that our son will become everything I ever wished I could be. A good man deserving of a woman like his mama.

Owen will be that man for you and the father my son deserves, because in another life, I would be like him, worthy of your love, a father for my son to be proud of.

Your everything.

Be happy, mi amor. You and our son deserve the world. I just wish I could be a part of it.

All my love, Carlos.

I won't tell our son any of that; I refuse to lie to him. Carlos may have wanted those things, and deep in his heart, I know he did, but they never happened. The reality couldn't be further from the truth. Too consumed with the power that possessed him. The unraveling of his demise turned him into the man he was always destined to be.

Only now do I see it.

Carlos Andreas was never my everything.

He wasn't even my beginning.

FORTY-THREE

OWEN

"Are you sure that you can manage? We don't mind staying another day." Ava sighs, and my lip twitches. Anyone would think she doesn't want to go home.

"They're fine." Tate waves his hand toward me and Romeo. The dark circles under his eyes are testament to the past twenty-four hours.

"We're fine," I parrot, gifting my boy with a kiss to his soft hair.

Ava scoffs. "They're not fine. Need I remind you they've just been through hell?"

Tate rolls his eyes, and for the first time since his self-imposed sleepover, I want to punch him in the balls.

"Morning," Laya declares from the doorway, and I scan over her face to gauge how she truly feels. I take note of the way her cheeks redden, then latch onto the makeup that covers my marks, and my cock twitches hungrily.

Tate steps forward, and my spine straightens, preparing for battle. "Laya—"

Laya holds her hand up. "Whatever is about to come out of your mouth, save it and listen."

"I..."

Her eyes drill holes into his, and he steps back.

"Me and Owen ..." She slides her hand into mine, and the racing of my pulse lessens under her touch. "We're getting married."

Tate's eyes dart from me to Laya, then she elaborates.

"We're having the wedding I always wanted." She turns to face me. "Marrying the man I always wanted."

My lip curls into a smile. "Yeah?"

She bites on her lip, and I swear I almost combust.

"Congratulations!" Ava declares, rushing toward Laya like she's not heavily pregnant. She almost knocks Laya off her feet.

Tate clears his throat, and I pull my attention away from Laya as he holds out his hand. "Congratulations, brother."

His words cause my heart to skip a beat, and when I slide my hand into his and he pulls me against his chest in a tight embrace, finally having the acceptance I so desperately craved, I have to clear my throat to hide the emotion begging to escape.

He saves me from doing so. In typical Tate fashion, he pulls back, then narrows his eyes. "You need sound proofing, just so you know." Laya tenses on his words. "You sound like wounded animals begging for help after being torn apart."

Holy shit, he did not just call out my wife like that. Anger sends my temple pulsating as my muscles coil tight.

I'm snapped from my death glare when an awkward laugh erupts from Ava. "Time for us to leave." She pats him on his chest, and they make a quick exit, my eyes not leaving the door they exit out of.

"Your brother is a dick."

"I know." She smiles up at me like I hung the moon and stars in the sky.

"You want to marry me again, huh?"

She bites on her lip, and it takes everything in me not to tug it into my mouth.

"Yes." She strokes over Romeo's head, and I love how my boy sleepily nuzzles into my chest.

My lip twitches. "What do I get in return for this dream wedding of yours?"

"All of me," she whispers as she steps up on the tips of her toes to deliver a soft kiss to my lips.

"I want you to place that ring on my finger, again." *Kiss.*

"Chain me to your bed." *Kiss.*

"And put a baby in my belly." *Kiss.*

My cock stiffens, and I fidget from side to side.

"Deal," I grunt out while she slides her tongue into my mouth, and I plan in my head how quickly I can pull this wedding together.

FORTY-FOUR

LAYA

My gaze trails down my dress in the mirror. "You look stunning." My dad adjusts the veil, sliding it perfectly into place. "He's a lucky man, Laya, and I couldn't be prouder." I go to tell him I'm the lucky one, but he continues. "Of both of you, Laya. I'm proud of both of you." He looks at me pointedly, and my approving smile meets his. "Ready?"

Taking a deep breath, I nod.

The lakeside lodge I had on my Pinterest account has been transformed with white Calla lilies and matching drapes. It's everything I ever dreamed of, and today, I marry the man who always had a starring role in those dreams.

Stepping through the double doors, my eyes meet Owen's and everyone else slips away.

Then I close my eyes as the music starts. "All of Me" by John Legend begins to play and memories collide with the here and now.

Every time he threw his head back on a loud chuckle that made his eyes twinkle when I told him a joke and he'd tell me I had a smart and sassy mouth. *"I don't know what I'd do without your smart mouth, Laya."*

The way his eyebrows would furrow as he studied me from a distance.

"What's going on in that beautiful mind of yours?"

Every sneaky glance he would take of me when I purposely dressed up, knowing he'd be at our home. The way his heated gaze would follow me around the room and leave me aching when he left.

"I'm sorry. I don't know what hit me. But you'll be all right."

All the gentle touches to my skin that felt like sparks of embers burning to erupt into flames, only to be dampened as he left me longing for more, like they never had a chance to burn bright at all.

Every memory of our longing comes rushing back with the words of the song as my feet sail toward him.

I mumble, "I love all of you" as my feet glide down the aisle toward the only man who ever held my heart.

The ceremony starts in a haze of tears. My son babbles happily on Tate's lap with Ava's hand in his, and a confident nod of approval in my direction has my chest filling with overwhelming happiness I never knew existed.

"I've got you, baby girl," Owen whispers, taking my

hand in his. He uses his thumb to draw reassuring circles on mine. He clears his throat. "You look beautiful." Tears swim in his eyes, and I choke back the emotion, and when a lone tear slips down his handsome face, it's my turn to swipe it away, causing him to chuckle.

"Thank you. You look gorgeous." He beams a smile that almost brings me to my knees.

The officiant works through the service, and our eyes never falter from one another. My chest tightens with the intensity of our love, so compounding it becomes difficult to see anything but him.

"Owen, I knew from the moment I saw you I wanted to marry you. I was a little girl with big dreams of making my brother's best friend my prince." Our family and friends laugh as I continue. "I knew people thought I'd grow out of this crush, but what they didn't understand was I was in love with you." I take a deep breath and place my hand over my heart. "I felt it in here and it never left me. Not once." I lick my lips. "When I kissed your bloody fists, I was grateful for your protection, but I saw the jealousy in your eyes. Gavin Jackson was going to steal my first kiss, and that was reserved solely for you." He chuckles, remembering the time. "I wish I could take back the time we lost and do it all over, but I will spend a lifetime making our stolen time up to you. You're everything I always knew I wanted. Romeo loves you, and I couldn't wish for a better father for our son. I love you, Owen James Stevens. Thank you for loving me, too."

Owen clears his throat. "Laya, my beautiful girl. You were always perfect to me, and I was never worthy." My eyes implore his as guilt swims in my stomach at the way he feels. "You gave me all of you, and it took me far too long to give you all of me. I'll always regret letting you slip through my fingers, but I will never regret falling in love with you. I wouldn't want to walk a day on this earth without feeling your love inside me. My heart beats for you and Romeo. Thank you for loving all my imperfections, for loving all of me."

My hand finds his jaw, and I pull him into a kiss, teasing of what's coming.

"I now pronounce you, man and wife. Again!"

Catcalling and wolf whistles happen around us, but I'm drowning in the sea of love for a man who was simply always meant to be mine.

FORTY-FIVE

LAYA

"Black Magic" by Little Mix plays as background noise when Owen kicks the bedroom door shut.

Then he goes over to the closet, and my eyes narrow. What the hell is he doing? We agreed no honeymoon.

When he returns, I latch onto the chain hanging from his palm.

He kicks off his shoes. "Owen, what is that?"

He crucks an eyebrow at me, "A chain, baby girl."

"A chain," I repeat dumbly.

"You said you wanted to be my wife, chained to the bed and pregnant. My wife gets what my wife asks for."

"You're chaining me to the bed?"

"Absolutely." He beams, and my gaze locks onto the solid length of his cock protruding from his pants. Oh, sweet Jesus.

"And I need to fuck my wife's bloodied cunt."

A choking sound traps in my throat. "I'm not." I wave

my hand down toward my pussy while he continues to undress. "I'm not bleeding, Owen."

"I know. You think I don't monitor your period?" He pins me with a glare. "You're two days late, by the way."

My mouth falls open. "But you said."

He ties the chain around the headboard, and my mouth waters to taste the pre-cum dripping from his heavy cock so close to my face. Then he opens a drawer on the bedside table, takes out a penknife, and holds it up to show me. The blade glimmers in the light, and I swallow hard.

Before I have a chance to question him, he slices through the palm of his hand, making me gasp at the sight of his blood dripping from him, but when he pumps his cock, my pussy pulsates with a familiar need for him to fill me.

"Oh god," I pant as he attaches my wrists to the chain.

"You're going to scream my name as I slam inside your bloody cunt, understand me, *wife*?" He bites out the latter, and I nod.

Dark Owen is in full control now, and I so desperately want him.

"Now I need to punish your tight little cunt for tormenting me with the good-girl act you've done all day." I gasp, wanting to argue. "We both know what a filthy little slut you are for your husband, don't we?" He pumps his cock vigorously while straddling my torso.

"Have I put a baby in here?" As he points his cock toward my stomach, I swear the possessive gleam in his eyes almost makes me combust. I want to beg him to do just that, to fill me so full I've no choice but to become pregnant.

"I'm going to force my baby inside you, Laya, and

you're going to be a good little wife and accept it. Understand?"

"Yes."

"I'm keeping you chained to my bed and full of my cum." He slams inside me. "Every fucking hour." *Slam*. "Filling you with my cum." *Thrust*. Sweat drips from him, and every vein on his body bulges, indicating the pure masculinity rolling off him in waves as I lie powerless beneath his powerful force.

The headboard bangs, and the chains rattle as I grip onto them like a lifeline. "My dirty"—he grunts as he plows into me—"cum slut"—*slam*—"of a wife." Snarling, he palms my aching tits, then pushes them together as I stare down at him and revel in the roughness of his hand. "That's it, feed me." He grunts with each deep thrust of his strong hips. "Fucking. Feed. Me." My milk flows from me, coating his mouth and chin, and the delicious bite of his rough hands teasing over my nipple has my pussy clenching around him. "Such a beautiful baby girl." He groans as his movements become stuttered, a telltale of his orgasm.

"Take all of me!" he roars with every ounce of his domination, filling me to my core.

I close my eyes with the familiar touch of his fingers wrapping around my necklace, my chain forever tying me to him, and I willingly allow it, knowing we're only just beginning. I place my hands on his, tangling them in the chain, and encourage him to press harder. His lips part, and the stars dance in front of my eyes as I willingly float away.

"I finally have my everything," he whispers as my vision blackens, and I couldn't agree more.

EPILOGUE

OWEN

I cast my eyes around Shaw's office, unable to wipe the smug grin off my face.

His eyes bore into mine in his lame attempt to chastise me. "So, let me get this straight. We now owe Oscar O'Connell a favor because you shirked duties?"

"His duties were to my sister," Tate snaps out in my defense. After being given the green light by Nico to orchestrate Carlos's death, it meant me having to pass workload on to a Mafia family, notably Oscar O'Connell. The only problem was the workload in question was to track down Rafael Marino's evasive girl. I grimace at the thought of upsetting Rafael, but then I remember the knowledge I hold in the palm of my hand, knowledge his family would love to be privy to involving the police commissioner.

"I just don't think you realize how dangerous some of these people are, Owen." Shaw drags a hand through his hair, and I want to scoff. He seems to forget it was me and my contacts that helped save his little Mafia princess from having their child cut from her stomach.

My best friends may not know everything about my past, but they know I had a different upbringing than them.

"What the fuck ever." Tate waves his hand toward Shaw like he's wafting a bug and changes the subject. "How's Laya doing?"

"Good." I smirk, remembering how well she took my cock this morning and at lunchtime when I made a trip home.

"Ava says she hasn't returned her text message yet."

I take a drink of my water while I contemplate my reply.

"Give him some slack. They're newly married. He probably has her chained to his bed. Right, Owen?" Shaw jokes, and the water I'm swallowing becomes clogged in my throat at how true that is.

I wheeze like an idiot, trying not to splutter the water over my desk but fail miserably.

The office door opens, and our attention is drawn there as our mouths simultaneously fall open with the disheveled appearance of Reed. His normally well-put-together appearance is in complete disarray. His hair is a ruffled mess, his shirt is open to the middle, and his tie is nowhere in sight.

Last I knew, he was attending a community event.

"What the fuck happened to you?" Mase asks as his hands rest on his hips.

"Please tell me you didn't kill someone." Shaw pinches the bridge of his nose, having a sly dig toward

Reed's younger brother, who is incarcerated for doing just that.

He drops down on his chair, and his dazed expression deepens.

Tate rolls a ball of paperwork up and throws it at his head, but Reed doesn't so much as flinch.

Mase stares down at him, then steps forward while we watch on, each of us baffled. He snaps his fingers in front of his face. "Reed."

"Tell him Lucinda has genital warts and he might have them." Tate points toward Mase. "That'll freak him out." He chuckles to himself.

"You do realize he can hear you himself, right?" I tilt my head toward Reed.

"Shut the fuck up," Tate grumbles, then throws himself back into his chair like a petulant child.

"I found her," Reed mumbles, and we all sit forward dramatically. "The woman. I found her."

"And?" Mase queries, studying Reed as if checking he has all his limbs.

"That's good, right?" Tate's face lights up, and I grin at how much he reminds me of an excitable puppy.

"It's awful." Reed laughs, but it lacks humor. "Fucking awful." He drags his hand over his head and blows out a deep breath.

"Is she married?"

Jesus.

My hand whips out and I clip Tate on the back of the head in warning while he glares back at me.

"Worse."

We all wait with bated breath for what could possibly be worse...

. . .

THE END

You can preorder REED's story here:
Would you like to discover how much worse it could get for Reed?

Join my newsletter to see more...

Extended Epilogue to REED'S story

ALSO BY B J ALPHA

SECRETS AND LIES SERIES
CAL Book 1

CON Book 2

FINN Book 3

BREN Book 4

OSCAR Book 5

CON'S WEDDING NOVELLA

O'CONNELL'S FOREVER

BORN SERIES
BORN RECKLESS

THE BRUTAL DUET
HIDDEN IN BRUTAL DEVOTION

LOVE IN BRUTAL DEVOTION

THE BRUTAL DUET PART TWO
BRUTAL SECRETS

BRUTAL LIES

STORM ENTERPRISES
SHAW Book 1

TATE Book 2

VEILED IN SERIES

VEILED IN HATE

CARRERA FAMILY

STONE

MAFIA DADDIES

DADDY'S ADDICTION Book 1

POSSESSION Book 2

ACKNOWLEDGMENTS

Tee the lady that started it all for me. Thank you for an eternity.

I must start with where it all began, TL Swan. When I started reading your books, I never realized I was in a place I needed pulling out of. Your stories brought me back to myself.

With your constant support and the network created as 'Cygnet Inkers' I was able to create something I never realized was possible, I genuinely thought I'd had my day. You made me realize tomorrow is just the beginning.

SPECIAL MENTION

To Kate, my amazing PA and bestie. Thank you for pushing me to be the best version of BJ Alpha I can be.

Jaclyn and Libby, thank you for all your comments, support and help.

Lilibet, thank you for all that you do. I'm incredibly grateful to you.

Jo, thank you for your support, I appreciate you!

My Incredible ARC, Street and TikTok Teams.

Thank you for every share, every comment and message. I'm so very grateful you find the time to support me.

My Reckless Readers!

You mean the world to me. This group of ours is my

sanctuary and the reader friends I have in there are the best I could ever wish for.

To my world.

Boys, another book. Thank you for understanding and all your support. I'm so very proud of you both.

To my hubby, the J in my BJ.

My man. You're the best. THANK YOU for everything. Without you I wouldn't be BJ Alpha. Love you trillions!

And finally…

Thank you to you, my readers.

Thank you for helping make my dreams a reality.

Love Always

BJ Alpha. X

ABOUT THE AUTHOR

BJ Alpha lives in the UK with her hubby, two teenage sons and three fur babies.
She loves to write and read about hot, alpha males and feisty females.

Follow me on my social media pages:
Facebook: BJ Alpha
My readers group: BJ's Reckless Readers
Instagram: BJ Alpha

Printed in Dunstable, United Kingdom

65232000R00221